Praise for RACHEL LEE

"A magnificent presence
in romantic fiction, Rachel Lee
is an author to treasure forever."
—*Romantic Times*

"Rachel Lee deserves much acclaim for
her exciting tales of romantic suspense."
—*Midwest Book Review*

RACHEL LEE

has always been a dreamer. If she couldn't find a book she wanted to read, she tried to write it. To this day, she's still trying to write the books she wishes she could read. Her life is certainly not the stuff of novels. She does her skydiving from her keyboard, where every time she faces a blank screen she wonders if the parachute is going to open. Boredom, however, is not in her lexicon. With five kids and two dogs, there's no time for that. Chaos and Murphy pretty much rule her life, much to her chagrin—and that of her editors. Perfection always seems to be beyond her grasp, but she's not going to quit trying to reach it. She considers herself blessed that she lives to write, and is fortunate enough to be able to write to live.

RACHEL LEE

An Officer and a Gentleman

TORONTO • NEW YORK • LONDON
AMSTERDAM • PARIS • SYDNEY • HAMBURG
STOCKHOLM • ATHENS • TOKYO • MILAN • MADRID
PRAGUE • WARSAW • BUDAPEST • AUCKLAND

To Mom,
with thanks for nagging me into it.

ISBN 0-373-81078-4

AN OFFICER AND A GENTLEMAN

This edition published by arrangement with Harlequin Books S.A.

www.eHarlequin.com

Printed in U.S.A.

Chapter 1

"You okay, cowboy?" The voice was cool, light.

Alisdair MacLendon's eyes snapped open. Blue lights flashed intermittently, giving an unearthly look to the youthful face that was bent over him. Too young to shave, MacLendon thought groggily, and nobody calls me cowboy, least of all some snotty kid.

Moving was a mistake. Shooting stars slashed across his vision, and some idiot with a jackhammer started trying to take a chunk out of the side of his skull.

"Hey! Cowboy!" The kid's light voice became sharper. "Open those eyes. Tell me where it hurts."

"My head, damn it!" His eyes flew open again. *Nobody* called him cowboy.

"Sergeant!" The light voice took on authority as the kid called to someone Alisdair couldn't see. "We've got a head injury over here. What have you got?"

"This idiot wasn't wearing his seat belt. He's got the windshield in his face. Can't tell about the rest."

"Radio the hospital."

The youthful face turned back to MacLendon, who was thinking that if he puked now it would be perfect. What had happened? Oh, yeah, some turkey in a blue hot rod had run the stop sign at about ninety miles an hour. He remembered the sickening thud as his head slammed into the door stanchion.

"Just going to check you out a little, cowboy," the kid said, voice pitched soothingly. Fingers moved through his hair lightly, feeling the side of his head.

"Ouch!" The fingers found the place where the jackhammer was working.

"You're gonna have one hell of a goose egg," the kid said. "Does anything else hurt?"

"No."

The kid backed off a little, squatting. For the first time MacLendon was able to identify the components of an Air Force security police uniform: nylon winter jacket, beret, holstered gun. Captain's bars winking at the shoulders. Captain's bars? This kid was too young.

"You cold?" the too-young captain asked. "I'm afraid we don't have any blankets, but the ambulance will be here in a couple of minutes."

"I'm okay." If okay was a knife in the brain, spots before the eyes, and a heaving stomach. "What's a captain doing on patrol?" he asked. Anything to keep from thinking about his discomfort.

A grin, a one-shouldered shrug. "Keeps the troops on their toes if I show up at odd hours. Midnight on Friday seemed like a good time to pull a little inspection."

This baby-faced captain was a man right after MacLendon's own heart. And God, he must be getting older than he thought if a captain looked like a baby to him. He closed his eyes against a sudden wave of nausea.

"Hey, cowboy!" The voice sharpened. "Stay awake. Talk to me!"

"I'm not a cowboy, damn it!" His sudden glare was convincing enough to cause the captain to blink.

"Sorry. Sure are dressed like one, though." Cool eyes took in his jeans, boots, and shearling jacket. "Could've sworn that was a Stetson over there on the seat."

Spunky young idiot, MacLendon thought, and in spite of his irritation and pain and wooziness, a corner of his thin mouth twitched. He wondered if he should tell this youngster who he was, then decided against it. He would enjoy it a whole lot more when he felt better.

The young head tilted. "I hear the ambulance, *sir*. Two more minutes." Leaning forward over him, the captain reached to release the seat belt.

Something soft pressed against MacLendon's chin, and he drew a sharp breath.

"Did I hurt you?" The captain's concern was swift.

Ever afterward, MacLendon wondered what had caused him to say something so outrageous and could only conclude that he'd been more rattled by the accident than he thought. He said, "You have breasts."

The captain blinked, and then a quirky, humorous grin spread across her face. "Yes, *sir*," she said smartly. "Standard female issue, one pair."

God, MacLendon thought, closing his eyes. This captain was going to be a handful. He could see it coming.

Suddenly a radio crackled. "Alpha Tango Niner."

The captain stood up and reached for the radio that hung on her left hip, its weight a balance to the pistol on her right hip. Security cops called those radios "bricks." They ate with them, slept with them, and all but showered with them.

"Alpha Tango Niner," she said.

"Intruder alert at Zulu Bravo," said a tinny voice.

"Charlie? This is Captain Burke. Alert the team. What have you got?"

"An alarm. No visual yet."

"Roger. I'm tied up at a traffic accident for a couple more minutes, but I should reach Zulu Bravo in fifteen to twenty minutes. You know the drill."

Flashing red lights joined the flashing blue ones of the security truck. Captain Burke turned and was saying something, but MacLendon couldn't make it out. The nausea in his stomach suddenly roared into his ears, and the last pinprick of light disappeared into utter darkness.

The row of B-52 bombers were hulking eerily in the pinkish light of mercury vapor lamps that turned their camouflage colors into muddy shadows. Looking like monstrous science fiction mosquitoes, their sleek bodies faced the runway. The long wings sagged beneath their own weight, saved from touching the tarmac only by the wheels attached to the undersides of the wing tanks. As the planes rolled down the runway, however, those wings would lift and the planes would no longer look awkward. Soaring, these birds became elegant creatures of the air.

Captain Andrea Burke never ceased to marvel that anything so ungainly could fly. The B-52 pilots claimed utter faith in their planes. Like the Flying Fortresses of World World II, the B-52s could limp home even with massive damage, and having seen some of that damage, Andrea Burke could well believe the stories she'd heard. More than once during her Air Force career, she'd seen one of these bombers land safely with an injury that would have toppled a commercial airliner from the skies.

They were old, they were creaky, many of their parts now had to be manufactured by their repair crews, and they were being replaced with the technical marvel of the B1-B. Like old horses about to be sent to pasture, they had served well and faithfully. With their passing, Andrea thought, an era would end. Since earliest childhood, she'd watched these babies fly. Soon they would fly no more.

"It has to be a fault in the sensor system, Captain," Sergeant Halliday told her, breaking into her thoughts. "There's absolutely no evidence that someone crossed the perimeter."

Andrea's men had searched every nook and cranny of the controlled area in the last three hours, and she was inclined to agree with Halliday's assessment. An optical sensor had been tripped, setting off an alarm at the monitor station, but a lot of things could trip a sensor, from debris blowing in the ceaseless North Dakota wind to a voltage drop.

It was nearly four in the morning, and Andrea very badly wanted to rub her eyes. Refusing to let her growing fatigue show, however, she repressed the urge. "What if someone was leaving the area, rather than entering?"

Sergeant Halliday was Andrea's electronic security expert. A man around her own age of twenty-eight, Halliday had joined the Air Force at seventeen and promptly displayed an awesome genius for anything through which electricity flowed. He was tall, painfully thin, and even more painfully shy—except when he talked about electronics. Then, and only then, he acknowledged no superior.

"Well, ma'am," he said easily in his lazy Georgia drawl, "if that's the case, we've got serious trouble. That means someone gained access to a controlled area without tripping any of the security systems. To do that, they'd either have to know the system inside out, or they'd have to pass the sentries. Either way, it's not good."

"That's what I figured." Andrea leaned back against the wall and looked out again at the hulking B-52s. "Well, I think we're safe in saying there're no unauthorized personnel in the area now."

"Yes, ma'am." Halliday's eyes were faded-looking behind his thick glasses.

"So find me a fault in the system, Halliday. Pin it down so I can get my butt into bed." She tempered the words with a faint smile, and Halliday returned it.

"You got it, Captain." Bending again to his terminals and displays and oscilloscopes, Halliday continued his diagnostics.

"Do you know anything about the new commander the Bomb Wing's getting?" he asked as he worked.

"Only what everyone else has heard, I guess," Andrea replied. "I hear he flew bombers in Nam, that he's some kind of hotshot jet jockey—some even say he was in the Thunderbirds—and that he's up for brigadier general."

"That's what I hear, too. I suppose he'll stick his nose into everything."

"That's his job," Andrea replied noncommittally. Privately, she wasn't looking forward to the change of command any more than anyone else.

The commander of the 447th Bombardment Wing was the commander of the base's host organization, and as such he was very definitely top dog. It was a fact that the personality of the man on top had repercussions all the way down the ladder. As commander of the 447th Security Squadron, Andrea reported directly to him, as did all the other commanders on base except the Missile Wing commander. The current Bomb Wing commander was a man content to let his subordinates do their jobs. The new man might have very different ideas.

"We'll survive, Halliday," she said after a moment. "Frankly, I'll start surviving a heck of a lot better when the change of command ceremony is over. I hate those affairs."

Halliday glanced up with a grin. "You could always get sick."

"Great first impression." Returning her gaze to the planes outside, she fell into uneasy reflection. Not everyone would be pleased to find one of his commanders was a woman. Command opportunities were limited, and despite the equal opportunity environment of the Air Force, those opportunities were even more severely limited for women. Because the Air Force had made some public relations hay out of her appointment two years ago, Andrea understood her uniqueness. She wasn't the only woman in her position, but the others were few and far between.

"Captain?" Once again Halliday's voice called her from thought. "I think I found it. We're measuring an intermittent voltage drop on that same circuit. Unless somebody's jumping back and forth through the beam at intervals, it's an equipment failure."

Andrea straightened and pulled her beret into place. "Thanks, Halliday. How long will it take to pinpoint?"

He shrugged. "Maybe a couple of hours."

"Okay. I'll tell the sentries to look sharp in the meantime. Call me when you've got it repaired."

"Yes, ma'am."

When, Andrea found herself wondering, was the last time she'd gotten a decent night's sleep? Being a squadron commander was something like being a mother, a priest, a judge, and a jury all rolled up in one, and there was no such thing as an eight-hour day or an uninterrupted night. She loved her work, but sometimes she thought she just ought to move a cot into her office and catnap round the clock in fifteen-minute snatches.

The predawn air of late October was cold, presaging the coming North Dakota winter. Almost time for survival gear again, she thought. Not since she graduated from the Academy six years ago had she seen anything approaching a warm climate. The wind nipped at her ears and tugged at her beret as she trudged to her blue security patrol pickup truck. Always the wind. She couldn't remember when it had ever stopped.

When Andrea Burke finally collapsed on her bed in the BOQ, Bachelor Officers' Quarters, it was five-thirty in the morning. She spared just enough time to shed her jacket, boots, and pistol, and then fell fully clothed across the blankets. Like it or not, she was going to have to go to the office today and write a report. So much for Saturday. But first a couple of hours of blessed sleep.

She was just spiraling down into the reaches of a warm place where alerts didn't exist when the phone rang. Cursing vigorously, she rolled over and considered not answering it. Business would come crackling over the radio on her night table, not over the phone. Groaning, she picked up the receiver anyway. You never knew.

"Burke."

"Captain, this is Sergeant Nickerson."

Nickerson. The auto accident. She'd sent the sergeant to the hospital to clean up the details while she raced over to the airfield.

"Shoot," she said, rubbing her eyes.

"I thought you should know," he said. "That guy who was in the vehicle that was hit?"

"Yeah, the cowboy. What about him?"

"Ma'am, he ain't no cowboy. He's a bird colonel, name of Alisdair MacLendon. Captain, he's the new Bomb Wing commander."

The expletive that escaped Andrea's lips was both unladylike and expressive. Nickerson chuckled.

"Thought you should know, ma'am," he said again, and rang off.

For the moment, all hope of sleep was forgotten. The new commanding officer, so of course she had called him cowboy. And naturally she had managed to shove her chest into his face, making it unalterably certain that he was aware of her sex, which was one thing she absolutely didn't allow to intrude on her job.

Well, she was just too damn tired to worry about it now. That knock on the head would keep him cooped up in the hospital for a couple of days, anyhow. In the meantime, she *had* to sleep.

The groan that escaped her this time was satisfied, as her head landed on the soft pillow. Nor was sleep shy. It caught her instantly in a warm embrace.

Noon found Andrea staring at her bleary-eyed face in the mirror. She'd always looked a little like Huck Finn, with her reddish blond hair and the smattering of golden freckles across her nose and cheeks. Her short haircut did nothing to dispel the illusion.

Sticking her tongue out at herself, she turned from the mirror and headed for the door. Today she was off duty, and dropping by the office to write a report didn't mean she had to wear a uniform. The people in her squadron had gotten used to the sight of her in her Air Force Academy sweat suit and jogging shoes. She'd grown up as the middle child in a family with six boys, and it was easier for her to be one of the guys than anything else. Pretty soon, everybody who was around her for a while realized she was just that: one of the guys.

Picking up her radio, which was exactly the size and shape of the brick for which it was nicknamed, she stepped through the door and set out at an easy jog.

The front office at the Security Police Headquarters building was at its usual Saturday afternoon ebb. The radio crackled with quiet static: two cops sat drinking coffee and looking bored. Andrea trotted past them with a nod.

As commanding officer of the squadron, she had the largest office in the building. Entering it still gave her a thrill, even after two years. Here the majesty of the United States put on a moderately impressive display, ensuring that anyone who entered was reminded of the authority residing in a commanding officer. The floor, elsewhere tiled in nondescript beige, here was carpeted in Air Force blue. To the rear and either side of her massive, polished desk, on stands topped with brass eagles, hung the U.S. flag and the squadron's flag. Large, framed photographs of historic Air Force planes adorned the walls on either side of the room. On the wall directly behind her desk hung the emblem of the Strategic Air Command, an iron fist holding crossed lightning bolts and an olive branch. Beneath it was the motto: Peace is our Mission.

Actually Saturday and Sunday were the best days to take care of paperwork, she thought as she settled behind her desk in her deep leather chair and pulled out a report form. Distractions were few, if any, and heaps of paper disappeared as if by magic.

She was scribbling away industriously when she became aware that she was no longer alone.

"Just a sec," she said and poked her tongue out between her teeth. "How do you spell circuit?"

"C-I-R-C-U-I-T."

"I-T, huh? Sure doesn't sound like it." Suddenly her head snapped up. She knew that voice.

Colonel Alisdair MacLendon stood on the other side of her desk. He was resplendent in a Class A blue uniform, rows of ribbons on his chest. There was something about broad shoulders, a wide chest, and narrow flanks in Class A blues that made Andrea feel not at all like one of the guys.

Up, up her eyes traveled—good grief, he was tall—and finally reached a face that was craggy, weathered, and set in an expression of patience. His eyes, however, did not look patient. The color of blue ice, they were at this moment narrowly assessing.

"Ah..." The sound escaped her like a strangled sigh, and she leapt to her feet. Throwing back her shoulders, she snapped to attention with a ramrod stiffness she hadn't needed since the Academy.

MacLendon opened his mouth to put her at ease, then stopped, a glimmer of amusement in his cool blue eyes. When she stood at attention in that sweat suit, there was absolutely no question that the captain had a pair of standard female issue breasts. In fact, he thought, a little better than standard issue. He rather liked the view.

He also found he rather liked the way her hair was tousled. Not quite red, not quite blond, it was almost exactly the color of a new penny. Was it strawberry blond?

"Captain Burke, I presume," he said. The name was on a plaque on the front of her desk, but he couldn't resist giving her a hard time.

"Yes, sir!"

"Do you always come to work in civvies, Captain?"

"No, sir. I'm off duty."

He glanced at the inscription on the shoulder of her sweatshirt. "Academy graduate?" He still had some difficulty adjusting to the idea of female service academy graduates.

"Yes, sir."

"At ease, Captain," he said, finally relenting. Amusing as it was to watch her respond like a plebe on parade, the workaday world of the Air Force was a relaxed one, in most ways exactly like its civilian counterpart. He understood why Burke had resorted to military formality, but he wasn't the kind of officer who required it.

Andrea at once slipped into parade rest, feet spread, hands clasped behind her back. The view thus provided was no less disturbing. MacLendon sighed.

"I'm Alisdair MacLendon," he said. "Monday morning I'm taking over command of the Bomb Wing."

"Yes, sir." Something flickered in her hazy green eyes. Humor? Doubt? He couldn't tell.

"From the moment I take command, Captain, I will be grateful if you refrain from addressing unknown persons as cowboy. *Sir* or *ma'am* are the appropriate forms of address." Was that laughter twitching the little minx's lips? he wondered.

"Yes, sir," was her only response, however, and a clipped one at that.

"Sit down, Captain. I want to talk to you."

Andrea immediately plopped into her chair. MacLendon followed suit, taking one of the three chairs that faced her desk. He crossed his legs loosely, right ankle on his left knee.

"How long have you been in security?" he asked.

"Since graduation, sir. Over six years." Andrea found herself wishing his eyes were any color but that particular icy blue that seemed to see right through her. She hadn't felt this nervous since her plebe days at the Academy. Of course, she'd never gotten off to quite this kind of start with a new commander before, either. Worse, she had the feeling that her excessive use of military formality was amusing him rather than soothing any ruffled pinfeathers he might have.

"So you're career law enforcement?"

"Yes, sir."

MacLendon rubbed his chin. Clearly she was an exemplary officer or she wouldn't be sitting where she was. Why, then, was he so convinced she was going to be a handful?

"Did you ever finish your unannounced inspection last night?" he asked.

"No, sir. We had that intruder alert out in the Zulu Bravo section. It took us until almost 5:00 a.m. to locate the cause of the alarm."

"Not a faulty circuit, by any chance?" he said drily.

Just the faintest tinge of color came to her cheeks. It was so slight he almost missed it.

"Yes, sir, it was. I plan to perform my inspection tonight."

"How often do you do this?"

She gave that one-shoulder shrug. "Whenever the mood takes me. Often enough so that my troops know I can show up anywhere at any time. Sometimes I hit everybody, sometimes just a few. I try to keep it random, so they can't predict."

"What time are you going tonight?"

"About nine."

He stood up, and Andrea immediately rose with him.

"Pick me up when you leave," he said to her. "I'll go with you. I'm in room 221 at the BOQ." He narrowed his eyes slightly. "Unless you object."

She did object, strenuously. This was something she always did by herself, or with one of her noncoms. But this damn cowboy was going to be her CO in less than forty-eight hours, and even though she had every right to refuse him, at least until he took command, it wouldn't be politic.

"I recommend you wear field dress, Colonel MacLendon," she said coolly.

He turned quickly so she wouldn't catch the sudden glimmer of amusement in his eyes. "I'll be ready." He headed for the door.

"Ah, Colonel?" Her cool voice halted him and he looked back. "How's your head?" she asked pleasantly.

His lips twitched appreciatively at her veiled implication that the blow to his head had affected his judgment. "Just fine," he answered in an equally pleasant tone. "You were right, though. I did get one hell of a goose egg."

Minx, he thought as he walked away. He had the strongest feeling that with Captain Burke most people never knew what hit them. Or even that they'd been hit. A handful indeed.

Slowly, Andrea released her white-knuckled grip on the arms of her chair. Inside, she had that same slightly fluttery, slightly edgy feeling she always got before she did something dangerous. It had to be because he'd gone out of his way just to reprimand her about her conduct last night. What a great start!

After drawing a deep breath, she expelled it through pursed lips and closed her eyes, only to stiffen anew as she recalled with unexpected vividness exactly the way his eyes had settled on her breasts. Back in the Academy she'd had a drill instructor who'd had a problem with his female cadets. Sergeant Harrison had been so obvious in his refusal to let his gaze stray that some women had taken to teasing him mercilessly by thrusting their breasts out as prominently as they could manage. One girl in particular had possessed the ability to render Harrison nearly speechless.

"Oh cripes," Andrea groaned, gifted with a sudden insight as to just how she had looked standing at attention like that. Not once but twice she'd thrust her chest to MacLendon's notice. Was she doomed to do everything wrong around the man?

Just as MacLendon reached the front office of the squadron, the glass doors opened to admit three men. The two in front looked as if they'd been through one heck of a barroom brawl. Their cheeks were bruised, one had a rapidly blackening eye, and the other had dried blood in a streak from the corner of his mouth down his chin. Bringing up the rear was a Master Sergeant, the man MacLendon remembered from last night in the emergency room. Nickerson? Yes, Nickerson. Just a little above average height and whipcord lean, Nickerson exuded tough competence.

"Move it, Butcher," Nickerson said, his voice a whispery rasp, when one of the men ahead of him appeared to hesitate. "The CO's gonna hear about this even if you pretend to be molasses."

"What's up, Sarge?" asked one of the men at the desk.

Nickerson opened his mouth as if to answer when his eyes

fell on MacLendon. "None of your business, Schuler," he said, and in one sweeping glance he took MacLendon in from head to foot. MacLendon knew that look. An experienced noncom could take a man's measure in a single glance.

"Ten-hut!" Nickerson barked, bringing everyone in the room to attention.

"As you were," MacLendon said immediately. "Carry on with your business, Sergeant Nickerson. You're obviously occupied." And you just as obviously don't want me to know what's going on here, he thought. Stepping aside, he watched the man urge the two others down the corridor toward Captain Burke's office. Well, it was a good sign that Nickerson was loyal to his CO, and that spoke well of Andrea Burke. He didn't imagine that Nickerson had found it easy to accept a woman in command. Few thirty-year veterans did.

Alisdair MacLendon was a man who liked to get the measure of his officers, who liked to know what was happening in his bailiwick. It might not be his bailiwick yet, but he had a very good notion he could get the measure of Andrea Burke if he poked his nose into this affair.

So he followed Nickerson back down the corridor at a discreet distance. By the time he reached the open door of Andrea's office, she had risen from her desk and come around it.

"So," he heard Captain Burke say, very, very softly. She stood before the two battered airmen, several inches shorter than either of them. Her feet were splayed, her hands clenched into fists behind her back, her narrow chin thrust out like a bulldog's. But her voice was calm, deceptively cool. As he moved into the room, MacLendon could see the white lines of fury stamped around her mouth, and her hazy green eyes were sparking with fire.

"So," she said again, quietly. "You couldn't have waited until you got off duty to act like a couple of animals in rut?"

"Ma'am," one of them started to say.

"Zip it, Butcher," she said coldly. "I don't give a hooker's damn if that woman sleeps with one of you, both of you, or half the men on this base. I don't even care if the two of you want to go off base on your own time and beat each other to a bloody pulp like a couple of overgrown roosters. What I do give a damn about is the security of this site. You two were assigned to protect the weapons depot. You were assigned to protect *nuclear weapons.* You were entrusted with the security of the United States of America."

A short silence followed her words. The two men's heads sank lower.

"Did you hear me, Butcher? Frankel?"

"Yes, ma'am," two voices mumbled.

"I said entrusted, and I meant entrusted. You were trusted by the people of this country to stay awake and do your job for a few lousy hours. You have betrayed that trust. You have disgraced yourselves, and you have disgraced your uniforms. I don't particularly give a hoot about your personal disgrace, but when you disgrace your uniform, you disgrace *my* uniform, too."

"Yes, ma'am."

"I want you back here at 0800 tomorrow morning. In the meantime, maybe the stockade will cool you off. Maybe *I* will cool off. Nick, take 'em out of here."

Never taking his eyes off Andrea Burke, MacLendon once again stepped aside to let Nickerson and the two airmen pass. "What will you do?" he asked her.

Only then did Andrea become aware of MacLendon's presence in her office. *Damn!* she thought, feeling her face tighten even more. Wouldn't you know every blasted thing in the world would go wrong with MacLendon there to hear about it?

MacLendon watched her face tighten, watched her back stiffen, saw Andrea Burke vanish behind a cool, expressionless facade.

"I'll hang their hides out to dry," she said flatly. "It's dereliction of duty."

"Demotion?" Under Article Fifteen of the Uniform Code of Military Justice, a unit commander had the right to summarily dispense nonjudicial punishment for infractions of regulations. The stiffest penalty allowed was demotion by one grade in rank.

"Probably." Unfolding the fists that were still clenched behind her back, she consciously relaxed her posture. "Was there something you needed, Colonel?"

"No." He regarded her steadily for another moment, thinking

that he'd learned what he'd come to learn, and that he liked what he saw in this spunky young woman. "No, Captain. I got what I came for. I'll see you this evening." With that reminder, he nodded his head and left.

Chapter 2

Andrea was still objecting strenuously when she walked up to MacLendon's door that night and rapped smartly on it. She couldn't escape the conviction that if she'd been a man he wouldn't be proposing to observe her in the field. What annoyed her even more was the feeling that he had every right to question her professionalism. Whatever had possessed her to call him cowboy?

If Colonel Alisdair MacLendon was imposing in Class A blues, he was intimidating in field dress. The loose cut of the green field jacket added about four inches to his shoulders. His pistol was strapped to his waist, accentuating its narrowness. The rakishly tilted field cap had surely been designed just to give his face a dangerous look. In all, Andrea thought irritably, he made every other man she'd ever seen look like a wimp. At five foot six, she'd never felt small, but just now she felt positively diminutive. The feeling annoyed her to no end.

''Ready, sir?'' she asked, managing to keep her voice expressionless, although her chest seethed with hot emotions.

Looking down at her, MacLendon wondered if he was losing his marbles. There was no way on earth he would ever have believed a woman could look appealing in fatigues, but somehow Andrea Burke managed to look *cute.* Impossible. That concussion must have unbalanced him. There was nothing cute or feminine about the way she looked at him, however. Her gaze was straight and steady, man to man.

"Ready." He closed the door behind him and followed her down the stairs to the dark blue Air Force pickup truck.

Andrea left rubber on the asphalt of the parking lot. MacLendon looked quickly out the window so she wouldn't catch the suppressed laugh on his face. She was furious with him, he knew, but before the night was out he figured he'd have her measure. He always got the measure of his officers.

After her quick, hot-blooded start, which embarrassed her a little, Andrea settled down to the speed limit. What the heck, she told herself. He's stuck with me, too. And she had it on the best authority that she wasn't great to be stuck with.

"What's on the agenda tonight?" he asked.

"I figure on poking around the perimeter of the weapons depot. Sir." She added the last word punctiliously.

"Do you ever have a problem with the men passing the word that you're on the prowl?"

"Communications are monitored. The first idiot who tries to pull that stunt is going to answer to me."

"I see." Tough little cookie, he thought. "By the way, Captain, I'm here tonight strictly as an observer. Anything I see or hear won't go any further."

There was a moment's silence. Finally Andrea answered, hating having to say it, "Thank you, sir."

MacLendon half smiled into the dark. Spitfire, he thought. "Mind if I smoke?"

"No, sir. My whole family smokes."

"You?"

"No, sir."

"How'd you miss it?"

Again there was a pregnant silence. Turning, he saw the struggle on Andrea's face. It was over quickly, but he caught it.

"Girls," she said finally, "don't smoke."

"Oh." He lit his cigarette and cracked the window to let the smoke trail out. "But they go to the Air Force Academy and become regular officers?"

"No, they don't do that, either. But if you want something badly enough, that doesn't hold you back."

"I guess not." He felt another inkling of real respect for her. It didn't mean he was necessarily going to like having her around, or that she wouldn't be a headache, but it gave him some of her measure. "Married?"

"No, sir. Are you?"

She turned the personal question back neatly, and he decided it was time to change tacks. "No," he replied. "How long have you been at the base?"

"Two years come December." She paused, then decided to make an effort to be friendly. Only God and Uncle Sam knew how long she was going to have to put up with this cowboy. "December is a wonderful time to arrive in North Dakota. No chance to acclimate. Winter hits you like a ton of bricks."

"This is my third tour here," he offered. "There's something about surviving a North Dakota winter that leaves you feeling a little smug."

"Smug?"

"Like you went eyeball to eyeball with Mother Nature and came away whole."

She surprised him with a throaty chuckle.

"Where are you from originally, Captain?" His question was a traditional military icebreaker, a perfectly legitimate query from one transplant to another.

"All over. I'm an Air Force brat."

"Who's your father? Maybe I know him."

"Charles Burke. He retired four years ago as Chief Master Sergeant."

MacLendon suddenly swiveled to look at her better. "Charlie Burke. Was he air crew chief at Mather in '74?"

Such coincidences no longer surprised Andrea. Everywhere you went in the Air Force you met old friends or friends of friends. It was, at heart, really just a large family. "Yes, sir."

MacLendon's brain clicked. He hadn't spoken to Andrea Burke at Mather, but he'd seen her. A teenage girl in a ridiculously frilly dress at chapel on Sundays. Thin, leggy, coltish. He'd seen her a couple of times rough-and-tumbling at football and basketball with a gang of boys who all had her hair and freckles. He'd noticed her because she'd struck him as out of place in both those situations. And he knew Charlie Burke. No girl would have found it easy growing up under his thumb. Another piece of the puzzle fell into place.

He stubbed his cigarette out in the ashtray and let the subject drop. Pursuing it any further would require getting more personal than he chose to get with his officers, or than she would like to get with her CO. Nonetheless he could still recall some of Charlie Burke's more outrageous statements about God's whys and wherefores in creating women. The worst of it was, the man hadn't been joking.

So he knew her dad, Andrea thought. She waited to hear all the hearty male things men always said about her father and was surprised when they didn't come. Could it be that somebody in the world didn't think her father was the best mechanic, the best sergeant, the best good ol' boy, in the Air Force?

Everything MacLendon learned about Andrea Burke raised his opinion of her another notch. A pretty remarkable young woman, he thought, as she turned off the truck's headlights and proceeded slowly down a narrow access road toward the perimeter of the weapons depot. She was approaching from the base side of the huge, hangarlike building that sat near the Main Gate, the side from which security would least expect an illegitimate approach.

Turning the truck to one side, Andrea pulled onto the grass and switched off the ignition. In front of them, to the right, lay the alert shack where B-52 crews spent a week at a time waiting for the war they all hoped would never happen. In the old days of the cold war, they often hopped aboard those planes and flew to the Fail-Safe line. These days such alerts were much rarer, but from time to time, when a chip failed in the computers at Cheyenne Mountain, or when international tensions raised the country's defense status to a war footing, they raced to their planes and took to the air.

To the left was the weapons storage building, where nuclear warheads from both missiles and bombs were stored and repaired. Most warheads were in place on their launch vehicles or in the bellies of the bombers, but maintenance had to be performed on a rotating basis, and it was here the work was done.

Unarmed, those weapons were safe, but MacLendon always felt a swift clenching in his gut when he was near them. More than once in his career he'd taken to the air with his bomb bay full of these weapons and his blackout curtains drawn, not knowing if this was the big one.

If Andrea Burke felt a similar reaction to the destructive forces nearby, her face betrayed nothing. She looked at MacLendon. "How are you on stealthy approaches, Colonel?"

"I used to be fairly good. After I was shot down in Nam, I evaded the Vietcong for six weeks."

Andrea didn't want to be impressed. For some reason she didn't understand, she didn't want to like this man. She didn't want to respect him. She was impressed anyway.

"Well, sir," she said, "the idea is to get up to the depot without being detected."

"And if you get that far?"

Andrea's expression turned grim. "I damn well better not. If I do, there'll be hell to pay." At the back of her mind was the belief that tonight, of all nights, she was going to make it through security. Why not? Everything else had gone wrong since Alisdair MacLendon had set foot in her life. And what kind of name was Alisdair, anyway? Did people actually call him that?

"What kind of security is there inside the building?" MacLendon asked her.

"None. Once you get inside, it's assumed you have a right to be there." Seeing the dubious look on his face, she explained. "I didn't set up the security arrangements, Colonel, but I assure you they're excellent. There's only one way in or out, and as long as you guard the access adequately, you don't need internal security. The inside of the building is entirely open. The warheads sit on high platforms that allow them to be viewed clearly from any place within the hangar. It also makes it impossible to move them surreptitiously. Maybe you should arrange to take an escorted tour."

"Maybe I will."

Andrea pulled off her beret and opened the glove box. Taking out two black ski masks, she tossed one to MacLendon. "Terrorists are a big concern," she said automatically, as she pulled a mask over her head. "They'd love to get their hands on one of those little babies.'' From behind the seat she brought out an M-16.

MacLendon looked at the ski mask in his hands and then at Andrea, who sat, M-16 in her hands, head tilted questioningly. He'd trespassed far enough, he decided abruptly. He'd learned what he needed to know about her, and he had no business involving himself in her actual functioning.

''I'll wait here, Captain,'' he said. ''I'd just increase the chance of alerting the sentries.''

After the briefest hesitation, she nodded. ''Yes, sir.'' So the man knew when to back off. Well, that would make the next few years a lot easier to take. Moving silently, she climbed out of the truck and closed the door without a sound. A moment later, she'd vanished into the shadows.

MacLendon lit another cigarette and settled back to wait. Beyond any doubt he liked the cut of Andrea Burke. He'd been known to pull just such stunts as this one to check on his troops, was in fact doing precisely that by accompanying her tonight. Unless he unexpectedly found evidence to the contrary, he was pretty well convinced he could leave her to run her squadron and not worry about it. He hoped he was as fortunate in his other officers.

The door at his elbow suddenly flew open, and MacLendon found himself looking down the business end of an M-16. Lifting his eyes higher, he looked into the face of a young, somewhat nervous security policeman.

''Please step out of the truck, sir,'' the airman said. ''And don't try anything. My partner has you covered.''

Over the airman's shoulder, MacLendon saw another SP, his rifle also at the ready.

''I'm not doing anything wrong, Airman,'' MacLendon said easily. ''Sitting in a truck, smoking a cigarette, isn't a crime.''

''No, sir. Please raise your hands and step out of the truck, sir.''

Shrugging, MacLendon climbed out of the truck, keeping his hands in plain sight. The second SP, balancing his rifle in his right hand, raised his radio with his left and called for backup.

''I need to see your identification, Colonel,'' the airman said, focusing on the eagle on MacLendon's cap. "Where do you keep it?"

"In my right hip pocket. I'll get it."

"No, sir, keep your hands high. Jerry?"

"Go ahead. I've got him in my sight."

MacLendon suffered the indignity of having his right hip pocket invaded and his wallet pulled out. At the same time, the airman removed his sidearm from its holster. With a flashlight, the airman examined his ID.

"It looks valid," he said after a moment. "Sorry for the inconvenience, Colonel, but this isn't a good place to stop for a smoke. You're sitting on the edge of a controlled area."

"Is it all right if I lower my arms?"

The airman hesitated just an instant. "Go ahead. Colonel, I don't recognize you."

"I just arrived on base on Friday. You'll be seeing quite a bit of me from now on."

"Well, sir, you'd better take the truck and park someplace else."

"I can't."

Both cops stiffened. "Sir?"

"I'm waiting for someone."

The muzzles of two M-16s rose again. "Perhaps the Colonel will explain who he's waiting for at this time of night beside a controlled area," said the second cop.

MacLendon smiled. These kids were good, and he was beginning to enjoy himself. "I don't want to spoil her surprise."

"Her—holy cow! Burke's on the prowl again."

"Something tells me she won't find anything she doesn't want to," MacLendon remarked. "You two are clearly doing your jobs."

For an instant pride showed on the younger man's face, and MacLendon realized that Andrea Burke had successfully instilled in these men a recognition of the importance of their work. His respect for her took another upward hike.

"Sorry, sir," said the elder airman, a staff sergeant, "but we'll have to ask you to come with us to the security station."

"But why?" Annoyance flared in him. A colonel wasn't used

to this kind of treatment. "I showed you my ID, and I wasn't doing anything wrong."

"No, sir, but you *are* acting suspiciously," the sergeant replied.

"Suspiciously? Smoking a cigarette?"

"Refusing to move on, sir. That's suspicious."

Much as he disliked to, MacLendon had to admit they were right. This was a SAC base, Strategic Air Command, and he *had* been sitting at the edge of a controlled area right between nuclear weapons storage and the airfield where battle-ready B-52s stood waiting. Refusing to move on *did* constitute suspicious behavior, and these men clearly didn't know who he was beyond his ID. Frankly, if he hadn't been personally involved in the situation, he would have wanted the hides of these SP's for doing anything else.

Sighing, he shrugged. "Which way? And do you mind if I light another cigarette?"

"Just move slowly, sir, and light it now."

So he moved slowly, pulling the pack and lighter from the breast pocket of his field jacket. Then, with two M-16s pointed at his back, he marched toward the security station at the front of the weapons depot. Behind him the staff sergeant spoke into his radio, announcing that he was bringing in a suspect and requesting someone to cover his leg of the patrol. All very efficient and correct.

Just as they reached the front of the depot, Andrea stepped out of the front door, M-16 slung over her shoulder. She caught sight of MacLendon and the two SP's at his back, and a grin split her face.

"Well, well, well," she said slowly, the grin deepening. "What have we here?"

"You know perfectly well what 'we' have here," MacLendon snapped, his patience flying out the window at the sight of her amusement.

Andrea blinked slowly, and while she wanted to continue teasing him—his annoyance made it almost irresistible—her brain advised her it would be foolhardy. Her grin vanished.

"It's okay, Stewart. Colonel MacLendon was out there waiting for me. The Colonel is the new Bomb Wing commander."

The rifles were lowered instantly, and the two men snapped to attention.

"Actually," Andrea continued, her entire demeanor growing cool, "you made an excellent decoy, Colonel. These men were so busy moving in on the truck that I slipped right past them in the dark."

A quiet, dismayed oath escaped the sergeant. Andrea's eyes flicked over him.

"However," she continued just as coolly, "the backup you radioed for caught me, Stewart. You and Mallory get a six-pack, and so does the backup."

Six-pack? MacLendon wondered. She awarded six-packs for a job well-done? Well, it was certainly a unique command style, but he wasn't entirely certain he approved.

"Make it Coors, please, ma'am," said Stewart, relief drawing a grin from him.

"Coors it is." Andrea returned her attention to MacLendon. "Shall we go now, sir?"

"Not without my ID and sidearm," MacLendon said.

"Oh! Right, sir!" The younger airman—Mallory, he guessed—became awkward in his embarrassment, but he managed to dig MacLendon's wallet out of his pocket and the pistol from where it was tucked into his belt.

"Thank you," MacLendon said, his humor rapidly returning at the sight of a very good cop reverting to an awkward, embarrassed young man. He doubted the kid was older than nineteen. "You men did a very good job."

He was immediately rewarded with two under-arms salutes: arm straight across the chest, palm down, hand opened flat. He returned them and then looked at Andrea. "Captain?"

Not until they were in the truck and headed back to the BOQ did MacLendon speak.

"I'm favorably impressed, Captain Burke," he told her, watching her in the dim glow of the dash lights.

"Thank you, sir."

A cool customer, MacLendon thought. A very cool customer indeed. He wondered if she were naturally cool or if the glimpses of annoyance and humor she permitted to show from time to time were a more accurate clue to her nature.

For the very first time in his life, MacLendon found himself wondering what price a woman paid to succeed in a man's world. Andrea Burke was clearly succeeding, but perhaps she'd had to sublimate herself to do it.

And maybe this was really who she was and what she was. He didn't think he would ever find out, but for some odd reason he'd sure like to know.

"It's not very late," he heard himself say. "Shall we stop at the O-Club for a drink?"

Not very late, and it was Saturday night. It crossed Andrea's mind that she was leading a very unnatural life. She didn't think one other woman in the entire country spent Saturday night skulking in the shadows to check up on her subordinates.

Because she was a woman, she hesitated before answering. A man in her position would have accepted immediately, recognizing the political necessity and recognizing also the honor inherent in being asked to share a drink with the future CO. But she *was* a woman, and she had to consider appearances and the possibility of gossip. Still it was the Officers' Club, not some night spot in town. Deciding it was safe enough to accept, and wise to do so, she agreed.

"Thank you, sir."

"You're welcome, Captain." His tone faintly mocked her punctiliousness. "Loosen up, will you? I'm convinced you're an excellent officer, so relax a little."

"Yes, sir."

MacLendon sighed. "Have it your way, Burke. Maybe a couple of beers will help."

Andrea fully intended to drink ice tea, but she didn't tell him so. A wise junior officer didn't get drunk in front of bird colonels who were up for general. Heck, a junior officer didn't dare loosen up even a little bit.

Her uneasy concern that they might be alone at the bar was vanquished the instant they set foot in the club. Better than twenty years in uniform had won MacLendon a lot of friends, and he was hailed immediately by a group of colonels and majors who were playing cards at a large, round table. He moved immediately to join them.

"I'll just leave," Andrea whispered to him, starting to turn back.

MacLendon looked down at her with those icy eyes as if he could see to her soul. "Chicken," he mocked softly.

It was like pushing a button, he thought with amusement. Captain Burke's chin took on a pugnacious, determined set, and she marched toward the table. Lips twitching, MacLendon followed. He'd figured anybody raised among a gang of brothers would have an automatic response to that challenge. Someday, he decided, he was going to find out what happened when somebody double-dared her.

Andrea had met all the colonels and majors at one official function or another and was greeted pleasantly enough, albeit a touch coolly. She was perfectly aware that she would never have been invited to join them under other circumstances. Some popular male captain, perhaps, but the subtle lines of sexual discrimination still existed in social matters.

"Captain Burke is showing me around," MacLendon said in answer to a question as he took his place beside her. "So far I'm very impressed with her handling of security."

Andrea shot a surprised glance at him. His blue eyes regarded her blandly.

"In fact," he added, "I predict that she has a very bright future."

Something shifted at the table. To Andrea it was an almost audible thunk as this group of men regarded her in a new light.

"You're an Academy graduate, aren't you, Captain?" asked the Missile Wing Commander, Colonel Adams.

"Yes, sir," she said, meeting his gaze forthrightly. She was floored by what MacLendon had just done for her and thoroughly puzzled by why he had done it. She was equally puzzled by the way his opinion was accepted. He must have one heck of a reputation.

"Shall I deal you in?" asked Adams.

"What's the game?" MacLendon asked.

"Five-card stud, for chips only, no money. You know regulations."

"Can't pass that up."

"Captain?" Adams's gaze settled on her. "Do you play?"

"Yes, sir."

"Deal her in, Hal," MacLendon said. "If Burke plays poker the way she runs the security squadron, we're all in for a run for our chips."

Laughter rippled around the table, and the uncertainty that had accompanied her arrival vanished.

When a white-coated waiter appeared at MacLendon's elbow, he looked at Andrea. "What'll it be? I'm buying."

"Beer, sir," Andrea said, gritting her teeth. No way was she going to blow this chance by looking like a prissy female. She'd just drink real slow. "Thank you."

Hal Adams pushed her a stack of chips. "Do you go by any name besides Captain Burke?"

"Yes, sir. Andrea, sir."

"Well, Andrea, let's see if you play poker as well as MacLendon thinks."

Picking up her cards, Andrea wondered if it would be wise to beat MacLendon, because she was looking at a royal flush.

"Andrea?" Colonel Adams was waiting for her bet.

What the heck, Andrea thought. The hand was one in a million and wouldn't happen again. "I'll see and raise ten," she said coolly, pushing her chips in.

By midnight Andrea was on her third beer and was holding her own in the poker game. A number of officers had departed, and there were only four players left: herself, Hal Adams, MacLendon, and a major named Lew Brimley, Adams's deputy commander. She was holding her own, Andrea thought, looking at her cards but wishing desperately for her bed.

The conversation around the table had been desultory but enlightening nonetheless. From it, Andrea had learned quite a lot about MacLendon. He'd served two tours in Vietnam and had ended the second one by being shot down. When he crawled out of the jungle after six weeks, he'd lost forty-five pounds and was suffering from so many parasites that it had taken the military doctors six months to get him back into fighting trim.

He'd never flown with the Thunderbirds, as rumored, but he'd test-piloted at Edwards Air Force Base for a few years and had flown SR-71 Blackbirds, the high-altitude spy planes, for three years. This would be his third stint as a wing commander. In all, MacLendon sounded like an ideal selection for general.

Andrea, her eyelids heavy from fatigue and beer, almost sighed. If she were a man, she'd be shooting for those stars, too. As a woman, however, she was aware she'd be doing well indeed to make full colonel.

"I'm folding," MacLendon said suddenly, putting down his cards. "It's been a long day. Burke?"

"Yes, sir." Relieved, Andrea laid down her cards. "It's been long for me, too." Mainly because of MacLendon.

He bid her good-night at the door of the enclosed walkway that connected the Officers' Club with the BOQ, and Andrea watched him walk away with a sigh of relief at being once again alone. She didn't tell him that her quarters were only two doors down the hall from his, even though it might create misunderstanding when he discovered it himself, as he inevitably would. At the moment she didn't especially care if he took it the wrong way. Right now she could even wish for preequal opportunity days, dinosaur days, when men and women had been relegated to separate floors. Rubbing her neck to ease the tension, she waited until she was certain he would have reached his quarters, and only then did she follow.

Shower and bed, she thought wearily. The radio on her hip reminded her that the night might be interrupted, but for once she allowed herself to believe that fortune would favor her.

Just as she was entering her room, however, she remembered Butcher and Frankel, the men who'd been arrested for brawling on duty. Damn and double damn! All sleepiness fled as she realized she had to deal with them first thing in the morning.

After flinging clothes this way and that in her annoyance, she stepped into the shower and turned her face into the hot spray. With her eyes closed, however, it was not Butcher and Frankel she saw, but Colonel Alisdair MacLendon. Why did he have to be so almighty attractive and virile? She couldn't afford to be attracted to him. He was her commanding officer, her superior, her…

Nemesis. The word floated into her weary mind like a whispered warning. So much for sleep.

Chapter 3

"How'd it go?"

Andrea turned from the window where she'd been staring out at the leaden sky and found Colonel MacLendon standing in her doorway, leaning against the doorjamb. This morning it was she who was decked out in blues, her tunic and skirt sculpting a lean figure, and MacLendon who wore civvies: gray slacks and sweater.

Irritation flared in Andrea. Couldn't the man leave her alone? He was sticking to her like a burr. What the devil was going on? She turned back to the window, folding her arms beneath her breasts, just plain not caring that tomorrow morning he was going to be her CO.

MacLendon saw her irritation, but before that he had seen her loneliness. There was nothing quite like the isolation of command, and when the decisions became tough, the isolation was virtually absolute. For a little while, when Andrea hadn't known she was being observed, her shoulders had slumped and her head had drooped. Just now MacLendon was feeling a little sympathetic.

"Demotion?" he asked.

"Yes."

"No other way?"

She turned, green eyes blazing, furious that he was questioning her judgment. "Does the Colonel see another way?"

"Is the Captain requesting my opinion?"

Her lips thinned. Funny, MacLendon thought, he hadn't noticed just how soft and appealing her mouth was until she made it thin and hard.

"Yes, sir," she said, the words falling into the room like a thrown gauntlet. The sharp lift of her chin defied him to criticize her decision. She'd lain awake half the night agonizing over this, well aware that she was about to stigmatize the careers of two young men. That enormous, frightening power was hers by virtue of her command responsibility, a duty to protect the security of the United States. No amount of sympathy or understanding could permit her to abrogate that duty. It sure hurt, though, she found herself thinking as she braced for MacLendon's answer. And all of a sudden she realized that it *mattered* what he thought of her decision.

"In my opinion," he replied quietly, "there was nothing else you could do. It wasn't the brawl, it was the situation they were in."

Something in her relaxed, and she turned back to the window to conceal her relief from him. She hardly knew the man, and it unsettled her to realize that his opinion was important.

"That's the devil of it," she said presently. "If they'd been on almost any other kind of duty..." She left the sentence incomplete. The military put up with a lot of things because many of its members were very young males. A brawl in the barracks would at most earn a reprimand. A series of brawls might lead to a day or two in the stockade. A brawl between two guys who were guarding nuclear warheads was something else altogether.

"Is there something I can do for you, Colonel?" she thought to ask, wishing he would just go away. She needed solitude to sort out her strangely tangled feelings. Worse, his presence seemed to be tangling those feelings even more.

"Actually, no," he answered, stepping farther into her office. "The fact is, I've been exactly where you are. Not every commander faces a decision like this, but too many of us do. I figured you wouldn't be feeling any too happy about it, so I dropped by. I realize I can't say or do anything to make it easier. Doing your duty isn't always easy."

"No, it's not." Why was he being so sympathetic? Andrea wondered. Yesterday he'd seemed determined to drive her crazy.

Staring at her rigid back, MacLendon decided this visit hadn't been one of his better ideas. "You know where to find me if you want to talk."

"The colonel is very kind," Andrea said stiffly.

MacLendon laughed. "Minx."

Andrea spun around. "I beg your pardon?"

MacLendon's lips twitched. "Just so you know, Captain, your little zingers don't pass me by unnoticed."

Hot color started to flood Andrea's cheeks, but MacLendon had already begun to turn away.

"Oh, Captain Burke?" He glanced back.

"Sir?"

"I also stopped by to tell you that I always thought your father was a horse's ass."

Andrea's mouth was still hanging open when MacLendon's footsteps had faded from the building. Only then did she start to grin. "A horse's ass?" she repeated out loud, and decided she liked that description a lot. In fact, merely imagining how Charlie Burke would have looked if he'd heard himself called that by a man of MacLendon's stature was enough to make the day a whole lot brighter.

Throughout the following week, winter edged more deeply into North Dakota. Monday morning there was the change of command ceremony for MacLendon, followed by a formal luncheon at the Officers' Club. That night there was a Hail and Farewell reception for the incoming and outgoing commanders. Colonel Houlihan, MacLendon's predecessor, practically danced through the whole thing, excited about his new posting to the Pentagon and eager to be off.

Andrea hated this kind of stuff and trudged her way through it grimly, hoping her radio would rescue her. For once the damn brick was utterly silent, issuing not a single squawk.

All week long her brick remained uncharacteristically silent. It was as if the fight at the depot had infused her sometimes reckless troops with a new sobriety. The pall of the demotion hung over everything.

MacLendon had left her alone all week, except to nod when he saw her. He was interested in other elements of his command, and the rest of the base's units had the dubious honor of his undivided attention. Evidently he had made up his mind about Andrea.

Friday night she worked late. Darkness arrived early in North Dakota in early November, and the temperature had edged down into the teens. Outside, the ceaseless wind moaned, a forlorn sound that suited her mood perfectly.

"Do you work all the time?"

Andrea looked up and found MacLendon standing in her doorway. The sight of him both surprised and amused her. She was glad of the distraction from her gloomy thoughts.

"Do I make you feel guilty, Colonel?" she asked.

His lips twitched. This time she saw it, and a small answering smile came to her face.

"I've been wondering," he said, "what you do with your free time." Actually, he'd been wondering a whole lot more than that about her, but this was the only question he felt certain wouldn't make her snap his head off.

"Free time?" Her tone was enough to answer the question.

"Captain Burke," he said, "I'm giving you a direct order."

"Yes, sir."

"Find somebody to replace you this weekend and leave that damn brick on your desk."

"If I can."

He straightened. "You do have a deputy commander."

"Yes, sir."

"Then call him. Now."

Standing there and waiting for her to obey, he left her no alternative. Mildly irritated, she picked up the phone and called Lieutenant Dolan. He sounded as thrilled as she felt. Then she called Operations and informed them. How the devil, she wondered, was she going to stand a weekend cooped up in the BOQ with nothing to do?

When she hung up the phone, there was a spark of defiance

in her green eyes. MacLendon was glad to see it. It had been missing all week. He began to zip up his parka.

"I'm going to the mall," he said.

She studied him in silence, wondering why he'd told her that. It was none of her business, surely, where he chose to go. There was something personal in his presence here, she realized with a fluttering sensation in her stomach. When he finished zipping his parka, his blue eyes locked with hers, and she saw something that made her feel oddly edgy, as if she were craving something but couldn't tell what.

"I have thirteen nieces and nephews," he remarked, "and it's almost Christmas."

"Don't you like Christmas, Colonel?"

One corner of his mouth lifted. "I like the idea of Christmas. I always think of roaring fires and brandy and good company. In my entire career, I haven't spent one Christmas like that. I've eaten more chow hall Christmas turkeys than I want to think about. The worst of it, though, is buying gifts for the kids. I just don't seem to know what they'd like. It's hell, Captain."

"It sounds like it," she managed to answer steadily, although the fluttering in her stomach now felt like rising bubbles of laughter.

He regarded her with an elevated brow. "Are you laughing at me, Captain Burke?"

"I wouldn't dream of it, Colonel." But she could feel the corners of her mouth tugging upward and knew he saw it by the smile that suddenly creased his cheeks and crinkled the corners of his eyes. It was, she thought with a swiftly indrawn breath, an unfairly devastating smile in a man who was already unfairly attractive.

"What about you?" he asked. "How many nieces and nephews do you shop for?"

Andrea ran a rapid mental check. "Nineteen."

"A fellow sufferer, I see. Do you find it difficult?"

"No, sir."

He looked at her steadily for a moment. "I don't suppose—" He bit off the sentence and turned to leave. "Good night, Captain."

"Colonel?"

Her cool voice caught him before he took his third step away. He walked back.

"Yes?"

Her face felt odd, and her stomach certainly felt odder, as she said, "My car's been acting a little funny lately. Could I possibly hitch a ride to the mall with you?"

He allowed himself another smile. "On one condition, Captain. That you help me figure out what to buy for all those kids."

"I'll be glad to help. I enjoy shopping for children."

The remark surprised him. He'd figured that Andrea avoided anything that sounded even remotely feminine, as if femininity were a plague.

"I'll pick you up in an hour, then," he said. "What's your room?"

"225," she answered.

Two doors down from him, he thought as he walked away. Interesting.

Andrea had learned enough about the loneliness of command, particularly in the past week, to recognize it in MacLendon when she saw it. He'd been about to make a simple, friendly request for her assistance, then had dropped it because she was his subordinate officer and under no circumstances could he make such a claim on her private time. Particularly when that request might be viewed as sexist, although it had been perfectly natural when she professed herself an experienced shopper for nieces and nephews.

Andrea sighed and picked up her parka. Sometimes being a woman in a man's world could be a royal pain. Most of the time she managed simply not to think about it, but other times it reared up and stared her in the face. Why did this tension have to exist? It had always been present with her father, but with her brothers it had been completely absent. Most of the time it stayed out of her relationships with her troops and fellow officers. Every so often, however, she was reminded that she was an anomaly, that what she was and what she wanted to be were not always how the rest of the world viewed her.

Damn! she thought, and slammed her office door behind her. Double damn!

When MacLendon knocked on her door an hour later, she

was ready to go. Dressed in jeans, wool shirt, and a commercial survival parka that was considerably warmer than government issue, she wasn't surprised to find MacLendon dressed similarly. Stepping outside with him, she pulled up her hood and tugged on her mittens.

"There's another cold front coming through tonight," he remarked as he turned onto the highway toward town. "Supposed to get down to around zero."

"That's warm for this place. Or would be, if it were January." The car's heater was beginning to catch up with the chill, and she pulled her hood off.

"What's wrong with your car?" he asked.

"Choke's sticking, I think. It stalls at stop signs and other convenient places."

"I'll take a look at it tomorrow."

Andrea swiveled her head to look at him. "Colonel—"

"Dare," he said patiently. "We're off duty, and you can call me Dare."

"Oh. I wondered about Alisdair. It's a mouthful."

"Old Scottish name," he chuckled. "There's one in every generation of MacLendons."

"About my car—"

"If it's a sticky choke," he interrupted, "I can fix it in about thirty seconds. No problem."

"No, it's not a problem," she agreed. "I can fix it myself. I just haven't gotten to it."

There was a pregnant silence. They seemed to share an awful lot of those, for some reason, Andrea found herself thinking irritably.

Finally he spoke, his voice silky. "Did I just step on your feminist toes, Andrea?"

"No, sir. It's just that I can't see letting my CO do something I'm perfectly capable of doing for myself, especially when it involves his free time."

"And I suppose you think your CO is incapable of deciding for himself how to spend his free time?"

"No, sir." Her cheeks were growing warm. "It never entered my head." She seemed to have an absolute genius for saying the wrong thing to this man.

"Did it occur to you that since you're doing your CO a favor he might want to return it?"

"I thought you were doing me a favor. You're giving me a lift to the mall."

"Andrea..." His voice had grown dangerous.

"Sir?"

"Shut up."

"Yes, sir."

And damn it, he thought, if she didn't stay silent as a clam all the way to the mall. It wasn't until they were strolling to the toy store that he realized she was going to stay quiet all night because he'd told her to. He glanced at her with frustration.

"Andrea."

"Sir?"

"Talk."

"Yes, sir." She cocked her head, and he caught the gleam in her eye. "About what, sir?"

"Anything that takes your fancy. And stop calling me 'sir.'"

"Yes, sir."

A muffled sound escaped him. She was utterly unable to tell if it was rage or laughter. Certainly the ice in his blue eyes was suddenly replaced by fire.

"Andrea," he said, drawing up short to face her.

"Sir?"

"Has anyone ever told you that it can be dangerous to drive your CO crazy? He just might be tempted to make your life miserable."

Her expression became one of perfect innocence. "I'm only trying to follow orders."

"We're off duty, Andrea."

"Yes, sir."

"Act like it."

"Yes, sir."

He took a menacing step toward her. "I told you to stop calling me 'sir.'" Her mouth opened, and for an instant he thought the imp in her would drive her to say 'yes, sir' anyway, but suddenly a laugh escaped her, and humor filled her hazy green eyes with warmth.

"Okay," she said.

"Thank God," he said with exaggerated relief. "I was beginning to think I'd have to strangle you to get you to stop that."

"No, sir," she said, and darted away laughing just as he turned on her. "I promise," she said, grinning, holding up a hand and backing away from him. "Not again. I won't do it again!"

"If you do, I'll leave you to walk back to base," he growled, his anger belied by the twinkle in his eye.

"Scout's honor. I won't say the s-word again this evening."

Her eyes sparkled, her cheeks glowed pink, and for the first time since he'd met her, Andrea Burke didn't look like a woman who was trying her damnedest to be someone else. No, he corrected himself, she'd also been herself the night she aided him after the accident. Her imp had come out then, too, and her concern for him had been genuine and warm. Too often, however, she appeared to be inhibiting her natural liveliness in favor of some sexless, sterile image of her role. But then, he reminded himself sternly, how well did he really know her? Just because he'd spent the better part of his evenings for a week wondering how to get behind that facade...

Andrea's attention was suddenly caught by the sight of a small artificial Christmas tree in a shop window.

"Maybe I should get one of those for my quarters," she said almost wistfully. "I really miss having a tree."

"Just once I'd like to get out of having to put one up."

Andrea glanced up at him in question.

"I'll be moving into family housing in two weeks," MacLendon explained. Rank had its privileges, like a three-bedroom house for a bachelor colonel. "I'll be expected to do the usual holiday entertaining, so I'll have a tree and all the rest of the trimmings."

"Don't you like Christmas trees?" He was beginning to sound like Scrooge, Andrea thought with amusement.

"The trees are okay. All of it's okay. It's just that it's a pain to do it alone, and it always makes me so damn blue."

"Couldn't you spend the holidays with your family?"

"I could, but then my deputy would be stuck here. He wants to visit his family in Georgia."

Andrea nodded, understanding. As a bachelor officer, she'd

always felt obliged to work through the holidays so men with families and others who wanted to go home could do so. She sent Dare MacLendon a glance from the corner of her eye. "You need a wife. Then *she* could do all the decorating and plan all the entertaining."

"That's usually how it works, isn't it?" he agreed, never missing a beat. "A woman who marries an Air Force officer might as well enlist herself."

"I hear it's the same in corporate America," Andrea said after a moment.

"Is that why you haven't married?" MacLendon asked, taking her by surprise.

Andrea blinked, speechless.

He looked down at her, smiling faintly. "Yes, I asked a personal question. Are you going to answer me?"

Andrea glanced down at the terrazzo floor and then back up. "Truthfully, I just haven't *wanted* to get married."

Dare thought he could understand that, considering how Charlie Burke had treated his wife, like some beast of burden.

"What about you?" Andrea asked unexpectedly, her cheeks pink again.

"A personal question for a personal question, huh? I was married once, long, long ago. It didn't survive my second tour in Nam. Maureen discovered that the reality of being a pilot's wife didn't live up to the imaginings." Deliberately he returned his gaze to the artificial tree in the window. "Come on, Andrea," he said, "let's go get you your tree."

"But I—"

Icy blue eyes glanced her way. "You want it, don't you? Then buy it."

Once again annoyed, Andrea followed him. She didn't like being maneuvered into something, even if it was something she'd been about to do anyway. The man was clearly so used to ordering everyone around that he did it even when he was off duty. He most definitely needed a wife, one who didn't have a docile bone in her body, to keep him in line. Overbearing, that was what he was.

Dare thoroughly enjoyed the next half hour. Watching Andrea trying to remain cool and distant because of her irritation with him, while at the same time she was so clearly enjoying herself, amused him. She kept her remarks to monosyllables, but her hazy green eyes sparkled with pleasure as she selected delicate ornaments.

When her purchases were made, MacLendon insisted on carrying them out to his new Bronco himself and told Andrea he'd meet her at the toy store.

She was hovering over the stuffed animals, trying to decide which one would most thrill a two-year-old niece, when a hesitantly cleared throat drew her attention. Looking up, she saw a young man in jeans and a military survival parka, the one uniform item that was permitted to be worn with civvies. Focusing on the young, nervous face, Andrea struggled to identify him.

"You're Jones, aren't you?" she said after a moment.

"Yes, ma'am." He shifted nervously from one foot to the other.

Andrea smiled. "Are you Christmas shopping, too?"

"No, ma'am. I'm here with some friends to see a movie. I saw you come in here and—" He licked his lips and looked down at the floor.

"Do you need to talk to me?" Andrea asked gently.

"Yes, ma'am." The airman looked relieved. "I know you're off duty, but..."

"But it can't wait till Monday."

"I don't want anybody to know I talked to you," he said miserably. "I heard some things."

"Where are your friends?"

"They just went into the movie. I said I had to use the latrine."

Andrea nodded. "Can you talk here?"

Jones glanced around. "I guess...."

He sounded so nervous that Andrea decided they'd better find a more private place. "You know the coffee shop around the corner? The one that's so dimly lighted you can't see the menu?"

Jones nodded.

"I'll meet you there in a few minutes. I'm here with somebody, and I'll have to tell him where I'll be."

"Yes, ma'am." Looking immensely relieved, Jones scuttled off.

MacLendon had entered the store in time to see the encounter and, recognizing the young man's nervousness, had hung back at a discreet distance. When Jones vanished around the corner, he approached Andrea.

"What's up?" he asked.

She looked at him, her smoky green eyes puzzled. "I'm not sure. He's got something to tell me, but he doesn't want anyone to know about it. I said I'd meet him at the coffee shop."

MacLendon nodded. "Go ahead. I'll potter around here."

"Thank you."

Was she never going to call him Dare? he wondered as he watched her stride away. She walked with a boy's easy gait, he noticed, but because she was a woman, it made her rear sway in a fashion that was definitely not boyish. Sternly, MacLendon called his eyes to order and turned them to the stuffed animals. Maybe little Jenny would like a stuffed koala.

Jones had picked the coffee shop's darkest corner, and in his olive drab parka he was almost invisible. Andrea took a moment to locate him. When she slid into the booth across from him, he started like a frightened deer.

"Relax, Airman," she told him. "I almost couldn't find you, and I was looking for you. Nobody else will ever notice you." Glancing at the waitress, she ordered two coffees and two crullers.

"What happened, Jones?"

He looked up, his expression anguished. "I feel like a rat fink."

"Sometimes we have to be rat finks. It's never fun."

He nodded and drew a deep breath. "I heard a couple of guys talking at the barracks. They weren't sure what to do about it, but I remembered those security briefings we get, about how it's not up to us to make decisions about things, but to follow the rules."

"That's right," Andrea said encouragingly. "If everybody makes up their own rules about the handling of classified information, pretty soon there are no rules at all. That's why you always have to report a violation. Has there been a violation?"

"I think so."

"Tell me about it," Andrea prompted.

Just then the waitress brought the coffee and crullers, and Jones sat back, obviously still waging his internal battle. When the waitress left, he seemed to make up his mind.

"As near as I can tell, it happened at a missile site last week during the change of crew. The crew in the hole came up and were on the helipad before the relief crew even got off the chopper."

Andrea drew a long, deep breath and expelled it slowly. "So the code book was unguarded during that time."

"Yes, ma'am."

Cupping her hands around her mug, Andrea looked down into the dark brew. Missile crews, two-man teams, spent a week at a time buried deep beneath the earth in the command capsule, or hole, as their crews called it. While there, they waited for the code from Cheyenne Mountain that would tell them to turn the key and launch their Minuteman missiles. In that hole with them was the so-called code book, a highly secret document that contained the active launch codes for each day of the year. Andrea didn't even want to think about what could happen if those codes were compromised and no one knew about it.

The book, it was true, was kept locked in a safe, but because of its extremely high classification, mechanical safety measures were considered insufficient. In fact, the codes had to be guarded continuously by persons with an equally high security clearance. The missile crewmen themselves fulfilled that function, which meant that one crew could not leave the capsule until the relief crew entered to take over.

"Jones," she said, "you did absolutely the right thing in telling me. Now I've got to know who was talking about this so I can pinpoint the missile crew that was involved."

Ten minutes later she rejoined MacLendon in the toy store. He didn't ask what had happened, and she didn't volunteer.

"I'm afraid I need to get back to the base, Colonel," she told him.

"Let's go, then."

Walking quickly beside him, trying to keep up with his much longer legs, Andrea flirted with the thought of how nice it was to be out with a man who didn't question the demands of her job. On those rare occasions when she dated, she avoided military men simply because she couldn't afford to stir up any kind of gossip in the tight-knit community that was an Air Force base. While she wasn't dating MacLendon—that was out of the question—it was still a pleasant experience not to get any arguments.

Falling a little behind, she got a good look at his tight backside and long legs in those snug jeans, and it caused the oddest tightening sensation in her belly. She blinked and missed a step, astonished by her reaction to the view. She'd never looked at a man like that before. In fact, she'd always believed only men looked at women like that.

"Andrea?"

MacLendon drew up short and looked back.

"Sorry, I'm walking too fast for you," he apologized when she caught up.

"No problem, Colonel," she answered expressionlessly, thinking she was glad he had, because she wouldn't have missed that view for the world. On the other hand, the world would have remained a distinctly more comfortable place without that sudden, unwelcome awareness.

Halfway back to the base, Andrea became aware that MacLendon was talking and she hadn't heard a word he'd said.

"—always invite a group of bachelor officers," he was saying.

"Colonel? I'm sorry, I was woolgathering and didn't hear you."

"I was talking about Thanksgiving."

"Oh."

"I was saying that I always invite bachelor officers from my command who don't have other plans for the holidays."

"Yes, s—I mean, yes."

"Will you join me for Thanksgiving, Andrea?"

Something flickered in her hazy green eyes, and she looked quickly away. Her heart had just developed a disturbing tendency to leap into her throat.

"Andrea." His voice had grown quiet. "Bachelor officers do what they can to get through the holidays. That's all I'm saying. I've always made it a policy to share the holidays with any of my officers who don't have family and aren't going home. I expect there'll be a half-dozen or so this year."

She managed to look up, her Huck Finn face composed. "I like to cook Thanksgiving dinner, but it seems like so much trouble just for me."

And impossible in the BOQ, he thought. "Then let's cook Thanksgiving dinner together and tell war stories so we don't get blue and lonely. Deal?"

She smiled suddenly. "Deal."

Chapter 4

"What I want to know," Andrea said to the two security policemen who sat across her desk from her later that evening, "is why you didn't tell me the missile crew left the hole and came above ground to the helipad before the relief crew went down."

Sergeant Nickerson stood off to one side, his lean, lined face expressionless as he watched the two young airmen exchange unhappy looks.

"Well, ma'am," said the elder of the two, a buck sergeant named Wilson, "the book was unguarded, but nobody went into that hole. We were both at our posts, and nobody could have gotten past us to go down into the hole. So nothing happened, not really."

"Except that the missile crew violated security, several regulations, and their orders. Who set you two up as judge and jury, Wilson?"

"No one, ma'am," Wilson answered miserably. "But you gotta understand."

"I have to understand what? Make this clear to me, Wilson, because you're skating on very thin ice right now."

Wilson shifted uneasily in his chair. "Well, ma'am, it's about Lieutenant Cantrell."

"Who is Lieutenant Cantrell?"

"The commander of the crew that was in the hole, Captain."

"The man primarily responsible for this escapade, I take it?"

"I guess so. You see, his wife was in an auto accident just a couple of hours earlier. I expect he was half out of his mind worrying."

"Very likely," Andrea said coolly. "I have to question his fitness to be in a missile crew if he can't think any more clearly than he did in this instance. I imagine he reached his wife's side all of five minutes sooner by leaving the hole before being relieved. And during those minutes the code book was uncovered, and all the Minuteman missiles he was responsible for were effectively out of action, as surely as if they had been sabotaged."

"Yes, ma'am, but Hart and I was there. Nobody got to the codes."

"That brings me to another point," Andrea said sternly. "You two aren't cleared to guard that book, yet you were effectively responsible for it during that time period. While I don't doubt that you would have protected it with your lives, right now I'm doubtful about *your* judgment, as well as Cantrell's. You should have told me about this *immediately.*"

"Yes, ma'am," two voices mumbled.

"I'm afraid you're both going to receive a written reprimand under Article Fifteen for this. Don't give me cause to write you another one."

After the two SP's left her office, Andrea looked up at Nickerson. "You have something to add?"

Nick shook his head. "No, Captain. You're absolutely right about the gravity of what happened. I'll see that those two yo-yos write a complete report on this."

"And now," Andrea sighed, "I've got to call Colonel Adams. Boy, is he going to love this."

"Better him than us," Nick said with a faint smile. "Are you still leaving Dolan in charge for the rest of the weekend?"

"What weekend? I think this little mess just put paid to that.

How much do you want to bet Adams wants to handle everything right now?''

''I'm not a betting man, Captain.''

''Smart, Nick. Really smart.'' Sighing again, she reached for the blasted phone.

Andrea was right: Adams wanted to handle it immediately, and his mood wasn't improved by the fact that he'd just climbed into bed when Andrea rousted him out. She had to escort Wilson and Hart over to Colonel Adams's office and wait while he questioned them. Then they had to wait again while he radioed the relief crew, who were still out in their hole somewhere in the barren reaches of wintry North Dakota, to confirm the cops' story. Once he had the confirmation, Adams asked Andrea to send out a truck to pick up Lieutenants Cantrell and Morrell from their nice warm beds so they could personally explain their actions.

Though it was well past three when Andrea at last tumbled into bed, sleep stubbornly eluded her. She told herself she was just keyed up from all the activity and excitement, but some part of her acknowledged that she was more frustrated than excited. The simple fact was that she'd been enjoying herself immensely at the mall with Dare MacLendon. For the first time ever, she resented the intrusion of her job into her private time.

What might have happened if the evening had drawn to a normal close?

Aw, cut it out! she told herself, and pounded her pillow into a more comfortable shape. She'd avoided any entanglements of that kind in favor of her career for a long time now. Besides, nothing could or would happen, given that Dare was her commanding officer. It wasn't that such things were forbidden by regulation, because they weren't. Andrea was acutely conscious, however, of how a relationship with her commanding officer would appear. A woman simply couldn't afford such appearances.

But a woman could, and did, lie in the dark and wonder what it would feel like to be held by a certain pair of strong arms against the warmth and strength of a certain body. And she could wonder just how much a person was supposed to sacrifice for a career.

By Monday morning the entire base was buzzing about the missile crew that had abandoned its post and was facing a general court martial. A good month for the legal business, Andrea thought glumly as she trudged her way over to the Bomb Wing for the Monday morning staff meeting. The Judge Advocate General's corps, or JAG, were probably tap-dancing with delight. If so, the lawyers were the only ones. It never ceased to amaze her how drastically a whole life could be altered by one moment of foolishness. It also never ceased to amaze her how fast gossip could pass among fifteen thousand people. Military communications should only be as effective as the base grapevine.

The officers around the conference table all sprang to attention when MacLendon entered the room. He looked gorgeous again, Andrea thought sourly, as she watched him make his way to the head of the table. This morning he wore the long-sleeved light blue shirt with dark blue shoulder tabs and necktie, and there was no question in Andrea's mind that he'd had that shirt specially made to fit his broad shoulders and narrow waist. Nobody else in the room had a fit like that. Of course, nobody else had quite his build, either.

As she'd expected, her unit's conduct in the affair of the missile crew was the first item on MacLendon's agenda. His icy blue eyes showed no hint of warmth as he questioned her closely about how events had unfolded and how she had handled them. And finally he asked the question she'd been dreading.

"Why didn't you tell me about this Friday night, as soon as you knew what was happening, Captain?"

Her chin lifted. "When I had ascertained the facts in the matter, sir, Colonel Adams was the commander most directly involved and the one who most immediately needed to be notified. As soon as that was taken care of, I wrote a report, which was on your desk by 0830 Saturday morning, detailing the conduct of my troops and my actions. I did not imagine that a couple of Article Fifteens needed your immediate attention."

Dare leaned back in his chair, rubbing his chin, never taking his eyes from her. Not another soul at the table stirred, sensing a confrontation.

"I suppose," Dare said presently, "that Colonel Houlihan would have agreed with you?"

"I believe so, sir."

"Ordinarily I would agree that an Article Fifteen doesn't need my immediate attention. In this case, however, something greater was involved, namely the possible compromise of the launch codes and the related conduct of airmen under my command. I don't expect to hear about every brawl and AWOL, but a matter of this nature should be brought to my attention immediately."

"Very well, sir." Her gaze met his steadily and unwaveringly.

Dare nodded. "Other than this very minor complaint," he continued more pleasantly, "I commend your handling of the matter, Captain. Now, on to other matters."

For the next half hour MacLendon listened to reports and fielded complaints from his staff. Most of the matters under discussion had little to do with Andrea, so she listened with only half an ear, the rest of her longing for an end to this meeting so she could get back to her own office and away from Dare's disturbing presence. Why the devil had she been stupid enough to agree to spend Thanksgiving with him?

It was with relief that she heard her radio squawk. Since the squadron knew where she was, it must be urgent.

"Alpha Tango Niner, this is Bravo One, do you read?"

Andrea looked up at Dare. "By your leave, sir?"

"Go ahead, Burke."

She started to rise to leave the room, but MacLendon motioned her to remain, so she answered the call.

"Bravo One, this is Alpha Tango Niner, go ahead."

"Alpha Tango Niner, we have an electronic security system failure—repeat, system failure—at Delta Three Zulu."

"Roger, Bravo One. Who's out there? Over."

"Sergeant Nickerson, ma'am. When the call came in he took a squad out. Over."

"Tell Nick I'll be there in twenty minutes. Alpha Tango Niner out."

Andrea looked up at Dare. "With your permission, sir."

"This needs your immediate attention?"

"Sergeant Nickerson evidently thinks so, sir."

"Evidently. Go ahead, but this time I want a report as soon as you know what's happened."

"Yes, sir." Steaming and barely able to conceal it, Andrea hurried from the room. Damn the man! she thought. Houlihan had trusted her enough to handle things her own way. Why did MacLendon have to be so damn nosy? Nosy and attractive. The combination was going to drive her out of her mind. Maybe she ought to put in for a new assignment at a base far, far away. Like maybe the moon.

By the time she reached Nickerson, who was on the far side of the airfield alongside the perimeter fence that separated the flight-line controlled area from acres of open land, Andrea had decided Alisdair MacLendon was a jinx. In the entire two years she'd commanded this squadron, she hadn't had as many major problems as she'd had in the weeks since Dare arrived. Just when she didn't need a nosy CO, she had one. There had to be some kind of cosmic connection there.

"What's up, Nick?" she asked the master sergeant as she climbed out of her truck.

The lines in Nick's face deepened. "Did you get roasted?"

"Only as much as I expected. What's wrong now?"

"You're feeling that way, too? Well, ma'am, somebody cut the fence."

"Last night?" Andrea scanned the chain-link fence but couldn't see the damage. "Where?"

"That's the thing, ma'am. Whoever did it is planning to come back. He fixed it so it wouldn't show, and none of the pressure sensors, trip wires or infrared detectors were triggered at any time, so we have to assume he didn't try to go any farther."

Andrea cursed under her breath and followed Nickerson to the fence, where he showed her the careful cuts in the links and the way they'd been wrapped with lead wire so the weight of the fence didn't pull the links apart, exposing the hole.

"If Lattimer hadn't been paying close attention," Nick said, "he'd never have spotted this. Frankly, this could have been here a while." Pulling his hat from his head, he ran his fingers through his hair and peered up at the barbed wire that topped the fence.

The fence wasn't electrified, because its purpose was not so much to keep an intruder out as to prevent anyone from stumbling accidentally onto the carpet of sensors that lay beyond, and to leave physical evidence if someone crossed the boundary. Security experts had long ago realized that it was impossible to stop a skilled, determined intruder. What had to be avoided at all costs was the possibility that an intruder could gain access and leave no sign of his presence. As long as the intrusion could be detected, the damage could be controlled.

"I don't believe this," Andrea muttered. "I absolutely don't believe this." Looking past the fence to the airfield where the B-52s stood in their hulking line, she shook her head. "Why would anybody want to get in there?" The question was purely rhetorical; offhand she could think of twenty or so reasons ranging from sabotage to intelligence collection to sheer curiosity.

"Unless we've become a terrorist target, I can't imagine," was Nick's sarcastic response.

"Gee, Nick, what a great thought."

He gave her a humorless half smile. "You got a better one, Captain?"

"I wish I did. Kids. I like the idea of kids playing a stupid game."

"Me, too. I ain't buying it."

"Me either." Andrea gave in and rubbed her neck. "Kids wouldn't have wired up the cuts that way. I'm beginning to wonder if I'm going to spend the rest of my life standing on Colonel MacLendon's carpet trying to explain things. Hellfire. Now I've got to recommend that he make sure those planes are checked out real good. He's going to love this!"

"About as much as you do, ma'am."

"Well, post a couple of sentries out here, get somebody out to repair the fence, and send a squad to check the rest of the perimeter."

"Yes, ma'am."

Andrea, already on her way to the truck, looked back. "And, Nick, say a prayer that that cut isn't just a decoy."

Nick's faint smile faded. "Gee, Captain, what a great thought."

"Yes, I think so, too."

* * *

Thirty minutes later, Andrea stood at rigid attention on the carpet in front of MacLendon's desk and watched the frown form on his rugged face as she explained what Nick had found. When she fell silent, Dare remained silent, too, so long that she began to get uneasy.

Finally he stirred and waved a hand. "Sit, down, Andrea. Is life here always this exciting?"

"Only the last few weeks," she replied as she perched on the edge of a straight-backed metal chair.

"Well, we're batting close to a thousand, aren't we."

Relieved that he was shouldering the responsibility along with her, rather than trying to place blame somewhere, Andrea nodded. "Yes, sir, it seems that way."

"Well, I'll send the maintenance crews out to look for anything suspicious, and I guess I'd better cancel the generation scheduled for this afternoon."

A generation was an exercise when the entire bomber fleet took off at thirty-second intervals, as they would have to in time of alert. Andrea always found it impressive.

"I think that would be wise," she agreed.

MacLendon, who'd been staring thoughtfully at a pencil he was rolling between his palms, suddenly looked at her. "You don't think there's any connection between this and that intruder alert you had the night I arrived?"

"That was a faulty circuit."

"But what caused it?"

Andrea shifted on the chair. "We don't know. We never did manage to pin it down."

"It wasn't a component failure?"

"No, sir. Halliday—he's my electronics expert—said a PCB, printed circuit board, had come loose from a connector. It's impossible to determine how that happened. It may never have been seated correctly, and a small jar could have loosened it."

"Or *someone* could have loosened it."

Andrea said nothing, merely met his gaze steadily.

Dare leaned forward, tossing down the pencil and resting his elbows on the desk. "In light of this incident, maybe we'd better consider the possibility that that board didn't come loose by accident. I'm not paranoid, Andrea, but I think it's time to assume the worst until we find out what's going on."

"Yes, sir." She wished he wouldn't lean forward on his arms like that. The posture pulled his sleeves tight across his upper arms and revealed some very respectable biceps. For the first time she realized that Dare not only had a great shape, he had great muscles, as well. Once again she experienced that odd tightening in places she seldom thought about.

"Andrea?"

Blinking, she raised her eyes from his arms to his face. "Yes?"

"Are you with me, Andrea?"

No, but I'm beginning to wish I were. "Yes, sir." For an instant, she had the horrifying feeling that he knew where her thoughts had strayed, but he stood up and continued talking business, so she dismissed the notion.

"You're tired," Dare said with unexpected kindness. "I imagine you worked all weekend again. Look, for now just bring your squadron to a higher readiness level and let me know about anything unusual that happens. And take some time off, Andrea. You won't be a damn bit of good to me if you work yourself to death. Let Dolan handle things for the next few days."

"But, sir—"

MacLendon came around the desk, perched on the edge, and looked down at her. "I know, Andrea," he said gently. "I've been there, too. You want so badly to prove yourself that you're afraid to leave anything to anyone else. But you're only one person, and you'll kill yourself this way. Or, worse, you'll get so tired you'll screw something up. Let Dolan earn his keep. Tell him to let you know if there's any more funny business, but otherwise just let him handle it. Let *him* deal with the fistfights and AWOLs and personal problems. That's what you have a deputy for. How will Dolan ever learn to be a commander if you don't give him a chance to practice?"

"Yes, sir." He was right, of course, but she didn't like it.

"You're a damn fine officer, Andrea. I know that already. I'll hardly think less of you if you delegate. Now, go take care of your readiness level and then let your subordinates do what they're here to do."

Standing, he indicated that the interview was over. "You know, Andrea, the hardest thing a commander has to do is trust a subordinate to do the job right."

Rising, Andrea looked him right in the eye. "Yes, sir, it seems to be a common failing."

Dare astonished her with a laugh. "You're wrong, Andrea. I trust you to do things right. I just prefer to be informed. Now, go handle it."

At eight Thanksgiving morning, Andrea pulled up to Dare's house as prearranged. His house was on a quiet, tree-lined street in the older section of base housing. Snow had still not fallen, although the skies kept threatening it. It wasn't unusual, though. North Dakota didn't get much snow, maybe twenty inches over an entire winter. The same twenty inches, however, stayed dry and continuously blew in the wind, rearranging themselves into huge drifts that had to be shoveled almost daily. Twenty inches might as well have been two hundred.

Dare opened the front door to her just as she stepped onto the stoop.

"I saw you drive up," he said with a smile. "Come on in."

She stepped into an entry hall that opened into a large living room. Wood floors gleamed with polish and were decorated with Navaho rugs. Sandy colors, accented with blues and an occasional touch of sunset and terra-cotta, brought the desert Southwest to North Dakota.

"It's beautiful," Andrea breathed, completely forgetting herself as she stepped into the living room. And it *was*. Not decorator beautiful. Home beautiful.

Dare was pleased. "Glad you like it." He took her coat and hung it in the hall closet. When he turned around, the wonder was gone from her face. She once again looked brisk and efficient. He felt a pang of loss but swept it aside.

"Kitchen's in here," he said, leading the way.

"Where are the others?" Andrea asked as she followed him.

"They'll be coming later."

Later? Her pulse shifted into high gear as she realized he had deliberately arranged for them to be alone together. Why had he done that? Only one reason occurred to her, and it made her mouth go dry. Surely he couldn't be interested in her as a *woman.* And if he were? Oh, God! She nearly bolted at the thought. Only years of self-discipline kept her moving after him into the kitchen.

It wasn't a very big kitchen, but it was adequate. A turkey sat in a roasting pan on the counter, waiting to be stuffed. Bags of bread cubes sat beside it. Andrea pulled an apron out of the bag she'd brought with her and tied it over her slacks with hands that trembled slightly. Together they went to work.

In a very short time Andrea realized that Alisdair MacLendon knew his way around a kitchen. Without the least difficulty, they worked in an intricate, silent ballet that yielded mince and apple pies by ten o'clock. When the pies came out of the oven, the stuffed turkey went in.

Suddenly there was a hiatus in the activity. Andrea was at once relieved that she didn't have to be constantly on guard against bumping into him and worried about how to fill the time. Where were the others?

Dare disappeared for a moment and returned with two glasses of wine. "It's early, but it's Thanksgiving," he said. "Sit down at the table and relax a minute."

So she sat at the kitchen table and watched while he cleaned up the baking mess. Her offer to help was refused. Andrea thought back to all the Thanksgivings she'd spent in the kitchen with her mother while her father and brothers watched football and lazed around, and decided that her commanding officer was a pretty unique guy.

And that wasn't necessarily a good thing, she found herself thinking ruefully. What she needed were reasons *not* to like the man, reasons to quell the growing attraction she felt. This was almost as bad as—no, it was worse than—her one and only high school crush. Not since the age of fifteen had she followed a man's every movement with her eyes, as if she could somehow physically satisfy her hunger just by looking, yet here she was filling her eyes with Dare's every movement. He'd always been attractive to her, but when had he started to look perfect?

When the last of the mess had disappeared, just as rich aromas of turkey were beginning to issue from the oven, he joined her at the table with his wineglass.

"To future holidays," he said, raising his glass.

Andrea lifted her glass and managed what she hoped was a casual smile. "No football?"

"Do I have to?"

"Don't you like it?"

"Sometimes. I can take it or leave it. Why? Is there a game you want to see?"

Andrea shook her head, the faint smile still on her lips. "I watch it because it's expected. I have to be able to talk football with the guys. I'd rather scan the sports section in the morning and pick up the highlights so I can sound intelligent."

He chuckled. "Me, too. But don't ever tell anybody."

"Personally, I'd rather play it."

"Don't tell me you were on the Academy squad."

She laughed then. "Not likely! Equal opportunity didn't go that far. I fenced."

"You're very good at thrust and parry," he said.

Their eyes locked, and something happened. While some corner of her mind acknowledged the thrust of his teasing remark, the ground seemed to shift beneath her. She blinked quickly and looked away, feeling panicky.

The conviction formed in MacLendon then that, although he was going to wrestle with himself about it all day, some time before he said good-night to Andrea Burke he was going to kiss her. Only as the idea took root in his mind did he realize that he'd been wanting to kiss her for weeks.

Looking down at his wineglass, he considered the idea. It would be dangerous, no question of that. They had to work together every day. He wished the thought had never occurred to him. He liked Andrea, damn it. He liked her and respected her and felt that they had arrived at a uniquely comfortable working relationship. She was, in fact, among the best of the officers he had worked with in his career. She took her job seriously and was unquestionably skilled at both security and command. Her no-nonsense approach to matters kept her unit running like a well-greased machine. Unlike so many other female officers of his acquaintance, her femininity never came to work with her. She was a good man.

So why the hell was he proposing to upset what surely must

be a delicate balance for her? Because he had to know what she tasted like? What she felt like against him? What his name sounded like on her lips? Never yet had she called him Dare. It was beginning to look as if she never would. So for the sake of a little male curiosity, he was going to risk it all?

He looked up and found her misty green eyes watching him warily. He could have sworn she knew what he was thinking. He wished he could read her mind. Was she sitting there wondering how she would handle the sexual harassment if he touched her? Because it could be considered sexual harassment. Off duty or not, he was her CO.

"Damn," he said suddenly, startling them both, and rose from the table. He couldn't touch her. They would never, ever be off duty enough for it to be all right for him to touch her. One of them would have to get a transfer first.

"Dare?"

The sound of his name on her lips for the very first time drew him up short halfway across the kitchen. "It's okay," he said, not daring to look back. "I just remembered something. Won't be a minute."

When the other guests, four very young lieutenants, arrived that afternoon at two, they were obviously nervous at the prospect of having dinner with the CO. All four were ROTC graduates, summer soldiers who were just getting their first taste of the real Air Force. Dare took pity on them and poured them all a stiff drink. By the time they sat down to dinner an hour and a half later, the alcohol was doing its work, and Dare kept it flowing freely, figuring he could sober them up over dessert.

Talk and laughter began to flow just as freely, and MacLendon told a few of his funnier war stories. Around five, when they cut into the pies, Dare cut off the alcohol and Andrea started pouring coffee. After pie, they settled onto the living room couches and somebody noticed that a light snow flurry had started.

"We had that briefing last week," one of the lieutenants said. Davis was his name. "The bad weather briefing, about carrying supplies and blankets and things in your car. It really gets that bad?"

"Absolutely," Andrea and Dare answered in one voice. They looked at each other and laughed.

"This is my third tour here," Dare said, "and I still take it seriously. We get these storms called Alberta Clippers, which are breakthroughs of polar air. Inside of twenty minutes the temperature can drop sixty degrees, and the wind kicks up so bad that if there's a quarter inch of snow on the ground, you get what's called a whiteout. You can't see the hand in front of your face for the blowing snow."

Hardy, another of the lieutenants, whistled softly.

"You know that saying about thirty-thirty-thirty?" Dare asked. "At thirty degrees below zero in a thirty-mile-an-hour wind, exposed flesh freezes in thirty seconds. When we're talking about an Alberta Clipper, we're talking about temperatures that can be sixty degrees below zero, with forty- to sixty-mile-an-hour winds. If you're out in one without shelter, you can expect to be frozen to death in under five minutes. It happens. It *has* happened. So you carry survival gear in your car, and if you go off the road, you stay put until rescue comes.

"And even on a sunny day in February, it's dangerous. There are about six weeks every winter when the daytime high doesn't get over thirty below. And the wind here never blows less than thirty miles an hour. Believe me, you want that stuff in your car."

"I guess so," said Davis.

"And come March," Andrea said, "when the daytime highs rise above zero, you'll be outside in sweaters talking about how warm it is."

The lieutenant gaped, and Dare chuckled.

"This reminds me of a funny story," Andrea said. "A funny *true* story that happened my first winter here. A couple of my cops were on their way out to the missile fields when they got caught in a whiteout and went off the road into a ditch. In almost no time at all they were buried in drifting snow. We found them, of course, but it took a good twenty-four hours, and all that was showing when we located them was their radio antenna."

"My gosh," said Davis. Coming from Florida, he really couldn't imagine it.

"Anyhow," Andrea continued, "they were okay except for

being thoroughly chilled and thoroughly scared. After they were released from the hospital, I called them to my office to see how they were doing. One of them, I can't tell you his name, said to me, 'I'm scared to death, Captain.' I thought he was joking, but he shook his head and said, no, he was even more scared than he had been when they were trapped. So I asked him why, and he said, 'I keep remembering all the promises I made to God.'"

When Dare walked the lieutenants out to their cars around seven that evening, Andrea went to the kitchen and started doing dishes. It had been a nice day, she thought, a very nice day, except for that one awkward moment this morning where something had happened. She wondered what it was, then shrugged it aside. She was getting used to awkward moments around Colonel MacLendon.

"Andrea, leave those dishes alone. I'll do them tomorrow."

He had returned to the kitchen, and as he came up beside her, she could feel the outdoor cold that clung to him.

"I can't do that," she answered. "I was raised to believe that leaving dishes overnight is a sin."

"Then I'll do them, and you go sit down."

"No, sir."

"Are you refusing to obey a direct order?" His voice was teasing, but there was another element, one that disturbed her. She looked up at him and green eyes met blue. The world stood still.

"Andrea."

"Yes?"

He closed his eyes. "If you don't get the hell out of here now, I'm going to do something unforgivable."

"Sir?" Her voice took on a note that made him open his eyes. She was looking up at him unwaveringly, the mist in her eyes deepening, swirling.

"Andrea, it is unforgivable of a superior officer to make a pass at a subordinate."

"A pass?" Some corner of her mind registered that she was sounding incredibly stupid right now, but it hardly seemed important when indefinable feelings were flooding her in alternating waves of heat and cold. A pass. The notion at once thrilled and terrified her.

"A kiss, Andrea. I want to kiss you."

"Oh!" The word escaped her on a sharply expelled breath, and she cocked her head, straining to find some vestige of common sense in a mind that had turned to mush. "Why?"

Damn, he thought, she was going to take this right to the bitter end, by which time he'd probably be a raving lunatic. "Why what?" he asked.

"Why do you want to kiss me?" Somehow the answer to that was incredibly important.

"Curiosity. Sheer male curiosity."

"Oh." That was safe, she told herself. Curiosity could be appeased quickly, and then they could get back on a safer footing. She refused to analyze the strange pang of disappointment his answer had given her. All she knew was that she had to kiss him. Something deeper than thought drove her. "I guess it would be best to get rid of that curiosity before it affects our working relationship," she said finally.

It was the best rationalization he'd ever heard. For a moment he let it resound through him as the mist in her eyes darkened, as the ice in his melted to the warmth of a blue fire. She was forthright always, he thought, and realized how much he admired the honesty with which she approached life.

He walked right up to her until their bodies almost touched, and not once did her gaze leave his. There was trust there, he realized. She trusted him not to do more than kiss her, not to let this come between them at work. And, surprisingly, he trusted her just the same.

Looking down at her elfin face, it suddenly crossed his mind that he was about to kiss a woman who was utterly without experience in these matters. There was something in the wideness of her eyes, in the rapid way her breasts rose and fell, that spoke more of nervousness than excitement. Surely she couldn't be inexperienced. He dismissed the notion as ridiculous. She was twenty-eight, after all, and a liberated woman.

You're crazy…crazy…crazy. The word pounded in Andrea's head in time with the thud of her heart. This was playing with fire of the worst kind. This man was her commanding officer! She watched him step nearer, and the whole focus of the universe suddenly narrowed to that tiny kitchen, to the hammering of her heart, to the blue of the eyes that moved closer…closer….

He bent slowly and closed his eyes only when his lips settled on hers. Her mouth was soft, warm, welcoming, as he had known it would be. There was no artifice or coyness to her, and she would have scorned such things even had she known about them. She simply received his touch as if it pleased her as much as it did him.

With his mouth nestled on hers, he very carefully brought his arms around her and drew her against him in a gentle embrace. His big hands traced soothing patterns on her back as his tongue traced her lips, tasting brandy, apples, cinnamon.

Oh, God, it felt so good! Andrea moaned softly at the sheer pleasure of his embrace. The pressure of his hands on her back and the strength of his arms around her satisfied an ache so deep it was rooted in her very soul. She could have luxuriated forever in the sensation and warmth, except that the flick of his tongue against her lips shot ribbons of fresh hunger toward her center. She wanted, needed, a deeper possession.

And then came the heart-stopping moment when her lips parted for him, separating as if they had just discovered something new and wonderful and couldn't wait to try it.

Dare drew her closer, deepening the kiss. He found smooth teeth and then, at last, her tongue, a trembling, shy tongue that didn't quite know what to do. Blazing across his mind like a meteor was the realization that she was genuinely inexperienced, and that he'd better stop now. Inexperienced women were too easily hurt.

But at that instant, just as he decided to break gently away, Andrea's tongue found his bravely in a coiling stroke that just about deprived him of reason. Inexperienced, yes, but instinctively skillful, with a thirst that suddenly seemed to match his own. And against his better judgment, Dare met her stroke for stroke, thrust for thrust, teaching her an erotic rhythm that caused her to go weak and trembling in his arms. It was complete and total surrender to the moment, and Dare recognized it with a sense of male triumph and an aching sadness.

Gently, regretfully, he raised his head. Her eyes opened slowly, hazy and heavy-lidded. Sparks of passion glowed there like green fire. His own passion was undeniable, pressed between them. Unconsciously her hips made an instinctive seeking motion, and he almost lost control. Almost, but not quite. Closing his eyes a moment, he drew several deep breaths. The kiss hadn't ended anything, he realized. It had only started it.

When he was able, he stepped back a couple of inches. Andrea opened her mouth as if to say something, but he stopped her with a finger on her swollen lips.

"Hush," he said. "I know."

Andrea's eyes became unreadable. She turned and went to the hall, taking her coat from the closet.

"Good night, sir," she said, betrayed by the faint quiver of her voice, and then she was gone.

Chapter 5

Andrea understood masculine curiosity. Her brothers had always talked freely around her, and on more than one evening she'd shared an illicit beer with them while they frankly discussed some girl's charms. In a way, back in the teen years, they'd proved their mother's warning to Andrea that guys were out for only one thing.

On the other hand, she'd seen them sweat over asking some girl out for the first time, had seen them heartbroken when a girl dumped them. Before she left for the Academy, she'd even watched two of her brothers fall in love and marry. She'd seen them moon-faced and starry-eyed, hangdog and desperate, and had long ago concluded that when you chipped away the macho veneer, you could often find mush. In spite of her parents' best efforts to convince her to the contrary, Andrea figured that, underneath, men and women weren't a whole lot different.

The sexual curiosity part was one of the differences, however. Unlike her brothers, who mentally undressed every attractive girl in the high school, Andrea had never wondered what was in a guy's jeans. Having six brothers, she'd concluded at a very early age that all men had pretty standard equipment. No curiosity in that. Men, however, looked upon women as a series of greener pastures, unexplored territory to be conquered. Her brothers had roared with laughter when a sixteen-year-old Andrea had told them she couldn't see what the big deal was: all cats were gray in the dark. Over the years she'd dated casually, kissed because it was expected, and found not one reason to change her mind on the subject.

Until Alisdair MacLendon. He'd aroused her curiosity, although she wasn't quite sure how or why. At odd moments she'd caught herself wondering what his chest looked like. Was it hairy or smooth? Was it flat or rippled with muscle? His thin, hard mouth that could look so dangerous when he was annoyed, did it feel warm and soft? How did it taste? Would the invasion of his tongue repel her the way all others had? Once, at a staff meeting, he'd been writing on a chalkboard, and she'd found herself staring at his hard, flat buttocks.

But such thoughts were fleeting and easily dismissed. Just curiosity, she told herself, and having grown up with six curious boys, she gave the matter no further importance.

But then he'd kissed her. Mountains moved, the earth trembled, and Andrea Burke stood shaken by the realization that the simple touch of lips and tongue could halt the planets in their courses. Just curiosity, but she knew how Pandora felt when she opened the forbidden chest and unleashed all the woes of the world.

By the time she went to work the following morning, Andrea had put a huge mental off-limits sign on Colonel Alisdair MacLendon. He didn't need it, and she certainly didn't, either. She had her career to consider, and any kind of involvement with her commanding officer would hang a vicious label on her that would ruin her future. Nor did he need people whispering that he took advantage of subordinate officers. Had he been in any other unit, there would have been no problem. As it was, the incident must never be repeated.

Firm in her decision, Andrea wondered why she felt so sour. Sitting behind the large desk that was a symbol of her achievement, between the flags she served, with life for once quiet, she ought to be feeling pretty good. In a couple of years she would make major, and there was no doubt in her mind that eventually she'd be selected for lieutenant colonel. That was what she wanted, wasn't it? To do all the things she'd always been told a woman couldn't do, instead of all the things she'd been told a woman should do?

Of course that was what she wanted. So why did she feel so restless and irritable? It was with relief that she greeted Nickerson when he showed up with the incident report.

"Morning, Nick. Help yourself to coffee and grab a seat."

When he'd filled a white foam cup, Nickerson sat, crossing his legs loosely, and gave her a knowing look. "If I didn't know better, ma'am, I'd say you were out of sorts this morning."

Andrea couldn't prevent a grin. "But you know better."

"Sure do." Nick set his cup on the edge of her desk and opened the folder in his lap. "Well, Captain, Airman Greene tells me she's three month's pregnant and she wants to separate."

"She's sure about that? Has anyone counseled her?"

"I tried." Nick looked wry. "Captain, I might as well be honest. I started in the Marines back when women in the service belonged to a separate corps and any who got pregnant were out. Now, I think I've done a passable job of adjusting to this equal rights business, but counseling pregnant females is about the hardest task I have as First Shirt. Heck, I ain't ever been married or pregnant myself, so what do I know? I can counsel a recruit about condoms and social diseases, I can handle domestic quarrels, but a pregnant female—well, I'm not real sure I'm very convincing. Thing is, Greene is a good cop. Pregnant or not, I'd *like* to see her stay in. Maybe you could ask somebody else to counsel her."

"I'll think about it, Nick, but I'm sure you did just fine."

"I'm not. I haven't blushed so much since I lost my ch—since before I shipped out to Nam."

Andrea felt her own cheeks heat. "You never told me why you transferred out of the marines into this outfit, Nick."

He shrugged. "I wanted to fly. And I did. And I discovered I get airsick, so here I am."

Andrea had to grin at his forthrightness. "I, for one, am glad you're right here."

Nick looked faintly embarrassed. "I'm not exactly upset about it myself. Anyhow, back to business. We got six new and very raw recruits in this morning, fresh out of Law Enforcement school. I looked 'em over, and I figure we got the bottom of the class."

Andrea had heard that before. "I guess you'll just have to break them in right."

"Well, I sure won't let 'em carry a gun until they know the barrel from the butt." He flipped a page in his folder. "We had a little to-do in the dorm last night, and I had to knock a couple of heads together. Nothing out of the ordinary.

"Hanson got picked up off-base for DWI last night," Nick continued. "The local mounties dumped him back on us. The usual?"

"Of course. That can't be tolerated."

Nick nodded. "What else? Oh, yeah, Mitchell phoned from Syracuse and said he's snowed in and won't be back from leave until tomorrow or Sunday. I called out to Rome Air Force Base, and sure enough he's lying. They haven't had a fresh snowfall since last Thursday. I told 'em to go pick him up and ship him back." He closed his folder and looked up. "That's it."

"That's enough. Drink your coffee, Nick, and take a break. How's Dolan been doing?"

Nick sipped his coffee and smiled faintly. "We-e-ll," he said, drawing the word out, "for a first looey who's never commanded anything except a latrine detail, he's okay. He has enough sense to know what he doesn't know, which is more than I can say for some lieutenants."

Andrea chuckled. "Hey, Nick, we were all green once."

"Sure. I guess you just spoiled me."

Andrea didn't quite know how to respond to that. When she'd first taken command of the squadron, she'd feared Nickerson was a man cut from the same cloth as her father. Instead, he'd proved to be a bulwark and a friend.

"No more intruder alerts or suspicious events?" she asked, needing to change the subject.

"Not since you walked out the door Wednesday afternoon."

"So maybe that fence business was just kids."

One corner of Nick's mouth lifted. "You a bettin' man, skipper?"

Andrea flashed a smile, then leaned back in her chair, sighing.

"I'm uneasy, Nick, like I'm waiting for the second shoe to drop, but I don't know why. I just don't like it."

"Me neither. That fence is buggin' the sh—beg pardon, ma'am. That fence is buggin' me." Draining his cup, he stood. "Time for a little look-see tonight?"

"Maybe." Andrea thought about it. "Yeah, Nick. Let's wander around the perimeter tonight. Around midnight."

"On foot?"

Andrea nodded. "On foot, with sidearms. We won't see a thing, but..." She shrugged.

"At least we'll know the beefed-up patrols are doing their jobs."

Shortly after midnight, Andrea and Nickerson split up and began to work their way silently from opposite ends of the perimeter fence around the airstrip. Andrea enjoyed this kind of activity, had enjoyed it ever since playing hide and seek with her brothers after dark. All the boys had admitted she could sneak more quietly than an Indian and blend into shadows better, and they always credited it to her small size. She liked to think she was just good at it. For her it was a challenge to step on the frozen ground soundlessly, to press so gently and carefully down on brittle grass and twigs that they bent rather than broke. And it was even more of a challenge to do that and still move swiftly through the dark.

When she'd worked her way along a third of the fence, she paused to tug up her parka sleeve and look at the luminous dial of her watch. She'd been moving for thirty-five minutes now. Surely a patrol should have come along?

Annoyed, she tugged down her sleeve, and it was then that she heard the sound. At once she crouched and grew perfectly still. It couldn't be Nick. Even if he'd moved faster than she had, which she doubted, he would still be too far away for her to hear his stealthy sounds. Well, if anyone was along the fence somewhere, they would be silhouetted against the lamps that lighted the area of the field where the alert planes waited.

Keeping low, she began to move at an angle to the fence, farther out into the empty fields. Where the devil was the patrol? When she felt she'd moved far enough from the fence, she again crept parallel to it, watching for a shadow against the lights. It was probably just some kind of animal, she told herself, but she didn't believe it. By now just about anything in the state had gone into hibernation.

Inside her parka she was perspiring, but her nose was beginning to grow numb from the biting cold, in spite of the black ski mask she wore so she wouldn't have to obstruct her vision with the snorkel hood of her parka. Pausing, she rubbed her nose vigorously and felt it tingle, then burn. Not frozen yet, she thought with satisfaction, and crept forward again.

She heard the sound again. Freezing into immobility, she held her breath and listened intently. Again. A quiet, stealthy sound, like a man's footstep. It was still too soon for Nick, she thought. Filled with tension, she very slowly and carefully released the snap on her holster, folding the flap in behind the belt.

The lights from the airstrip kept trying to draw her attention, but she forced herself to focus on the fence, following its cross-hatched length from left to right.

And then she saw it, the crouched shadow of a man against the fence. Rising, she put her hand on her pistol butt.

"Halt! Who goes there?"

The crouched figure spun about into a marksman's stance, and simultaneous with a loud crack, Andrea felt a hammer blow to her left shoulder. Without a thought, she yanked her pistol from its holster and fired at the fleeing shadow. She hit it. She saw it stumble just before darkness claimed her.

Alisdair MacLendon couldn't sleep. He'd reached the conclusion that it was wiser to keep clear of Andrea, more for her sake than his. He was perfectly aware that his attentions could destroy her career, and he had no wish to do that to her. None of these wise, mature, intelligent thoughts could prevent him from thinking about the way she'd felt in his arms, however.

In fact, he thought irritably, he felt as if he were on fire. He hadn't felt like this since he'd been fool enough to get the hots for Maureen and marry her. Then he'd had the excuse of youth. What was his excuse now? Andrea was twelve years his junior, for crying out loud. She was much too young, much too inexperienced, much too set on her career for his taste. Oh, he liked her and had a great deal of respect for her, but if he got involved with anyone at this late stage of his life, he wanted all those things he'd never had: home, hearth, and a couple of kids. Andrea most definitely wasn't in the market for that kind of thing. Yep, it was better for everyone if they kept things impersonal from here on out.

He was standing before his bedroom window in his skivvies, grateful that it was 2:00 a.m. Saturday and not a weekday when the phone rang. He reached for it with something akin to relief. Anything was better than a cold shower.

''MacLendon,'' he said into the receiver, already reaching for his pants.

A woman's professionally calm voice responded. ''Colonel MacLendon, this is Sergeant Danton of the Security Squadron. I'm calling to inform you that Captain Burke was shot this evening and is presently undergoing surgery. Shall I patch you through to Sergeant Nickerson?''

''Yes!''

The line went temporarily silent as he was placed on hold, giving Dare an opportunity to envision the worst. Vietnam had taught him what a bullet could do to human flesh, and he needed little imagination to heighten his anxiety. Eyes closed, mouth drawn in a thin line, he stood beside his bed, phone in one hand and pants in the other as he waited for the patch to be effected. This wasn't the first time in his life that time had slowed to a crawl, but it was one of the worst. Surgery. Damn it, she was in surgery, and that could only mean the worst. A fist squeezed his heart.

''Colonel MacLendon,'' said the expressionless voice of Sergeant Danton, ''you're patched through to Sergeant Nickerson.''

''Nickerson here, sir.'' Nick's voice sounded tinny, and wind could be heard whistling in the background.

''What the hell happened?'' Dare demanded. ''How bad is Burke?''

''Well, sir, I can't rightly say how the Captain is. She was wounded in the left shoulder. Entry wound and no exit wound, so I reckon it was a small calibre firearm that shot her. I was still a good half mile down the perimeter from her when it happened, but it sounded like a .22 report.''

MacLendon, who was intimately acquainted with the effects of an M-16, none of which could be termed minor, let his head fall back and released his pent-up breath as the size of the disaster scaled down a little. At least Andrea was still in one piece. "What about the perpetrator?"

"We're still looking." Nickerson went on to explain that when he reached Andrea he'd been unable, by the illumination of his flashlight, to see any sign of the assailant or to determine in which direction he'd fled. Given no sign to guide him in a pursuit, Nick had decided to await the backup he'd radioed for as soon as he heard gunfire. "We still haven't found anything, sir, but we're setting up floodlights right now. If there's anything to find, we'll find it."

Dare approved Nickerson's actions and disconnected. A call to the hospital revealed only that Andrea had gone into surgery a half hour before and the operation was expected to take several hours. For lack of any more useful activity, Dare decided to go over to the Security Squadron and keep his fingers on the pulse of matters. No way was he going to sleep until he knew Andrea was all right.

It was nearly dawn when MacLendon had everything pieced together. Nickerson and Andrea had gone out to pull one of their inspections and had separated. Forty minutes later, Nickerson had heard the report of a .22, followed rapidly by the report of Andrea's .38. He'd found Andrea out cold about twenty feet from the perimeter fence, a bullet in her shoulder. Investigation of the area with floodlamps showed that Andrea had grazed her target. A trail of relatively infrequent drops of blood led toward the highway, indicating that the intruder had fled by auto.

As for the patrol that should have passed through the area, they'd been held up at the other end of the airfield by evidence of an attempted break-in, clearly a diversion. Nickerson had advised area police and hospitals to be on the lookout for anyone with a bullet wound. Beyond that, there wasn't a damn thing anyone could do.

Rubbing his eyes, MacLendon glanced at the clock on Andrea's desk. Five-thirty. Too late to go home, and too early to start the day. The gallon of coffee he'd drunk while questioning the parties involved in tonight's fiasco had left a hole as big as the Grand Canyon in his gut.

Suddenly he stood and reached for his parka. He would go over to the hospital and check in on Andrea. If rank had any privileges, he was going to use them to look in on her. Damn it, he couldn't stand another minute of wondering.

Snow was falling lightly, and the sun was nowhere near rising yet. The wind had lightened, though, and it felt odd to step out into the bitter cold and not feel the wind claw at him. That wouldn't last. This little bit of snow would probably be whipping up a ruckus before the day was over.

Andrea was out of surgery but still in recovery when he arrived. The charge nurse hesitated only momentarily before leading him down the hall. Just as he thought, colonels who were commanding officers got what they wanted.

"She's recovering very nicely, Colonel," the nurse said. "Don't be afraid to wake her. It helps her shake off the anesthetic faster."

He was left alone with her, and for a long time he simply stared down at her, relief warring with worry. How fragile she looked, he realized suddenly. She was always so calmly confident and competent that he'd never really noticed just how small and delicate she was. The smooth shoulders, one bandaged heavily, which peeked above the sheet looked small and defenseless. She was so pale that her smattering of freckles stood out like beacons on her face. In the worst way he suddenly wanted to gather her close and assure himself that she would be all right.

"Andrea?" He contented himself with clasping her cool, soft hand.

Her head stirred restlessly, and she licked her lips.

"Andrea?"

Her hazy green eyes opened a little. She mumbled something.

"I can't hear you, Andrea." With his thumb he stroked the back of her hand.

Suddenly her eyes opened wide, and she reached full consciousness. "Is he dead?"

"I don't know, and I don't give a damn." He only gave a damn that *she* wasn't.

"I do."

"He got away, so the bastard is probably okay. You're going to get a commendation for this."

"I don't want a commendation for shooting a man."

"Andrea, you're a cop and a soldier. You were doing your job. You had to defend yourself."

"Then maybe I don't want to be a cop or a soldier." Her eyelids were drooping again. "Dare..." Her voice trailed away.

His grip on her hand tightened at the sound of his name, and the urge to hold her close became nearly overwhelming. So, he found himself thinking, when her guard was down she thought of him as Dare, not as her CO, not as Colonel MacLendon. Only awareness of her injury made him keep his distance. "Andrea, do you want me to notify somebody?"

"If you notify anybody in my family, I'll never speak to you again." Sudden tears sparkled on her lashes. "It hurts," she mumbled, and then sank back into the sleep induced by the dregs of anesthesia.

Disturbed, MacLendon straightened. Shooting somebody was never an easy thing to live with, even when it was done in self-defense. Andrea would probably remember that instant, relive it right down to the way the trigger had felt when she squeezed it, for a long, long time. Sighing, he went looking for a doctor to give him all the details.

It was the hospital commander, an old friend, who finally gave him the information he wanted. Andrea would recover without permanent damage except for a scar. She would probably get out of the hospital on Thursday, but full function wouldn't be restored to her arm for six to eight weeks.

But she *would* regain full function. Incredibly relieved, MacLendon stepped out into the halfhearted light of the North Dakota dawn and realized that just as it was too late to go to bed, it was too late to have all those wise and mature thoughts that had kept him awake in the first place. He cared what happened to Andrea Burke. He cared a lot more than was wise.

Andrea returned to work Friday morning. She didn't have a single uniform blouse big enough to button over the arm that was strapped to her side, so she wore her academy sweats as a temporary measure. When she walked into headquarters, the two cops at the front desk sprang to their feet and saluted. It surprised her, but she managed a wan smile. All the way down the long corridor, similar things happened. Enlisted men saluted; non-coms snapped to attention. In spite of herself, she was touched.

And then she opened her office door and stepped into a flower garden. Flowers everywhere. She started to sniffle.

"The men took up a collection for flowers," Nickerson said quietly behind her. She turned slowly, and he saw her reddened eyes and heard her sniffle. "Skipper, are you crying?"

"No." She gave a watery chuckle and then unleashed a huge sneeze. "I'm allergic to flowers!" She started to laugh, and after a moment Nickerson joined her.

A crowd of grinning faces had gathered at the door. Wiping her eyes on her sleeve, she said, "Gee, thanks, guys. They're beautiful. But next time, send a picture, huh?"

A chorus of laughs answered her as she gave vent to another sneeze.

"I hate to do it," Andrea said. "They really are beautiful. But—" She sneezed again. "Get rid of 'em, Nick. Take 'em to the pediatrics ward or something."

Nickerson grinned from ear to ear. "Yes, ma'am."

While the flowers were being removed from her office by grinning cops and Andrea was unleashing one chain of sneezes after another, MacLendon arrived.

"How the devil did I know you'd show up this morning, Burke?" he groused as he sidestepped a huge bouquet of pink azaleas, covering his concern with irritation. "Didn't the doctor tell you to take it easy? What's with the flowers?"

Andrea loosed another sneeze and pawed around her lower desk drawer for the box of tissues she was sure she'd stashed there during a cold last winter. Finding it, she scrubbed her itching nose until it shone red.

"Thank you, sir," she said, and sneezed again. "It's great to see you, too."

"She's allergic to the flowers, Colonel," Nickerson said as he carried a double armload out.

"Oh. It looks like you guys must have bought out every florist in the state."

"Had 'em shipped in special," Nick said as he disappeared around the corner.

MacLendon returned his attention to Andrea, who was hiding behind a wad of tissues.

She was pale, he noted. Too pale. And a fine sheen of perspiration covered her face. With a quick glance, he saw that her right hand was trembling. Damn it, she was trying to do too much too fast.

"My office is polluted," she muttered in an undertone into the tissues. "It'll be months before all the pollen is out of here."

MacLendon looked down at her and saw that in spite of her grousing mumble, there was a smile on her lips. She was neither as tough nor as gruff as she pretended. Feeling faintly amused by her predicament, he crossed to the coffee maker she kept on the file cabinet and started a pot brewing. At last the final flower was gone and the door closed, leaving them alone.

"You shouldn't be out of bed yet, Andrea." He sat in the armchair facing her desk and crossed his legs. Guessing she wouldn't want his overt concern, he masked it behind what he hoped was a professional interest.

She merely looked at him without arguing, an indication of just how weak she was feeling. Her smile was tight, her green eyes empty.

"You may be right, sir. But my own company is driving me crazy." She sneezed again, then sniffled. "Damn!"

"The man you shot got away, Andrea. Considering what a .38 slug can do at that range, you must have just grazed him."

"They told me." Her eyes were dark, unreadable.

"And you're going to get a commendation whether you want it or not."

"Yes, sir." She sounded hollow, uncaring.

MacLendon suddenly longed to seize her, shake her, force the tears out of her and then soothe away her pain. His knuckles turned white as he gripped the arms of his chair. He couldn't do it, couldn't bridge the gulf that had to remain between them for her sake. He'd known this woman was going to be a handful. He just hadn't guessed what kind.

"Andrea, you can't come to work in a sweat suit." It was a dumb remark, but all he could think of to say.

"No, sir. Monday I'll be in uniform. One of the nurses at the BOQ offered to help me dress until I can do it myself." Please, she thought. Please don't order me to take sick leave. Don't lock me away all alone with the memory of the way the revolver kicked in my hand. Don't leave me with the way I sighted him with perfect calm and deliberation. The way I never even hesitated.

His icy blue eyes were watching her, assessing, measuring. She really did feel as if he could see through to the barrenness of her soul, and she wondered what he thought of her, really thought of her.

"Captain," he said quietly, "you're not the first cop to shoot a man in the line of duty, nor will you be the last."

"No, sir."

"It's not easy to live with. I know. But we do learn to."

"Yes, sir."

"Moreover, you didn't kill anyone, so at least you don't have that on your conscience."

"But I do," she said grimly. "I aimed to kill."

"That's what you're supposed to do, damn it!" He jumped up in frustration. "The man had just tried to kill you! If he'd had something bigger than that peashooter, we'd be burying you in little bloody pieces. You had no choice."

"No, sir. And that disturbs me as much as what I did."

"I see." He rubbed his chin and studied her. There was no argument for that. Deeply troubled, he asked, "Will you resign?"

Her chin came up, a welcome spark of her old self. MacLendon was so glad to see it that he could have done a jig.

"No, sir," she said coolly. "I'm not a quitter. I'll get over this, or around it or under it, somehow."

"I'm sure you will, Captain." Thank God, he thought. Thank God.

"Well," he said when he had his relief under control, "I'll let you come back to duty on one condition."

"Yes?"

"That you take off and go home when you get tired. And that you don't take that damn brick with you. Give Lieutenant Dolan a chance to discover the joys of command responsibility."

She cocked her head. "That sounds more like two conditions."

"So it's two. Do you agree?"

Andrea smiled faintly, glad to know her recent escapade hadn't raised her to a level of holiness that prevented MacLendon from showing his irritation with her. Good grief, a couple of times he'd even looked at her as if she were *fragile.*

"I agree, sir."

"Now, promise me you'll take off when you get tired."

"I just agreed—"

"Agreeing and promising to obey are two different things. I want your word on it, Captain."

"Yes, sir."

"Andrea," he said silkily, "say it. In so many words."

She glared at him, then gritted out the words. "I give you my word to go home when I get tired and not take my radio with me."

"Thank you." One corner of his mouth lifted, and the fan of laugh lines by his eyes deepened. Rising, he went to pour himself some coffee. "Can I pour you some?"

"Yes, thank you."

He set a cup in front of her, then returned to his chair. "Now to the part that you're really interested in."

Stifling another sneeze, Andrea looked up quickly at him. "Sir?"

"The part about what we know and what we don't know, and what I've done about it. You know the intruder got away. There was actually no evidence that he succeeded in crossing the perimeter, because none of the electronic alarms were triggered. At first we assumed that you scared him off before he achieved his purpose. It appears, however, that he either evaded the electronic systems somehow, or he wasn't working alone, because something *did* happen."

Andrea was all ears now, aches and pains and sniffles forgotten. "What, sir?"

"On Monday, one of my bombers returned to base with a six-foot diameter hole in the cockpit. The pilot figures he hit a goose."

Andrea nodded. It happened frequently in the kind of low-level flying B-52s did, when they practiced bomb runs, or practiced flying into Russia beneath the radar beams. A goose might not be terribly big, but it packed one hell of a wallop when it collided head-on with a plane traveling at five hundred miles per hour. "So?"

"So, Andrea, I seem to remember the geese flew south quite a while ago."

So they had. She sat up straighter and winced when the wound in her shoulder pulled. "But...maybe there was a crazy goose, like that whale that got lost in Alaska."

"No goose feathers. No blood. I called in the OSI."

The Office of Special Investigations was the Air Force's FBI. Nobody liked the OSI. Andrea liked least of all the thought of them tramping around in her domain. Anger flared in her green eyes. "Was that necessary, Colonel?"

"I think so." MacLendon rose, sighing, and began to pace. "I figured you'd be furious, but I'm afraid I can't let that matter. If you're honest, you'll admit that they're a hell of a lot better trained and better equipped to conduct an investigation of this sort than the Security Police Squadron. It's no reflection on you, Andrea. None at all. It's just the truth. You know damn well that if something like this happened to a civilian plane, federal investigators would be called in simply because they've got the expertise and equipment local authorities lack. We're in the same boat here, and I expect your full cooperation."

Andrea eyed him grimly. "Yes, sir."

Dare came to a halt and looked across the desk at her with a faint, humorless smile. "And they're here undercover. Only you and I know about it, and only you and I and a couple of aircraft mechanics know it wasn't a goose that goosed that plane."

Andrea tried to smile at his attempted humor but failed miserably.

"Aw, Andrea," he said, his voice dropping. That valiant attempt at a smile was his undoing. He had just enough sense left to ensure that the door was tightly closed before he came around the desk to her side.

The next thing she knew, he'd caught her by the waist, lifted her from her chair, and gently tucked her right side against him. His left arm wrapped snugly around her back, and his right hand caught her chin, lifting it. He looked down into her startled green eyes.

"I swore," he said softly, "that I wasn't going to do this again. Tell me not to, Andrea."

But she didn't say a word. Instead she stared steadily up at him, and once again he saw the hazy mists swirl in her green eyes, drawing him down, closer and closer, until his mouth nestled against hers.

"Sweet Andrea," he muttered against her lips. "God, you haunt me."

She needed no coaxing this time. Her lips parted at once to his questing tongue, and he was drawn into a whirlwind of passion as smoky as her eyes. We're both too lonely, he thought, and then he stopped thinking.

Her mouth was warm, tasting of coffee, her tongue as eager as his. Right within the circle of his arms, as if by a wizard's magic, she was transformed from a cool, collected officer into a wild and wonderful woman, hungry, wanting, needing, and his hunger grew apace with hers.

He lifted his head briefly, drinking in her eyes, her swollen lips. He smiled, and she smiled back.

"Andrea," he murmured. "Delightful, wonderful Andrea." And then his lips sought hers again, wanting more and more.

"I wish I could hug you back," she sighed against his mouth, her right arm trying to find its way around his waist. She wanted, needed, to hold him, to press closer. He shifted so that her arm could slip around behind him, and groaned softly as he felt its pressure close around his waist. It had been so long since a woman had held him. So long.

His hand left her cheek, beginning a careful, gentle journey downward, wary of her injuries. The thick bandage and strapping guided him until, at last, he cradled her breast in his palm. Through her sweatshirt he felt the nipple harden instantly. She arched into the touch, her moan swallowed by his mouth.

"Andrea," he murmured, stroking lightly over her nipple, back and forth with his fingers. "You feel so nice, so soft." He dropped kisses on her eyelids, her cheeks, the tip of her freckled nose.

Andrea couldn't believe this was happening, hoped it would

never end. He smelled so good, tasted so good, and his hand was wreaking havoc with her, sending shafts of pure delight racing to her core until she thought she would die if she didn't feel his weight on her, pressing against her, covering her. Never had she dreamed this was possible. Never. "Dare," she whispered, her mouth seeking his, hungry to taste him again. "Dare, please."

"Please what?" He lifted his head and smiled at her, his blue eyes warm now, so warm that they seemed to cover her with heat. "I want you, Andrea. I want you desperately." A shuddering sigh escaped him, and he bowed his head lower, his scratchy cheek coming to rest against hers. Reluctantly he moved his hand from her breast, bringing it to rest gently on her waist.

"It's the wrong time and place," he said, and the regret was so sharp in his voice that she knew he felt it as deeply as she did.

A breath almost like a sob escaped her. "Yes, sir, it is," she said presently. "The wrong time and place."

She straightened. His arms slipped from her. Blue eyes glittered down into sad green ones.

"Someday, Andrea," he said. It was a promise.

Turning, he headed for the door. With his hand on the knob, he paused and looked back.

"You look like death warmed over, Burke," he said frankly. "Get your butt home before noon."

"Yes, sir!" There was enough irritation in her voice to make him grin as he walked out.

Chapter 6

Andrea awoke in the morning furious with Dare from the instant she opened her eyes. He had held her, kissed her and touched her, and aroused feelings she had never dreamed existed even in her wildest imaginings. He had created longings and desires where none had existed before. Sleeping Beauty was awake, unfulfilled and mad as the devil.

MacLendon, four blocks away, drank coffee and tried to read the morning paper. He was mad as the devil, too—at himself. He'd felt Sleeping Beauty wake in his arms and had a pretty good idea just where he'd left her standing. If he had seduced a virgin he couldn't have been any angrier with himself.

But he felt a kind of wonder and awe, too. Not even his young wife of five miserable years so long ago had ever blossomed under his touch as Andrea had. He couldn't help feeling a little as if he had been touched by magic.

Giving up on the paper, he carried his coffee into the living room and stared out the window at the bleak North Dakota winter morning. What had he done? What was he going to do about it? He'd acted like a damn—

—cowboy, Andrea thought as she walked into Dare MacLendon's office Monday morning. A damn cowboy. Her shoulder ached miserably, perfectly in tune with her mood. She still felt as if most of her energy had slipped down a black hole somewhere. Anger sustained her and drove her in to work, determined to show that damn cowboy just what he deserved for toying with her like that. She was going to—

—freeze him, Dare realized when his gaze met hers across the conference table that morning. The little minx gave him a look glacial enough to cause frostbite. While the other officers wandered into the room and poured themselves coffee, he met her stare for stare and allowed himself to imagine her lying naked and trembling on his bed, reaching out for him—

—touching his chest, Andrea thought; stroking her hands downward to grasp his buttocks and pull him—

—into her, Dare imagined, deeper and deeper.

Suddenly they both blinked, and reality returned with a crash. Major Francis was pulling out his chair at the far end of the table, the last one to arrive. Dare glanced around, taking attendance mentally. No one missing.

"Good morning, people." Since arriving here, he'd given up on the word gentlemen. It always left that awkwardness of what to do about the one lady. Gentlemen and ma'am? Lady and gentlemen? Gentlepersons? Screw it.

"First item on the agenda," he continued, drawing his pad closer and scanning it. "General Hamilton is coming next Tuesday on a routine visit. He heard about last week's events and specially requested to meet Captain Burke. We'll have a formal luncheon at the Officers' Club, and I need a volunteer to supervise arrangements."

As Dare's gaze swept around the table, he caught an absolutely adorable look of confusion on Andrea's face. Their earlier eyeball-to-eyeball session had evidently driven all her resolutions from her head. It tickled Dare to realize he could fluster his cool Captain Burke so easily, and he began to think it might be a lot of fun to have Andrea angry with him.

"I'll handle the arrangements, sir," Captain Bradley said after a perceptible hesitation. "I've done it before, and I know the ropes."

"I hate this kind of stuff," Andrea said. "It's one of the two things that make me wonder why I ever joined the Air Force."

Dare's lip twitched. Zinged again, he thought. From the gleam in her eye, he gathered he was the other thing. Mercifully, no one asked her what the second thing was.

"Well," he said pleasantly, "you were wounded. You can always claim weakness, Andrea."

Now she was glaring again, not obviously, just enough for Dare to pick up on it. "I'm not a chicken, sir," she said icily, accenting the I.

And I am? Dare wondered. The corner of his mouth twitched again, still with amusement. People were going to start thinking he had a tic if Andrea kept this up.

"Item two," he continued. "It's almost January, people. Time to make our pledges to the United Way. Pledge forms will be distributed this afternoon to all units. I respectfully request that we attempt to surpass this year's average of five dollars per month per person. Now folks, most of us can squeeze out a little more than that. Talk to your people, and get the forms back in no later than fifteen December."

He glanced around, saw the bored nods. "The pledge thermometer will be put out in front of our building again this year. I will see it every morning."

Chuckles ran around the table.

"Next item. Toys for Tots is still looking for toys. The drop box is by the base exchange. Remind your people. The Aid Society says we have several enlisted families that aren't going to make Christmas dinner without some help. Information will be posted on the bulletin board."

He looked up. "Now, I want all staff requests for Christmas leave in my office by the tenth. We'll follow last year's general holiday schedule through January third, unless we run into some kind of problem. The Wing Christmas party is scheduled for the NCO club on December twentieth. Lieutenant Tubbs is handling it. Lieutenant?"

Tubbs stood up and began to talk about tickets and menus and bands, and Dare allowed himself to tune out for a while. His own holiday schedule was so packed with invitations that he figured he'd be running in a continuous state of semihangover from the tenth through New Year's. What would Andrea be doing?

Andrea was thinking grumpily that maybe this year she would go visit one of her brothers rather than spend her holiday season sitting in the BOQ, attending an occasional party thrown by people she hardly knew, and sitting in the Officers' Club in the evenings, drinking with the other bachelors. She wouldn't, though. She always felt that as a bachelor it was only fair to stay on duty through the holidays so the married guys could be with their families.

Just as the meeting was breaking up, it occurred to Andrea that she wasn't usually this grumpy and gloomy, and that it couldn't all be her wound. MacLendon, she thought irritably. It's that damned cowboy's fault.

Ready to growl at the first person who glanced her way, she stalked back to the Security Police building and pulled out the troop schedule. It was all very well to say they would follow last year's schedule, but that provided only a general outline. A lot of her staff had changed during the year, and their marital status had to be taken into account. She'd have to prepare a blank schedule and then send it out to her various units to fill in the blanks. It was the last thing she felt like doing.

"Let me handle it, skipper," Nickerson said when she mentioned it to him. "Me and Lieutenant Dolan. In fact, I think it's a perfect job for the Lieutenant. He might as well learn that this job isn't all glamor. And didn't you promise Colonel MacLendon you'd go home when you got tired?"

Andrea glared at him. "Did he tell you that?"

"As a matter of fact, he did, and you're looking pretty peaked to me." Nickerson gave her his most inscrutable expression.

"Don't coddle me, Nick."

"Wouldn't dream of it, ma'am. I'd as soon coddle a two-headed rattler. I'm going over to the chow hall to pick up something hot for lunch. Anything sound good to you?"

Andrea forced herself to consider the question. "Soup sounds good. And maybe a sandwich or two."

Nick nodded. He was accustomed to Andrea's appetite. "How about dessert?"

She shrugged. "If you see anything that looks decent."

"Okay. Back in a jiff."

He *was* coddling her, and she knew it, but much as it annoyed her, it touched her, too.

Her shoulder throbbed steadily, and her stitches itched maddeningly, but the wound was still too tender to scratch satisfactorily. The worst part of being shot, she decided, was being unable to get comfortable no matter what she did. That and the troubling dreams that plagued her. Getting shot at made a person aware she wasn't immortal.

And Dare MacLendon, damn his blue eyes, had made her just as aware that there was more to life than a career. Never had she dreamed that it could feel so good to be held, or that it could be so wonderful to lean against someone else's strength. Not only had he awakened desires she didn't want, he'd awakened a need to be held. For those few brief moments he'd made her feel safe, secure and cherished.

She hated to admit it, but more than anything in the world she wanted to dive into those strong arms and let them shelter and protect her. Female foolishness, she told herself irritably. It had no place in her life or plans. She'd be damned if she'd let a man interfere with her future. No, henceforward she wouldn't let Alisdair MacLendon within arm's reach.

Her mind made up, she forced herself to sit forward and reach for the paperwork on her desk. Andrea Burke had more important things to do with her time than moon over a man.

For the next ten days she was quite successful in keeping her resolution, nor did Dare test her resolve. She told herself she was glad he appeared as eager to avoid her as she was to avoid him, but in a small corner of her mind there was a sad, nagging ache of disappointment.

And then, just a week before Christmas, she answered her telephone to hear a familiar voice.

"Good afternoon, Burke," said Colonel Alisdair MacLendon.

Andrea told herself that her heart was *not* doing a silly little tap dance at the sound of that voice. No, it was just a muscle twitching, a delayed effect of the wound in her left shoulder.

"Good afternoon, sir," she managed to reply coolly.

"I need a favor, Burke," he said. "I want you to take me out tonight or tomorrow and show me how security is handled at the missile sites.''

It was the last thing on earth she felt like doing. Did he lie awake nights thinking up ways to annoy people? ''Why?'' she demanded bluntly, and never mind protocol. ''Why this sudden interest?''

''Because I'm responsible for those sites just as I'm responsible for everything on this base. It behooves me to know how it's handled.'' His tone lay somewhere between sarcasm and exaggerated patience. ''Well?''

Well, if she couldn't get out of it, she didn't want to postpone it. In fact, the thought of spending some time alone with him caused her traitorous heart to leap and her blood to rush. ''This evening,'' she said when she felt she could trust her voice. Weak, Burke, she scolded herself. You're really weak. ''Say seven?''

''Good. Pick me up at my house. I'll be looking for you.'' He disconnected with a click.

Leaning back in her chair, she eased her arm from the sling and began the limbering exercises the doctor had given her. What the devil was going on? She winced as her healing muscles pulled. Well, if he really wanted to go all the way out to Romeo, the nearest missile site, he could damn well do the driving.

Dare was watching for her, and as soon as the blue truck pulled up in front of his house, he trotted down the walk and came around to the driver's side.

''I'll drive,'' he said. ''Scoot over.''

Andrea was glad to. It had been a long day—too long, really—and her shoulder was aching just about as bad as it ever had.

''Are we really going out to the Romeo site?'' she asked. The more the afternoon had waned, the more difficulty she'd had in believing he was really interested in security at the missile sites. It was possible, of course, given his predilection for sticking his nose into everything. Still, something felt odd about the request.

''No. We'll drive up the road a dozen miles or so and have coffee someplace.''

All her good resolutions faltered as something inside her went liquid and weak. Had he gone to all this trouble just to steal some time alone with her?

"How's your shoulder doing, Andrea?"

"You want the real poop or the polite answer, sir?"

"That bad?"

"That bad, sir."

He was genuinely sorry to hear it. "I thought by now it would be considerably better."

"It's better than it was." She wanted to change the subject. "I heard we're getting a storm tonight."

"Four inches of snow and a twenty-degree temperature drop," he agreed. "We'll be back before it gets bad."

She nodded. The storm wasn't supposed to hit until between eleven and midnight. She wondered, though, why he was heading away from town along a less traveled stretch of road. Did he think someone might follow them?

"Ah, Colonel?"

"Hmm?"

"Is there a point to all this James Bond stuff?"

MacLendon chuckled quietly. "Actually, yes. We'll talk about it over coffee."

Resigned, Andrea settled back and tried to find a comfortable angle for her shoulder. If there was one, she hadn't yet discovered it.

Dare pulled over at a truck stop about fifteen miles west of the base. The place was pretty well deserted, boasting only one interstate rig and a couple of pickups out front. Inside there were a counter and numerous booths with ragged plastic-covered seats. Dare chose a booth at the far end of the diner, away from the other patrons.

An elderly waitress with a Swedish accent hurried over to take their orders. Dare wanted coffee and apple pie. Andrea settled for coffee and tried not to think about how badly she wanted to be standing beneath a hot shower, letting the warmth steal the stiffness from her muscles.

Only when they'd been served did Dare speak.

"Well," he said slowly, "it wasn't a goose that put the hole in that bomber. It was plastique."

Andrea's head jerked up. Shock overrode her fugitive disappointment at learning he'd brought her here to talk business. For a moment she was simply speechless. "My God. But why? What could anyone possibly hope to accomplish?"

Dare shrugged. "Who knows? Simple terror? Something more complex? We won't know unless we find the culprit, which brings me to the point of all these James Bond tactics you asked about. Andrea, the OSI investigators say the perpetrator had inside help. Or that someone on the inside used someone on the outside as a diversion. Either way, we have big trouble."

For a long moment Andrea made no response. Dare saw the shock in her eyes, then saw her control it rapidly.

"Why," she asked finally, "do they think it's an inside job?"

"You're the security expert. You tell me what it would take for a terrorist to get into the nose of that B-52 to plant plastique. Hell, that's the easy part, I guess. The hard part is getting into the controlled area so he had access to the planes. OSI is very impressed with you and your squadron. You're doing a marvelous job, one of the best they've ever seen. And that's why they're convinced that the culprit had inside help. They believe that's the only way he could get past your security."

"A uniform. A badge. It's simple."

"Not that simple. OSI tried four times in the past two weeks to gain illicit entry to the area. Your guys stopped 'em every time."

"Since the shooting—"

MacLendon silenced her with a shake of his head. "Sure, everyone's on his or her toes, but they were on the alert even before you were shot, because of that business with the fence. You beefed up your patrols long before that incident."

Andrea shifted restlessly and winced as her shoulder pulled. Finally, frustrated by her own discomfort, she propped her chin on her right hand and stared glumly into her coffee. "An inside job. Damn. Who do they suspect? My people? The mechanics? The pilots?" It gave her a queasy feeling to realize she might actually know someone capable of such an act.

"Right now everybody's suspect. Everybody except you and me. You because of the shooting incident, and me because I called OSI."

Without moving her head, she raised her eyes to his. "What do we do about it?"

"Stay alert and pay attention. What else *can* we do? Plastique pretty effectively wipes out fingerprints."

Sighing, Andrea lifted her coffee cup and sipped.

"Andrea?"

"Mmm?"

"I've been meaning to tell you; you're one damn fine officer."

Color rose in a deep flush from her neck up. Dare watched in fascination. He wouldn't have believed Andrea could blush so profusely. The rush of color canceled all resemblance to Huck Finn, not that he had any problem with her looks. Her green eyes flickered and lowered, avoiding his gaze.

"Andrea?"

"Sir?" She retreated swiftly into formality, and his eyes gentled, although she was too busy fiddling with her coffee spoon to see it.

"We need to talk."

"I thought we were talking, sir." Her heart accelerated slightly. Instinctively she knew the direction he was taking.

"I know you're angry with me."

"Angry, sir?" She kept her face blank. Why the devil couldn't he leave this alone?

"I can't leave it alone," he said, as if he read her mind. "It's like a toothache. You keep poking it with your tongue."

Her hazy green eyes took on that gleam he knew so well. "I believe, sir," she said smoothly, "that this is the first time I've ever been compared to a toothache."

"Cut it out, Andrea. And drop the 'sir' business."

"We've tried that, sir," she reminded him. "You may have noticed it only works for a few minutes at a time. It also strikes me as being about as wise as playing catch with a live grenade." And if her heart pounded any harder, it was going to burst from her chest.

The mistiness was gone from her eyes, he noted. While her cheek still rested tiredly on her hand, her gaze had grown clear and unwavering. If he chose to pursue this, he was going to get the unvarnished truth from her. He wondered suddenly if he were up to it. Alisdair MacLendon had never been a chicken, however, so he advanced into the fray.

"What are your career plans?" he asked bluntly.

She ran her tongue along her upper lip, considering. "Two weeks ago I would have said I wanted to retire at the rank of colonel. I'm not sure now. I mean, I knew that if I played with guns there was a distinct possibility I might have to use one. I guess I didn't really believe it." She straightened and took a sip of coffee. "I just don't know anymore. I have to be able to live with myself, one way or the other." Suddenly her gaze transfixed him. "What about you, sir?"

"Me? I'm a year away from retirement, if I want to take it. And I'm thinking about it, Andrea. I'm thinking about it very hard."

"But you're up for general."

"I can retire as a general just as easily as a colonel. There are a lot of things I never got around to doing, and I find myself thinking about them."

She was softening. Captain Burke was slipping away like a veneer. Taking advantage of the moment, Dare charged ahead.

"About what happened between us, Andrea..."

Her head jerked up, and her eyes were suddenly snapping. "Yes, sir, let's talk about that. It's high time we cleared the air on that subject."

Uh-oh, thought Dare with amusement.

She saw the resignation pass over his face but didn't relent, even though she was tempted. She'd been having this argument with herself since Thanksgiving, and now that she was wound up, she wanted to cite all her reasons, to make him understand what she felt he'd failed to.

"I'm not sure you fully understand my situation. The simple fact is, my entire career can be destroyed by a single indiscretion. You're a man. You're expected to chase skirts. If the skirt happens to belong to a subordinate officer, it doesn't matter in the least unless she chooses to make some kind of fuss about it.

"On the other hand, I'm a woman. In these liberated times it's okay if I have an affair, but it will never be okay for me to have a personal relationship with my commanding officer. One whisper of something like that will label me forever as a woman who uses her body to get ahead. I can forget the whole idea of a career if that happens."

"Whoa, Andrea. Easy."

She shook her head, and her green eyes met his forthrightly despite the color that climbed up her throat. "It's not that I don't want to kiss you." Which was one heck of an understatement, she thought. It was about all she seemed to want anymore. "I think, however, that the price may be a whole lot higher than I'm willing to pay for a casual affair."

It was the last two words that got to him: casual affair. Was that how it looked to her, as if he were toying with her entire future for a few casual couplings? Casual was not the word for any of the things Andrea made him feel. He hadn't really examined those feelings, but he guessed it was time to do so. Before they decided how to settle this thing between them, he owed her that much, at least. And, he decided, he owed her equal honesty.

"Andrea, this isn't casual for me. I'm not sure what it is, but it's definitely not casual."

Her eyes widened; then she blinked in that way she had when she was momentarily taken aback. "Oh." Suddenly all her arguments fled from her head. *Not casual.* The admission at once terrified and elated her. She didn't want his interest to be casual, but she didn't know how she would handle it if it wasn't. Lord, she'd turned into a dithering idiot!

"I'm not sure you'll be grateful when you think about it," he said drily. "A casual affair is a lot easier to dismiss." Reaching inside his parka, he retrieved a pack of cigarettes and lit one. For a guy who'd nearly quit a couple of months ago, he was starting to smoke an awful lot.

"What are you saying, sir?"

"I've been where you are, Andrea. I know better than you think just how you view things and what you want out of life. Maybe in ten or twelve years you'll understand where I'm coming from. When you devote your whole life to an institution, you get very few personal rewards. You wake up one morning and find you've missed most of what life is about. It's not a happy experience. So I've reordered my priorities. That's why I kissed you, and that's why I'm going to kiss you again."

Andrea drew a sharp breath. Something deep inside her clenched pleasurably, but she tried to ignore it. "Sir..."

"Quiet, Captain. Don't worry. I have absolutely no intention of damaging your career. There won't even be a whisper of impropriety. But I *will* kiss you again."

Andrea found herself fascinated by his hands. Large, strong, long-fingered hands. Their backs were thinly sprinkled with fine black hairs, and it took no great leap of the imagination to picture that hair elsewhere. She swallowed. The truth was, she wanted him to kiss her right now, and it was getting harder and harder to remember why that was wrong.

"Andrea." One of his hands reached out to cover hers.

She looked up, and there was such an unconcealed wealth of longing in her eyes that MacLendon felt as if he'd been socked in the chest. Never had anyone looked at him that way.

He withdrew his hand and deliberately pushed up his parka sleeve to look at his watch. "What time would you get back tonight if you really had gone to Romeo?"

"About ten-thirty." The moment was shattered. Her answer was businesslike.

"We've got time for more coffee, then." He stubbed out his cigarette and signaled the waitress.

Andrea nodded, dropped her chin into her hand again, and let her eyelids droop. The day had been too long at two-thirty that afternoon, and now it was nearly nine. Her shoulder throbbed in time to the beat of her heart. How long would it be before she got her old energy back? And how long would it be until the sight of Dare's face stopped hurting worse than her shoulder? It was an almost physical pain that pierced her each time she looked at him.

When they stepped outside, it was immediately obvious that they had made a big mistake by staying so long. Snow whirled wildly everywhere, and the wind had strengthened considerably. Visibility was reduced to about ten feet.

"We've got a problem," Dare remarked when they were safely closed up in the cab of the truck. "Still, it'll be easier to explain what we're doing in a ditch five miles east of here than what we're doing out of our way at a roadhouse."

"We won't go into a ditch," Andrea said wryly. "There isn't

a single bend in the road between here and the base. You could tie a rope around the wheel and we'd get home all right.''

The corners of his mouth moved upward, and he turned on the ignition.

The state highway engineers had taken advantage of the state's flatness and unceasing winds. The road was somewhat elevated above the surrounding fields, so that the never-ending wind swept away the snow and kept the roads clean. Drifts and ice were not the danger; whiteout was. When they set out, it was still possible to see the white stripe at the edge of the road. Dare drove a cautious thirty miles an hour.

Before long, however, they were in a full whiteout, unable to see even as far as the front end of the truck's hood.

''Damn,'' Dare muttered. He slowed to five miles per hour, hoping their reduced speed would improve visibility. It didn't.

''Maybe we should pull over,'' Andrea said.

''Pull over where? I don't even know where the shoulder is now.'' He considered stopping right where he was, but even as the thought was forming, the truck tipped toward Andrea's side. They were off the road.

Chapter 7

The situation was quite simply one of survival. They radioed the base that they'd gone off the road and were told that visibility was zero and all travel had been stopped by order of Dare's deputy commander. No rescue would be forthcoming until the storm passed—around dawn, it was hoped. Neither Andrea nor Dare had expected anything else. Anybody who tried to come after them would probably wind up in precisely the same predicament.

Dare ventured out briefly to get the survival gear from the back of the truck, and soon he and Andrea were wrapped in wool blankets and staring at each other by the light of a single candle set safely in a tin on the door of the glove compartment.

Dare shifted suddenly, wedging himself into the corner between the door and the seat. He insisted that Andrea lean back against him and try to sleep.

"You're pooped," he said. "It's been obvious all evening. Just lean back, shut up and sleep."

Covered by layers of winter clothing, he made a comfortable pillow, and Andrea fell asleep with her back to his chest, fatigue taking her by surprise.

Dare didn't sleep. Sleep was dangerous in these subzero temperatures, and there was no guarantee you'd ever know that you were freezing to death. Instead he remained watchful. His right arm closed about Andrea's waist, covering the left arm that was strapped just below her breasts, and he let his chin rest on the top of her head.

Several hours later, Andrea came instantly awake. She was shaking, but she didn't feel more than a little cold.

"Dare?"

"I'm here." His rumble was reassuring, right above her head.

Suddenly she realized why she was shaking. "You're shivering!"

"I'm losing a little body heat through my back. It's right against the door."

Andrea shoved herself up immediately and looked at him in the light of the guttering candle. His teeth were clenched.

"I suppose you thought it would make me feel wonderful in the morning to find you frozen to death under me!"

"I'm not in any danger of freezing, damn it." He sat up and tried to pull the blanket around his shoulders. "I'm just a little cold. Shivering will warm me up in a minute."

Andrea made a disgusted sound and reached for the candy bars that had come with the survival kit. "Eat one of these. Eat them all. Damn, where are the candles?"

"In the glove box."

"You really amaze me," she scolded as she pulled out a fresh candle. "You know better than this. Every bit of body warmth is essential. You can't afford to let yourself get cold." After lighting the candle, she stuck it onto the stub of the old one. "Here. Take off your mittens and hold your hands right over the candle."

He tried to comply, but he was shivering so badly that he was unable to get much good from the flame. Andrea made a disgusted sound and opened the two middle buttons of her parka.

"Come on, cowboy, put your hands in here."

"Don't call me cowboy," he grumbled as his hands found their way inside the parka, inside her regulation cardigan, and into a nest of warmth and softness. If he hadn't been so cold, he might even have enjoyed it.

Andrea pulled the blankets up and over their hooded heads,

sealing in the heat of their breath, wrapping them in a dark cocoon. The light from the candle was dimly visible through the tight weave of the wool blankets. She made a small sound as her injured shoulder bumped into the seat back.

"This isn't going to work, Andrea," Dare said through chattering teeth. "You can't get comfortable."

"I'll get comfortable when you stop shivering. Until then, I'll survive."

But the shivering didn't stop. He'd gotten more hypothermic than he'd suspected. Gritting his teeth to stop them from chattering, he pulled his hands away from the warmth of Andrea's body and struggled to unfasten his parka. When it fell open, he reached for the buttons of hers. She helped him as best she could, and then his frigid hands slipped up her back, inside the stored warmth, and their chests came together, sharing heat. Shifting slightly, he managed to maneuver them so that Andrea rested comfortably against him, all pressure off her shoulder.

Gradually his violent shuddering began to taper off, and feeling began to return to his fingers, toes, and nose. He still felt cold, deeply, internally cold, but his body signaled that the worst was over by letting his muscles relax between bouts of shivering.

"Dare?"

"Hmm?"

"What have you got against cowboys?"

He almost smiled. "Nothing. I just don't like to be called cowboy. My ex-wife used to call me that when she was in one of her bitchy moods."

"How long were you married?"

"For five endless years way back when. Maureen wasn't cut out for either me or military life. She was a city girl, a socialite. Being a lowly lieutenant's wife drove her crazy. She should have married a general."

"Was she pretty?"

He considered. "I guess. I thought so at first. Later I thought she was pretty ugly. I got so I hated the sight of her, the sound of her. To this day I can't stand the perfume she used to wear."

"Must've been rough."

"There's nothing quite like the ugliness that can happen between two people who know each other well. You get so you know what really hurts and how to use it. Maureen was especially good at it."

"I'm sorry." Andrea's voice was soft.

"I recovered a long time ago. It's a mistake I'll never make again, though."

"Marriage?"

"Not marriage. Marrying somebody without thinking about just what they'll be giving up. If I met Maureen now, I'd know better. I'd know it would sour her. Love doesn't conquer all, you know. It doesn't conquer anything. Sooner or later you've got to deal with the real world. There's always a trade-off."

"How unromantic." With her cheek against Dare's chest, she listened to the sound of his heartbeat. He was hardly shivering now, and the earlier rapid rhythm had slowed to normal.

"Oh, I believe in romance," he said. "Moonlight, wine, roses—"

"Skip the roses."

He chuckled. "Quiet candlelit dinners, then. But I'm a realist, too, Andrea. Think about it. How would you feel if some man told you to choose between him and your career?"

There was a silence. "Yeah," she said quietly after a moment.

His hands began to move in slow, soothing circles on her back, and a kittenish purr escaped her.

"You're all tense," he said.

"It's the shoulder. I seem to be stiff all the time from trying to protect it. Mmm." His fingers were kneading gently, working the tension out.

"Andrea?"

"Sir?"

"I'm getting a nearly irresistible urge to kiss you again."

She surprised him with a low throaty chuckle. "I thought you'd never mention it."

It was crazy, it was insane, and he kissed her anyway. Outside, the wind howled and the snow whipped icily, but inside the blankets warmth began to grow.

It was a curiously sweet and tender episode. Between Andrea's shoulder, the confinement of the truck, and the deadly threat of the cold, their kisses could not evolve into passion. Instead they savored the warmth and closeness, the gentle, lingering comfort of lips and tongues. It was enough to hold and be held, to kiss and be kissed. They both began to realize what they'd been missing.

Finally they simply leaned against one another, content and comforted. There was a world of difference in Dare's mind between an embrace and a hug. He was hugging Andrea, and she him. It occurred to him he couldn't have picked a worse person to make the object of that kind of affection. Andrea was a career woman, determined to pursue her goals. There was pain waiting for him at the end of this road. Sighing, he drew her a little closer. He was old enough to understand that all good things had a price. You just had to decide whether something was worth it.

"Penny?" said Andrea from where she was nestled against his shoulder.

"I was just thinking how huggable you are."

"Mmm. I like the way that sounds. You're huggable, too."

"Am I?" He'd never thought of himself that way. It pleased him.

"You are." She snuggled closer. In their warm cocoon, cut off from the world, it was easy to forget everything, and Andrea let herself do just that. She understood that eventually reality would intrude, but for the moment she refused to care.

He raised his hand to cradle her cheek. "Was it rough being Charlie Burke's daughter?" he asked.

The perception of the question amazed Andrea. People who knew her father always assumed he was a great dad, that he'd encouraged Andrea's independence and her Air Force career. In fact, he'd seized every opportunity to try to grind her down and turn her into a submissive, dependent female. There wasn't anything personal in it. It was just the way Charlie Burke thought women ought to be. In fact, the only thing in the world tougher than being Charlie Burke's daughter was being Charlie Burke's son.

It was her brothers who had saved Andrea from her intended fate by treating her as one of them, by expecting her to play their games and take part in their escapades. Being kids, they just didn't know how else to treat a sister, particularly one whose competitive spirit was fierce. She never hesitated, so it never occurred to them to balk.

"Sometimes it was rough," she admitted, intensely aware of Dare's thumb stroking her cheek. His gentleness continually amazed her. He looked hard, tough, competent, yet when he held her, he made her feel precious and safe. He managed to treat her as if she were fragile without in any way diminishing her strength and independence. It was a dangerously addicting sensation.

"You have so many contrasts, Andrea," Dare said suddenly. "That night I was in the accident, you were so easy and boyish. I distinctly remember deciding that you were going to be a handful. Then there's the prickly pear cactus who glares at me when I step on her toes. And there's the smartmouth who slips her zingers almost unnoticed into the conversation. There's the cool, capable officer with a steady gaze, and there's the tough cookie who can dress a trooper down with all the punch of Patton. And then there's *this* Andrea."

"What's this Andrea?" There was a smile in her voice.

"This Andrea is a soft, warm, wonderful woman who can put her arms around a man and make him feel like he's come home."

Andrea lifted her head. "Dare," she said uneasily.

"Leave it alone, Andrea," he said gently. "I'm old enough to know what I'm doing. You'll forget your damn career long before I do."

She was surprised to realize that she believed him. He would be the last one of them to forget all the obstacles in their path.

For Dare, the night was endless. He had wadded a blanket and slipped it between him and the door to provide insulation, then stretched out, his long legs on the passenger side floor, his back wedged against the blanket and seat. Andrea lay half over him, her face burrowed into his shoulder, one hand tucked into the warmth of his armpit. His own arms were wrapped snugly around her waist inside her parka. Every time he drew a breath, her warmth and sweetly feminine scent wafted into his nostrils. They kept each other warm, but it was more than Andrea's body heat that raised Dare's temperature.

Andrea slept, but Dare kept watch over her, so there was no

escape from the tingling in his loins that kept trying to turn into a full throbbing. He'd never been a promiscuous man, had never indulged in casual relationships. Such things just didn't appeal to him. Consequently the span since his last relationship could be counted in years. Too many years, to judge by his present discomfort.

The fact that Andrea really wasn't his type made his attraction to her all the more serious. Like Andrea, he'd been raised in a large family of boys, but on a ranch in Montana, where life had been hard. His mother had died while he was still very young, so there had been no female influence in his life. It was the femininity of women that usually attracted him, their softness and gentleness, their ruffles and frills, their perfume and long hair. He was attracted to all the things that his life had always lacked.

Andrea enticed him with none of those things. In so many ways, his relationship with her was no different from his relationship with his male officers. He could easily see her becoming a poker buddy, or a drinking buddy, or even a hunting buddy. He could not, hard as he might try, imagine her in any typical female role. Yet on those rare occasions when they gave free rein to the man-woman urges between them, he found her incredibly feminine, irresistibly sexy. Why?

Why did she feel so right in his arms, even now, when it was sheer torment? Why did he take such delight at the spark of annoyance in her eyes, or the way she bedeviled him and zinged him? Why, when she was being cool, collected, competent Captain Burke, did she make him feel like he was a man in possession of a wonderful secret?

Sighing, he shifted just a little and then nearly groaned when the movement brought her hip into more intimate contact with him. If he weren't a gentleman, he would slip his hands up inside her uniform blouse and find out if her skin was as satiny as it looked. It probably was, damn it. And those better-than-standard-issue breasts were probably high and pink-tipped. And her fanny, which he'd eyeballed from time to time when she wore slacks, was gently rounded and ever so slightly fuller than average in a way that made him want to—

He muttered an oath and forced his mind from such thoughts.

He might be going crazy, but there was no point in being masochistic about it. The woman had made it clear that she would do nothing to risk her career, so he'd better just focus his thoughts on something safe, like work.

Rescue arrived before dawn. The winds had quieted enough that the blowing snow snaked along at ground level, leaving visibility unlimited. A drift had grown against one side of the truck, nearly covering it, but Sergeant Nickerson was able to walk around and open the door on Andrea's side.

He found the two officers shivering and exhausted but otherwise all right. Andrea never wanted to see another candy bar.

"We'll send someone out for the truck later, sir, ma'am," Nickerson said. "Right now, let's just get you two to the hospital."

"Forget the hospital," Andrea snapped. "Just take me to the chow hall. I'm gonna drink a gallon of coffee."

Dare and Nickerson eyed one another over Andrea's head, sharing a look of masculine patience.

"Chow hall," said Dare after a moment.

Nickerson nodded. "Yes, sir." He reached up to help Andrea down, but she brushed his hand away, insisting that she could get out of the truck under her own steam.

She managed it, too, in spite of nearly tripping over the blanket, being able to steady herself with only one hand and discovering that hypothermia had affected her coordination. When she climbed into the crew cab of Nickerson's truck, the blast from the heater was painful to her cold skin.

The sun was just beginning its slow rise when they cleared the main gate and drove onto the base. This far north, it didn't have all that far to lift. It was going to be a clear, bright, cold day.

Nickerson pulled into the parking lot near the chow hall, and the three of them went inside to begin the day the way Andrea thought it should begin, with a gallon of coffee, bacon, and eggs. She was still shivering somewhat, but it didn't take long for the coffee to thaw her.

Gradually the world began to return to normal. The night had been an aberration, she told herself. It was the danger that had brought her and Dare together in a brief time of openness and gentleness. It was over, and time to forget it.

"How come you decided to go out to Romeo, ma'am?" Nickerson asked.

Andrea looked up from her plate, telling herself that it was her tiredness that made Nickerson's question seem out of line. She lifted one brow and paused before answering. Nickerson had been working with her for two years, she reminded herself. Like a lot of high-ranking sergeants, he treated young officers in a somewhat fatherly fashion. Or maybe it just seemed out of line because she couldn't answer truthfully. Dare had made it clear that no one but he and Andrea was to know about the OSI investigation.

"Why do I ever go out to the sites, Sergeant?" she asked coolly.

Dare noticed that Nickerson didn't miss Andrea's zingers, either. The sergeant, who was accustomed to Andrea calling him Nick, retreated instantly.

"None of my business, ma'am," he said.

Andrea ate a piece of egg. "No, it's not," she agreed. "In point of fact, I hadn't been out to a couple of those sites in too long. My timing was atrocious, I guess." She was aware that that left the question of why Dare had gone with her. "Nick, have you heard anything about a crap game out at Romeo Four Two?"

Nickerson looked surprised. "No, ma'am," he said swiftly. "I can't believe—no, ma'am, I sure haven't. Wouldn't be much of a crap game with only a couple of guys."

"There are mobile units, too, Nick. It would be easy enough for them to get in on it."

Nickerson nodded slowly. "I'll sure keep my ear to the ground. But ma'am, I just don't think—"

"Unthinkable things happen, Nick."

Let him put that in his pipe and smoke it, Andrea thought. He probably figured she'd gone round the bend. That was fine. He would quit asking questions, and after a week or so he'd probably decide this had been a temporary aberration on her part.

She shoved back her chair. "I'm still starved," she announced and took her plate back to the chow line.

Dare saw the look on Nickerson's face and gave Andrea high marks for redirecting his attention.

Andrea returned with a heaping plateful of home fries and scrambled eggs. Dare's lips quirked in amusement, and he wondered how she stayed so lean if she ate like a football player.

"Do you always eat like this?" he asked her.

"Like what, sir?" She didn't even look up, occupied with peppering her potatoes.

"Never mind," Dare said. "Just finish so I can get you safely dumped off at the BOQ with orders to stay in bed today."

"That's really not necessary, sir," she said coolly. Of course, she couldn't see the purple rings under her eyes.

"I don't recall asking for your opinion on the subject, Captain." Dare's voice had suddenly taken on a note of command. It startled her; she'd never heard him use quite that tone before. He generally seemed to manage men with an easy style and didn't have to bring authority to bear.

"Sorry, sir," she said promptly.

Dare might have relented if Nickerson hadn't been there. As it was, he left the colonel and the captain once again firmly in their places. There was one advantage to being Andrea's CO, he thought ruefully. He could shut her up when he had a mind to.

The morning of Christmas Eve, Andrea arrived at her desk to find a summons from the CBPO, the personnel office. Her heart quickened at once. That kind of summons usually meant only one thing: a new assignment. She indulged a few moments of speculation, thinking that there could be worse Christmas presents. It would get her away from Dare, who continued to have the most devastating affect on her tranquillity in spite of the fact that they had kept strictly to business since the night they had gone off the road. In fact, they hadn't even discussed spending Christmas together, as he had once suggested, and she gathered he planned to spend the holiday in solitude, just as she did.

She was grateful to him for letting the matter drop. Grateful and annoyed. On the one hand, a relationship with him was impossible, given the circumstances, and she was honest enough to admit to herself that if he'd pushed the matter, she would have given in eventually. On the other hand, she wished he *had* pushed it. In all honesty, while she might have hated herself for it afterward, she would have loved to be swept off her feet, pushed past the decisions and problems, and brought to a fulfillment she still could only imagine. He had begun to invade her dreams, had Alisdair MacLendon, and she was getting tired of waking in the morning with an ache in her heart and soul that made her want to weep.

Dare. Even his name was a challenge, and she felt like a coward for not daring to meet it.

Sighing, she grabbed her parka and headed for personnel. With her luck, they'd probably be sending her to Alaska. She hadn't had a single warm assignment since joining this damn outfit.

It was an assignment. The sergeant she spoke with handed her a stack of rosters with a laconic, "Merry Christmas, Captain. You've won an all-expense paid trip to Minot, North Dakota."

Andrea looked down at the inch-thick stack of orders. "Somebody must love me."

The sergeant grinned. "If it's any consolation, ma'am, while the climate won't improve, you'll be in command of a larger squadron."

Andrea hardly knew whether to laugh or swear. She would be moving to the other end of the state to command the larger security squadron at Minot, but she'd have the same North Dakota winters to contend with, the same missile fields, the same problems. It hardly seemed worth the effort of moving her. Shrugging, she headed back to the Squadron HQ, telling herself that this was a big step up in her career. The climate didn't matter.

She walked back into the building and lifted the stack of papers as she passed the front desk. "I got orders," she said. The cops at the desk grinned.

"Where to, ma'am?" one of them asked.

"You'll never believe it."

"Hawaii?"

She shook her head. "Minot."

Their roars of laughter followed her all the way down the corridor.

Back in the privacy of her own office, however, she didn't feel like laughing, and a step up in her career suddenly seemed relatively unimportant. In five weeks she would be leaving. In five weeks Dare MacLendon would be gone from her life. She'd told herself that nothing could ever have come of it, but that didn't stop her from feeling cheated.

Resting her elbows on the desk and steepling her hands, she pressed her fingers against her lips and closed her eyes. She felt—and no amount of internal argument dispelled the feeling—that she was about to lose an opportunity that came only once in a lifetime. But what could she do? Orders were orders.

Twenty minutes later, Dare was on the phone. "You got orders?" he asked, hoping it wasn't true.

It never failed to amaze Andrea how fast gossip traveled. "Yes, sir. I'm leaving January thirtieth for Minot."

"Minot, huh." Dare forced a laugh into his voice. "Luck of the draw, Captain. Just one of the wonders of GI life. You could say you're so good at what you do that they just don't want to waste you."

"I could also say somebody doesn't like me."

"You could." He could say the same about her departure, but he figured she was in no mood to hear it. He doubted very much that Minot was on anyone's Dream Sheet of preferred assignments. He opted instead to tease her. "Next Christmas, I'll send you a set of red long johns. Just don't get caught in any ditches with any colonels."

A gleam came to Andrea's hazy green eyes. "I don't repeat my mistakes, Colonel."

The ensuing silence was so long that Andrea realized Dare hadn't liked her teasing remark. Good Lord, did he think she was saying *he* was a mistake? That the little bit of human warmth they'd shared was a mistake? Her mind began to scramble for a way to explain herself while a mocking little voice said, What's the matter, Burke? Isn't that what you've been saying all along? That it's one big mistake?

It was Dare, however, who broke the silence. "I've got this problem," he said. Quietly. Gravely.

Andrea's heart nearly stopped as she waited tensely. "Oh?"

"I've got a Christmas tree to decorate tonight. Funny how I

haven't gotten around to it yet. And I have a bottle of B&B, but I hate to drink alone.'' He sighed. ''That's the problem with giving twenty years of your life to your career. You wind up drinking alone.'' With that, he hung up.

And left Andrea to wonder if she had just been given an invitation.

She struggled with that possibility for the rest of the day and right through dinner. Along about seven o'clock, it occurred to her that her orders had just set her free from a whole boatload of problems. Some of the other bachelors stopped by to invite her to come along to the Officers' Club, but she turned them down, saying she had been invited to a friend's home for the evening.

Suddenly excited, she dug a seldom-worn royal blue jersey dress out of the closet, along with a pair of stiletto-heeled pumps. She even managed to find a little eyeshadow and mascara and a pale lipstick, left over from so long ago that she wasn't sure they were still safe to use. It was only when she stood at the door, parka in hand, that she questioned the wisdom of what she was about to do.

If she parked her car at Dare's place, the entire squadron would know it. The patrolling cops would recognize it. She might as well take an ad out in the base newspaper. And it was too cold to walk over there dressed like this, with nothing between her legs and frostbite but a layer of nylon mesh.

Sighing, she turned back, ready to relinquish the whole idea. And then she saw the telephone. Why not? said the daring voice that had carried her through the academy and into a career that was unusual for a woman. Why the heck not?

She dialed Dare's number and didn't begin to get nervous until she heard his voice.

''Hello?'' he repeated when she didn't immediately answer.

She found her voice at last. ''It's Andrea,'' she said.

''What's up?'' His voice told her nothing; indeed he sounded businesslike, as if he thought she were calling about work.

''Uh, I wondered if you wanted any help with the tree.''

''I'd love some.'' His voice grew warm, and it caused something inside her to quiver. ''Come on over.''

"Uh, my car—" She couldn't lie, but she couldn't explain her reasoning, either. It sounded so dumb.

"I'm on my way," he said briskly. "I'll pull up right out front."

Shrouded in her parka with the concealing snorkel hood pulled up, she darted through the empty hallway and down the back stairway to the parking lot. She might have been any of the thirty female officers in residence in the BOQ, and there was nothing about Dare's Bronco to set it apart from dozens of others on base. Five minutes later she was climbing into the warmth of his car, somehow feeling that she had just burned a bridge behind her.

Chapter 8

Dare's Christmas tree stood in front of the curtained patio doors. He had already strung the lights, and they were twinkling gaily. While Andrea admired the tree, Dare admired her.

A new side to his Captain Burke, he thought. She looked so soft and womanly in that clinging blue jersey that he didn't know how he was going to keep his hands off her. He had held her in his arms three times, yet he'd never really realized just how perfectly she was constructed. The full skirt and high heels accentuated a pair of legs that were long and exquisitely formed. All the boyishness she ordinarily presented had vanished.

Or maybe he was just besotted. He didn't care. Stirring himself, he poured a B&B and handed it to her.

"It's a lovely tree, Dare," she said shyly.

Dare? Pleasure swooped through him. This was promising indeed. He'd been feeling gloomy all day because she was leaving in a month. For the first time it occurred to him that those orders might be a blessing.

"I baked some cookies earlier," he said, feeling suddenly awkward. "I'll go get some."

"You baked cookies?" She looked surprised.

"Now who's being the chauvinist?" he asked wryly. "It happens I like Christmas cookies.'' He enjoyed the blush that suffused her cheeks for a moment and then forced himself to go get the cookies. Keep it cool, MacLendon, he warned himself, or she'll turn into Captain Burke again and start yes-sirring and no-sirring you to death.

While he was in the kitchen, Andrea set her brandy down and went over to the couch to peer into the ornament box. She noticed he had a new painting on the wall over the couch, a scene of the desert Southwest at twilight. Done in oils, it conveyed the texture of the scene, as well as its wildness and beauty. Forgetting the ornaments, she lost herself in the painting. One of the many things lacking in her life, she realized suddenly, was art. Good music, good painting, good books.

''Like it?'' Dare asked. He stood at her elbow, a plate of cookies in his hand.

''I love it.'' She smiled at him, her shyness forgotten. ''It's beautiful.''

''Have a cookie.'' His eyes were warm, making her feel warm, too.

He put a record of Christmas carols on the stereo and then handed her a box of ornaments. ''These are my favorite ones,'' he said. ''You do the honors.''

His taste in Christmas ornaments surprised her, too. Each was unique; all were handmade of wood or fabric or stained glass. There were sleighs and skiers, Santas and bells and trees. Some were shapes she didn't recognize, and he told her they were Indian good luck symbols. Before long she was as excited as a child herself, each new ornament a surprise.

Finally it was all done. Dare turned out all the lights, and they stood side by side in the dark, admiring the tree.

''It's so perfect,'' Andrea said in a hushed voice. ''I've never seen such a beautiful tree.''

As if it were the most natural thing in the world, Dare slipped his arm around her shoulders. And as if it were the most natural thing in the world, Andrea leaned against him.

''Andrea?''

''Hmm?''

''Who are we tonight?'' He had to know. There was no way he was going to stumble around blind tonight, perhaps offending her, perhaps losing her. He had to know where he stood. He heard the catch of her breath and tensed, waiting for her answer. After a moment, she turned slowly to face him. He looked down into her eyes, dark pools in the dim light.

She spoke steadily. "I left my uniform back at the BOQ, sir. Just for tonight, I'm nobody at all."

"You're not nobody, Andrea," he said huskily. "You're the most enchanting, bewitching woman in the world. Just for tonight," he added, seeing the sudden flicker of concern on her face. "Just for tonight."

She relaxed then, a small smile lifting the corners of her mouth. What a role reversal, Dare thought, with a brief sense of the wry humor of the situation. She was concerned that he might be hurt. She was the one who wanted no strings to interfere with her future, no obligations to bind her. Quite a man, his Captain Burke.

"I am so very glad," he said, spacing his words as his blue eyes fixed on her mouth, "that you left your uniform behind." It was such a soft, inviting mouth, he thought, and it had started to tremble ever so slightly at the corners. "You don't need to be afraid of me, Andrea."

"I'm not. At least, not exactly."

"Nervous?"

"A little."

Lightly, as if he were touching the wings of a butterfly, he brushed his thumb across her lower lip. "What are you nervous about?"

She blinked and gnawed the lip he'd just caressed. "Everything," she answered finally.

"Everything?" He moved a little closer. "That's an awful lot to be nervous about. Just how inexperienced *are* you?"

She blinked twice this time, rapidly, and had to clear her throat before she could speak. The low intimacy of his tone made strange things happen deep inside her, as did the feathery caress of his fingers on her cheek. "Very inexperienced," she croaked.

"Tell me, Andrea," he coaxed. "I have to know, for both our sakes."

Her courage failed her at last, and she closed her eyes tightly.

"Never," she whispered, and wondered how long her rubbery knees would hold her. She wouldn't blame him if he backed off right now, but, oh, now that she'd finally come to this point, she didn't think she could survive the disappointment.

A virgin. He'd suspected as much. As if she were glass that might shatter at a careless touch, Dare wrapped his arms carefully around her and drew her head into the comforting hollow of his shoulder. Hearing her shaky sigh, he sought to soothe her with a gentle kiss to her temple.

"I'm going to try very hard to seduce you, Andrea."

"Yes, sir." Her voice was little more than a choked whisper.

"But," he said softly against her hair, "I have very strict rules about seduction. Would you like to hear them?"

"Mmm."

"First of all, I won't do anything you don't want me to. That's a promise, Andrea."

She made a small sound of acknowledgment.

"Secondly, you can tell me to stop at any point, and I won't get mad."

She nodded.

"Finally, you have to enjoy this and want this every bit as much as I do, or I'll stop. This is supposed to be a mutually wonderful experience. I'll do my best to make it that way for you, but I don't want you to feel pressured in any way."

Slowly Andrea's hazy green eyes opened, and she looked up at him. "I believe *I* called *you,* sir."

Dare smiled. "So you did. You're still allowed to change your mind. I don't take this lightly, so I don't expect you to. I want you to be very, very sure about this."

Lifting her right arm, she wrapped it around his neck, looking at once shy and brave.

"Colonel MacLendon?"

"Yes, Captain?"

"I believe I'm already seduced."

His heart slipped into high gear at that admission.

"Oh, no, Captain," he whispered huskily, zeroing in on her mouth. "I haven't yet begun to seduce you."

He stole her breath in a kiss that left her shaken. He knew

her mouth now, knew just what to do to send electric shocks racing through her, knew just how to make her shiver and burn.

My God, thought Andrea, if he learns any more about me I'll be defenseless. But she wanted to learn those very things about herself as much as he wanted to discover them. Tightening her arm around his neck, she stood on tiptoes and murmured deep in her throat at the pleasurable feeling as her breasts were crushed against the hard wall of his chest.

Oh yes, thought Dare. Oh yes. It seemed as if he'd been aching all his life to hold this woman, and the thin jersey was little barrier to his hands as they stroked her back from neck to hip. Each time he held her, he was astonished anew at how small and delicate she felt. He'd seen the way she carried herself and talked with her troops and faced things straight on, and nobody in the whole world would think to call Andrea Burke either small or delicate.

Nobody except Alisdair MacLendon when he held her close and felt every delicate bit of her womanliness. That slender waist was almost small enough for him to span with both hands. Those shoulders disappeared in his grasp, and the curving line of her back and hips had all the grace of a swan. She was lovely, his Captain Burke, and he said so.

Looking down at her flushed face and dazed eyes, Dare swept his hands from her neck to her hips one more time. This time, however, he went farther, bending a little as he cupped that sweet, soft bottom that had been driving him crazy for months and pulled her snugly up against him. Andrea's breath caught in her throat as she felt his unashamed arousal hot against her abdomen.

"Dare..." she breathed in wonder. Her fingernails bit into his shoulder as slowly, slowly, he rocked his hips against her and groaned. Her breath stopped, and perhaps her heart, too, as the ache in her was at once answered and worsened.

Groaning again, Dare stilled himself, or tried to, but Andrea could still feel minute movements against her as if two forces were in opposition and one was just a little bit stronger. Why was he stopping? She didn't want him to stop. She wanted every bit of his hunger. The thought that she excited him so greatly thrilled her every bit as much as his kisses did.

"Dare?"

His face was hard with passion and self-control, but he heard the doubt and the edge of worry in her voice, and he responded with a crooked smile.

"It's okay, Andrea," he said huskily. "It's okay. I nearly blew it, that's all."

"Did you?" Slowly a very female smile dawned on her swollen lips.

A choked chuckle escaped him as he saw her satisfaction. "I *knew* you were going to be a handful."

"Yes, sir," she answered demurely, but her desire to tease him vanished as swiftly as it had been born. Green eyes wide, she looked up at him. "I never felt like this before."

He dropped another kiss on her cheek. "How do you feel?"

"Like—like every part of me aches so badly to be touched. I want—I want—" Words and courage both failed her.

"Me too," Dare said hoarsely, gathering her closer. "Me too. But I was close to forgetting my rules, and I don't want to do that. Not this first time."

"What rules?" she asked, dropping her forehead against his chest. "Did I ever tell you you smell good?" She nuzzled his shoulder and sighed.

"So do you. And you feel even better."

A laugh sparkled in her misty eyes as she craned her neck to look up at him. "Do I?"

Here she was again, he thought delightedly, his very favorite smartmouth captain who'd so pertly told him she had a pair of standard female issue breasts. He wanted this Andrea as much as he wanted the softer Andrea she so rarely allowed to show. He wanted *all* of her in his bed, not just bits and pieces of her.

"You know you feel good, you little minx," he retorted gruffly. Back firmly in control of his body, he was able to search out that sensitive place behind her ear and, with the tip of his tongue, send a shiver rippling through her.

"Dare?"

"Hmm?" He found an equally interesting spot where her neck met her shoulder.

"I think my knees are going to give out."

"Mmm. I like the sound of that." Lifting his head, he smiled.

"Are you brave enough to let me carry you to my bed? Or are you still unsure?"

Clinging to his shoulders, she cocked her head. "Why are you so sure I don't know what I'm doing?"

"Because until tonight you've been dead set against this. Because you're inexperienced, and that gives you the right to have second thoughts."

"I don't believe this," she said after a moment's thought.

"Believe what?"

"When I graduated from the Academy, my father had only one comment to make regarding my career. He warned me to look out for you pilots because you'd tumble anything that looked vaguely willing."

"I *told* you I always thought he was an ass." Dare tunnelled his fingers into her short, reddish hair, enjoying its silkiness. "Just what are you saying?"

She stepped back a few inches so she could see him better. "I may be inexperienced and nervous, I may even get a little shy and embarrassed, but I've made up my mind. I wish you'd just quit worrying about it."

"Sweet Andrea." Her jaw had that bulldog set he knew so well, and he had to smile. "Are your knees still rubbery?"

She shook her head slowly, looking him right in the eye. "No, sir."

"We'll have to do something about that." He closed the small distance between them.

"Yes, sir." Her eyelids fluttered in anticipation of his kiss, but he astonished her by scooping her up in his arms as easily as if she weighed nothing.

"I always wanted to carry a woman off to my bed," he remarked humorously as he started down the hall.

"Thank God," she muttered against his throat.

"For what?"

"We both finally agree I'm a woman."

He laughed. "And at the same time, no less."

Dare was still chuckling when he carefully lowered her to her feet beside the king-size water bed. "Off with your shoes, Captain." He kicked off his own, as well.

For just a moment he held her by the shoulders and studied

her face, as if verifying her resolve. "What are you wearing under your dress?"

Startled by the question, Andrea blinked. "Standard undergarments."

"Good." His smile was crooked. "In the books and movies, clothes just conveniently vanish. In real life there's no romantic, easy way to take care of them."

Drawing her into his arms once again, he reached for the zipper on the back of her dress. "Lean on me, Andrea."

She couldn't have done anything else. The instant he tugged the zipper tab, her knees turned to water again. Instinctively, she wrapped her arms around his waist and clung.

"Why does it matter what I'm wearing?" she asked shakily, trying to concentrate. Heavens, he was pulling that zipper slowly.

"Because you're not ready to be naked with me, but it's easier to deal with undergarments than a dress. Now, shut up, Andrea. Pay attention to what I'm doing to you."

As if she could pay attention to anything else. All the while he eased that zipper down, his mouth insisted on pillaging her face and throat. His tongue streaked lightning along nerve endings she'd never been aware of before. And then…then his hands slipped inside her dress, warm against the smooth, sensitive skin of her back. Andrea gasped with pleasure, and Dare took advantage of it to kiss her long and deep.

When he raised his head again, her dress had somehow slipped off her shoulders, and she could feel it sliding down, down. His mouth followed, trailing hot little kisses across her shoulder to the swelling rise of one breast above her bra. Andrea froze, her heart hammering painfully as she waited for what was to come next. She guessed, half in fright and half in hope, that he would kiss her there where no one had ever….

With a cool caress, her dress puddled about her ankles, and she stood within the circle of his arms clad in nothing but her bra, half-slip, and panty hose.

"Shh," Dare whispered when she gave a small cry of surprise. "Shh, sweetheart. It's all right. Everything's all right."

Of course it was all right, she thought hazily, unable to raise eyelids that had somehow become weighted with lead. What was he talking about? It felt so good to feel the warm skin of his arms around her bare back, to feel the fabric of his shirt against her stomach.

Gently, Dare loosened her hold on him, and then, lifting her once again, he tucked her into his bed, beneath a comforter. Startled, Andrea opened her eyes, and in the dim light from the hallway she saw that he was discarding his own clothes. For an instant she felt a pang of fear. This was really happening, and she must be mad, insane. She'd sworn she would never do this, not ever, yet here she was, and it was far too late to back out. She'd insisted she wanted this, and she couldn't possibly change her mind when he was so—so—*ready*.

Suddenly he was in the bed beside her, beneath the coverlet, the warm, furry skin of his chest brushing her arm. The sensation electrified her, and her doubts no longer seemed as important.

"Andrea?" Propped on one elbow, he leaned over her, brushing her hair gently back as he studied her in the dim light. "Second thoughts? Don't be afraid to tell me." Disappointment might kill him, but he didn't want to harm a hair on her head.

Andrea's eyes opened again, and she looked up into his concerned face. That face, she realized uncomfortably, had become very dear to her in ways she was afraid to examine. Drawing a deep breath, she unconsciously squared her shoulders.

"You were right," she said on a breath. "Clothes are very awkward to deal with."

Slowly, he smiled. "Ah," he said with understanding. "Not second thoughts but cooling fires. We can remedy that."

Bravely lifting her arms, she twined them around his neck. Well, Burke, she told herself, you wanted this. You've been fantasizing about it for weeks. Now you're going to find out. Don't be a damn chicken.

Dare accepted her invitation, claiming her mouth in a soul-searing kiss that made everything else seem insignificant. There, beneath the comforter, in the sheltering shadows, he warmed her with his hands and lips, and when her bra vanished, her only thought was to press closer, to ease the ache in her breasts against the hardness of his chest. When she felt him shudder in response, she was further emboldened to rub against him.

"Andrea, Andrea," he muttered, "oh, *yes!*"

Arching his body away from her suddenly, he ducked his head beneath the comforter. A cry escaped Andrea as at last, at last, his mouth found the swollen peak of her breast, closing on it gently. Each suckling motion of his mouth and tongue sent a shaft of need spiraling to her core, feeding the ache there. She wanted him never to stop, but she wanted more, too.

His hands suddenly slipped beneath her slip, panty hose, and panties, cupping her round bottom and kneading in a rhythmic motion that made her sway in time to the pulsing fires inside her. In fact, her whole body throbbed in time to his hands and mouth.

When he suddenly took his mouth from her breasts, she cried out in disappointment, only to freeze in renewed excitement as he sat up and dispensed at last with her remaining garments. In one sweeping movement he stripped them down her legs and tossed them onto the floor before pulling up the comforter once more and returning to lie half over her.

"God, you feel so good to me," he grated near her ear, and Andrea realized he felt good to her, as well. One whole half of her body was pressed intimately to his, and she was acutely aware of the wondrous differences between a man and a woman. With an instinct as old as humanity, she accommodated herself to him, parting her legs so that one of his fell between them. She was instantly rewarded with a renewed throb of sensation that led her to turn toward him, to seek him with her hands.

"That's it, Andrea," he said huskily, controlling himself with difficulty. "Do whatever you want, whatever feels good to you."

"I want to make you feel good, too," she said thickly as she nibbled on the flat muscles across his chest.

"Oh, baby, you do. You do."

Finding a small, hard male nipple in the fur, she nipped at it experimentally and heard a groan rip from deep within him.

"If you do that too many times," he said roughly, "this'll be over before it's started."

Liking the way he reacted, she did it again and felt him jerk from head to foot. "You like that, too?" she asked breathlessly.

"God, yes."

So she did it again, and for her sake Dare rolled on top of

her and kissed her into breathlessness. He'd been ready to go almost from the outset, but he wanted Andrea to be right at his side. With lips and tongue he suckled first one breast and then the other, while his hand foraged downward toward her silken secrets. His fingers didn't get much below her navel before she was writhing against him and sobbing something that sounded like a plea.

With each kiss his own control had grown weaker, and he knew he wasn't going to be able to keep his own promises about drawing this out, not this time.

"Andrea? Andrea, my timing is terrible, but this is important. You're not protected are you?"

Her hands were clutching at his head, holding him to her breast, and he felt them suddenly grow still.

"Andrea?"

"It's okay," she groaned. She took the pill to regulate her cycle, and never had she been so grateful for that little inconvenience.

"You're sure?"

"It's my career. Dare, please. *Please!*"

Slowly he slid over her, parting her legs gently with his hands, rising to his knees.

"Oh, baby," he sighed against her mouth. "Touch me, Andrea. Touch me."

With the instincts of the ages, she reached for his velvet hardness, felt him stiffen and groan with a pleasure equal to her own. The sound thrilled her, and she guided him closer, needing that hardness as if it were a lost part of her.

"Now, Dare," she begged. "Now. Now."

"Yes, honey. Yes."

He thrust slowly, hanging on to the dregs of his control, giving her time to accommodate him. She was so tight that he knew she must hurt, but when he felt the barrier and hesitated, she arched up suddenly and fully sheathed him in her welcoming softness. A cry escaped her, and Dare grew instantly still, lifting his head to look into her face. He knew there was no way to avoid the pain, but he felt suddenly helpless and ignorant. How long would it last? Was there anything he should do to help her?

Her eyes were closed, and her mouth was open on a gasp that told him nothing.

"Andrea? Are you all right?"

Her eyelids fluttered, and her hands tightened on his waist. "I'm fine," she whispered. "I'm fine." The pain was passing off, leaving her aware of a wondrous, satisfying fullness.

"So good," she sighed. "You feel so good." She arched toward him.

He needed no more. Pulling back, he thrust again, and she met him eagerly, long legs twining around his hips, hands gripping his shoulders. "Yes," she groaned. "Yes."

Higher and higher he took them, racing for a place she could only guess at. A hard, exquisite pressure grew in her, seeking his thrusts, until it filled her completely, and the universe focused in that small place where they joined together, meeting, retreating, seeking.

Suddenly Andrea shattered as she never had before, bursting into blazing fireworks of scattering sparks, convulsing just as Dare convulsed with a hard groan, his short sharp jerks answering the rippling contractions inside her. His head fell to her shoulder; her arms fell to the bed. Only slowly, however, did her legs release him, reluctant to give up the fullness of their sharing.

And only slowly did Andrea come back to herself. "If that isn't illegal," she said huskily, feeling dizzy and weak, "it ought to be."

Dare kissed her and rolled off her, drawing her carefully to his side so that her head was cradled on his shoulder. It was on the tip of his tongue to tell her that never had it been so good for him, but some instinct warned him not to. She could believe the wonder of it came from her inexperience, but she wouldn't be able to believe that about him. She wanted no strings, so he would give her none. But God, it wasn't easy. If he had wanted her before, he wanted her more now.

"Do you have any aspirin?" Andrea asked.

Dare, who was engaged in gently stroking her arm with his fingertips, paused. "Headache?"

"I think I overdid it with my shoulder."

"Bad?"

"Not really. Just a little too much to ignore is all."

He dropped a kiss on her temple. "I'll be right back."

Rising, he thoughtfully pulled the comforter to her chin before padding away on bare feet.

Andrea decided she liked water beds. This was her first experience of one, and she thought it felt like floating. No hardness to remind her of reality. Reality was that she was leaving in a month and would never see Dare again. Reality was knowing how much she was going to hurt.

Turning over, she pressed her face into the pillow. She tried to tell herself she felt this way because he had just set her free of a lot of misconceptions, had just showed her something so wonderful she was greedy for more. But she didn't believe her own rationalizations. It was more than the last couple of hours. It was the way his lips twitched and his eyes twinkled when she zinged him. It was the way he intuitively understood what it meant to be Charlie Burke's daughter. It was the way he was so firmly and squarely centered in himself that he wasn't threatened by her. It was the way he seemed to take pleasure in Andrea Burke just the way she was.

"Andrea?" His voice was quiet, his touch on her shoulder gentle.

She rolled over at once and tried to smile at him. Dare saw past the smile, however. In the smoky mists that swirled in her green eyes, he saw the shadow of longing and loss. He'd put that there. Suddenly he didn't feel so good about himself.

Andrea took the aspirin he offered, swallowing it with water. The scar on her left shoulder was an angry red, puckered. Dare touched it lightly with a fingertip and thought how incredibly brave she was. Not grandstand brave. Andrea wasn't a grandstander. Just quietly and continuously day-in-and-day-out brave. Bending forward, he kissed the scar.

She closed her arms around him, hugging him, fingers stroking the nape of his neck.

"Andrea?"

"Sir?"

He smiled against her shoulder. "When do you go back on duty?"

"What day is it?"

"It just turned into Christmas Day ten minutes ago."

"Then I go back on duty tomorrow. Lieutenant Dolan wanted an extra day at New Year's, so he's working today."

"Finally learning to delegate, I see."

"Yes, sir."

"Andrea?" She smelled so sweet.

"Yes?"

"Would I be imposing if I asked you to stay with me?"

She drew a deep breath. "No," she said softly. "You wouldn't be imposing at all."

He raised his head, looking into her hazy green eyes. "Do you want to stay with me, Andrea?"

"There's nothing I want more in the whole world, Dare."

He brushed the lightest of kisses on her lips. "Sweet Andrea. Tell me something."

"Yes, sir."

"Are you a Christmas morning person, or a Christmas Eve person?"

"How do you mean?"

"Do you like to open your presents in the morning or on Christmas Eve?"

"We always opened them in the morning at home. But I always thought Christmas Eve would be more romantic."

His fingers found their way into her short, silky hair. Before Andrea, he'd always preferred long hair on a woman. Somehow her strawberry blond boyish cut had become incredibly sexy to him. He liked the way it hid nothing of her face, her ears, her neck. He even liked her Huck Finn freckles.

"So you've thought about romance from time to time, Captain?"

"Once in a while it has crossed my mind."

"We missed Christmas Eve."

"I didn't notice."

"But it's still not morning. We can pretend it's still Christmas Eve."

She considered gravely. "I don't see any problem with that. I wouldn't find it difficult to pretend at all."

"Tell me what would be a romantic Christmas Eve for you, Andrea."

She smiled suddenly, a soft, melting smile. "I just had it."

His smile answered her. "But you didn't open your presents."

"But I did. The best present of all."

He couldn't help it; he had to kiss her, had to kiss her until her eyes glazed and she melted into softness in his arms.

"What if I told you," he asked huskily, "that there's a present under the tree right now for you."

"For me?"

"For you. I was going to risk your undying wrath and drop it by the BOQ this morning."

He gave her his robe to wear, a thick royal blue terry cloth robe that dwarfed her, but for once in her life Andrea didn't mind being made to feel small. Dare pulled on his jeans and a gray sweatshirt, and they returned to the living room hand in hand.

"Brandy?" he asked.

"I'd really like coffee, if it wouldn't be too much trouble."

"No trouble at all. But it might keep you awake."

The smile she gave him stirred the banked fires in his loins. It became a feat of willpower to walk the short distance into his kitchen and make the coffee.

Together they sat on the couch, Andrea with her legs tucked under her, sipping coffee and eating cookies.

"At my place in Montana," Dare said, "I have a fireplace. Two, actually. One in the living room and one in the master bedroom."

"You have a house there?"

"Yep. And right now we'd be sitting in front of a blazing fire. Outside, snow would be falling gently on the deck, and I'd have the floods on, so we could see it through the glass doors, behind the Christmas tree."

"Sounds nice." The words were a sigh.

"It is nice," he agreed. "I've had the house for five years now, and I spend my leave there. There's always enough snow for skiing. And the summers are super. I practically live outside when I'm there."

"Where are you from originally, Dare?"

"Montana." He kissed her, running his tongue along her lips. "You taste like chocolate chip cookies. Want your present?"

Her eyes looked dazed. It tickled him to death that his kiss could daze his cool Captain Burke.

"But, Dare, I don't have anything for you."

"Oh, yes, you do." He kissed her again, this time slipping his hand inside the terry robe to cup her breast. Andrea trembled, leaning into him. "You have plenty for me," he murmured against her hair, "and I plan to open my presents again and again."

He drew away reluctantly and went to the tree, picking up a medium-sized box. "I figured this would make you furious enough to splutter at me. Maybe now it won't."

He stood over her uneasily while she tore away the red paper. She could tell he was nervous about it, so she drew the moment out, glancing up at him with that devilish gleam he knew so well.

"Captain Burke," he said finally, "do I need to remind you that it isn't wise to keep your CO in uncomfortable suspense?"

"Why are you in uncomfortable suspense, Colonel? What is it? A chastity belt?"

He gave a muffled laugh. "Worse. I saw it at the mall, and from the minute I saw it I was possessed. I had to give it to you, even if you threw it back in my face. Go on. Open it."

"Sounds to me like you were the one being unwise, sir," she said primly, and then gasped as she opened the box.

Inside was green silk, beautiful, brilliant green silk. Lifting it gently from the box, she tested its softness and admired its loveliness. It was a peignoir, she realized.

"Will you put it on?" he asked huskily.

She raised her face slowly, and he saw tears sparkling on her lashes.

"Andrea? Andrea, if it offends you, throw it away." He was suddenly panic-stricken. Her spluttering fury was one thing. Her tears were altogether something else.

"It doesn't offend me," she said, a catch in her voice. Rising, she took the box with her to the bedroom.

He had touched her, she realized as she slipped into the peignoir, her hands trembling almost too much to manage the bows.

He had reached down inside her and found an Andrea that had never been allowed to exist. In there somewhere was an Andrea who wanted to be beautiful for a man, an Andrea who loved beautiful things, who craved the softness of silk and the heat of a man's need. Inside, buried in the tomboy, hidden in the officer, was a woman, and Dare had found her and touched her.

There was a full-length mirror on the back of the bedroom door, and Andrea stood before it, looking at herself in emerald silk. The peignoir concealed nothing, really. It was meant to be viewed only by a lover. She looked at herself and realized this was how Dare saw her, realized that he had guessed at something she'd never known about herself. To him, she was all the things she believed herself to be, but she was also more, much more.

He was right. Yesterday she would have thrown it in his face in fury. Tonight she hurried back down the hall to share her discovery with him.

Dare was pacing, scared to death he'd offended her beyond bearing. He called himself seven kinds of idiot for giving in to the compulsion to give her that gown.

"Dare?"

He turned swiftly. Andrea stood just inside the living room, wearing the peignoir. He sucked in his breath at the sight of her, her every curve outlined in clinging, soft silk. Her eyes were shining at him, as if he'd given her the most precious gift in the world.

"Is it...?" She hesitated. "Is it what you hoped?"

"You're everything I hoped for," he said huskily, deliberately changing the pronoun. "And more. Andrea, you're stunning."

She smiled then, and fresh tears filled her eyes. "I didn't know this was me, Dare," she said unsteadily, and then she flew into his arms.

He held her tenderly, kissing away the tears. "Andrea, sweetheart, you're not upset?"

"No, sir," she answered forthrightly. "Somehow I'm tickled to death."

"Quit calling me sir."

"Yes, sir."

He lifted his head, looking down into her gently smiling face.

"If you call me sir when I'm making love to you, I'm going to be very upset."

"Yes, sir." Her lips twitched, and her damp eyes gleamed wickedly.

"Andrea, you drive me to the edge of madness."

"Sorry, sir."

There was only one way to deal with this insubordination, he decided. Scooping her up easily in his arms, he carried her back down the hall to bed. In a very short while she was no longer sir-ring him. She was saying his name in a very satisfactory way indeed.

This time he turned the bedside lamp on, a warm glow across the silk of Andrea's peignoir. For the longest time Dare caressed her through the silk. It was little barrier to his hands, and the glide of its cool smoothness on her skin provided her with a newly erotic sensation.

"I bought this gown right after Thanksgiving," he told her softly as he shaped her breast with his hand and watched her nipple tighten against the silk. "I lost count of the nights I lay here in the dark and imagined you just like this."

She drew a soft, shaky breath. "Did you?" Her insides were turning liquid. It had never entered her head that she might be the subject of his fantasies. "I thought about you, too," she admitted unsteadily.

His blue eyes lifted to hers. "Did you?" With thumb and forefinger he teased an exquisitely sensitive nipple. "Did you imagine me touching you like this?"

Her eyelids fluttered heavily. "No."

His fingers paused in their caress. "Why not? Don't you like this?"

Her hand closed over his, holding it to her breast. "Don't stop," she sighed. "Dare…"

Lowering his head, he suckled her through the silk and groaned when he felt her twist eagerly toward him.

"How could I imagine this?" she asked breathlessly, hands grasping his head, hips rising toward him. "I had no idea."

"You still have no idea," he murmured, lifting his head to kiss her mouth. While his tongue stroked hers rhythmically, erotically, he slowly drew up the skirt of her gown. Only when his fingers gained unfettered access to her dewy core did he lift his head. Looking down at her, he smiled. "But I've got more than a few secrets to share with you, honey." Parting her moist petals, he stroked her deeply, gently, and listened to the catch of her breath. "Is that good?"

"Yes. Oh, yes." So good it almost hurt. Turning toward him, she flung her arms around his neck and pressed her face to his shoulder. "Dare, please..."

"Shh," he said soothingly. "Shh." He wanted this night to be as perfect as it was possible for him to make it. Eventually, though, he gave in to her pleas and his own needs. He rose above her and looked down at her as she lay in the pool of green silk that was bunched around her torso.

"It's better than I imagined," he said huskily. "*You're* better."

Before she could gather her wits enough to respond, his driving thrust carried them both away.

Chapter 9

It had begun to snow during the night, and Dare stood before the window of his kitchen looking out at North Dakota's all-too-common white whirlwind. Snow so dry and fine never had an opportunity to settle in the winds that never ceased. It was unlikely that they'd gotten more than an inch of fresh snowfall, but the wind had drifted it into a four-foot dune across his driveway and front yard. Snowed-in, he thought with pleasure. He couldn't even see the neighboring houses except as faint ghosts in the blowing snow. In all likelihood this meant no one would decide to pay a courtesy call on a lonely bachelor this Christmas day. He couldn't have planned it better.

The coffeepot made the loud gurgles that signaled it had finished brewing. Dare reached for it and filled two mugs, then put them on a tray beside two plates filled with coffee cake. Ordinarily he avoided sweets, but Christmas demanded things that were out of the ordinary or it would be just an ordinary day.

Strange things happened to him when he thought about the fact that Andrea was soundly asleep in his bed. His heart zipped into high speed, his loins ached, and his mouth grew dry. Reaching back through his memory as he poured two glasses of orange juice, he tried to remember the last time merely thinking about a woman in his bed had caused such a strong reaction. Adolescence?

He lit a cigarette and returned his attention to the white world outside. He was afraid to wake her, he realized. He was afraid she would regret last night and look at him with hurt or horror. It was very possible she might, because there was nothing as awkward as the bright light of morning after a passion-filled night.

Muttering a soft oath, Dare stubbed out his cigarette and picked up the tray. The best way to handle it, of course, was not to let her wake alone while he stewed out here in the kitchen.

Andrea woke the same way she'd fallen asleep in the wee hours of the morning, with a strong arm around her and fingers lightly caressing her bare arm.

"I brought you coffee," Dare murmured near her ear, his breath warm and tickling.

"Mmm." Stirring, she turned a little toward him. Her eyes remained closed, but he could see the beginning of a smile on her lips.

"And coffee cake," he added softly.

"Mmm." She sighed, and her smile grew a little wider.

"Orange juice."

"Coffee," she said on a mere breath. "Coffee and thee."

"Me?"

Her eyes opened sleepily, misty green pools. "Most especially thee."

Dare felt his own smile start to dawn. "In which order, Captain Burke?"

"That's the Colonel's decision, sir."

"The coffee will get cold."

"Too bad." Her arm slipped around his neck, causing her to wince slightly.

"Andrea? Your shoulder hurts."

"Just a little." Her eyes opened wider. "Don't let that keep you from waking me up."

He trailed a string of kisses along her smooth jaw. "Just how awake do you want to be?"

"As awake as it's possible to be."

Her hand found his cheek, tracing the strong bones and fine

lines, as she watched the blue flames begin to burn in his eyes. "The first time I saw you in uniform," she said, "that morning in my office, I knew I was a sham."

"Sham?" He ran his thumb lightly over her lower lip.

"Sham. I knew right then I was really a woman after all."

"And what a woman," he said roughly as her silken thigh rubbed against his.

Andrea's smile grew satisfied as she felt his building response to her light touches. "Yes, sir," she murmured. "There's something about the way you look in a uniform that makes me forget I'm wearing one, too."

Dare sucked in a sharp breath as she began to lightly pinch the kernel of his nipple. Inexperienced as she was, she was teaching him things he hadn't known about himself.

"Too much?"

"Not enough. What other tricks have you got?" His arm tightened convulsively around her.

"I don't know yet," she answered gravely. "Do you want me to experiment on you?"

He drew a ragged breath and looked down into her hazy, hot green eyes. "You go right ahead and try anything that occurs to you, honey. In the meantime, I'm going to try a few tricks of my own."

Bending his head, he kissed her deeply while his hand foraged along her length. When he was sufficiently pleased by the ragged, rapid way she breathed, and by the way her hips kept rolling gently toward him, he sat up, throwing the comforter aside.

Andrea made a protesting sound and her eyes fluttered open. "Dare…"

"Hush, baby. It's experiment time."

Gently he pressed her legs apart and knelt between them. Andrea was dazed enough to let him do as he wished while crazy half-thoughts ran through her head about how magnificent he looked, how big he was, how…

Dare sat back on his heels and drew Andrea's hips up onto his knees, pressing her legs yet farther apart. He knew the exact moment she realized how exposed she was to his eyes. Her breath locked in her throat, and her eyes flew open. He saw wild color flare in her cheeks and heard her murmured protest, but he also saw the unmistakable flare of excitement in her eyes.

And she *was* excited. No one had ever looked at her this way, and part of her wanted to hide, but another part of her was inflamed. Frozen, caught between conflicting impulses, she could only watch as he reached out with a forefinger and touched her. She jerked.

"Easy, Andrea," he whispered roughly. "Easy. It's okay. You're so lovely, so perfect. Don't hide from me."

She couldn't have hidden. His gently stroking, gently seeking fingers made a joke of her last inhibitions. Last night's hungers paled beside the desire he stoked in her now.

"Let go, Andrea," he crooned. "Do it for me, honey. Let it all go." He wanted it all, all of her, all of the wildly passionate woman she hadn't yet fully unleashed. Dare had always been a considerate lover, but never before had he wanted so badly to strip away the civilized veneer, to crack the last bonds of self-control in his partner. He wanted Andrea Burke, woman elemental, without a vestige of Captain Burke left to come between them. He wanted her complete and total surrender to the fires that raged between them. He wanted her partnership in this adventure.

And he got it. Suddenly, without warning, she sat up and straddled him, impaling herself on him, wrapping her arms tightly around his shoulders. Her short nails dug into his back, and her teeth closed on the soft flesh of his shoulder.

Grasping her soft rump, he almost shouted his pleasure as she groaned deeply. Lifting her, he let her settle slowly on him and watched as she threw her head back and gasped. His own needs were pounding at him, but he gritted his teeth, wanting to give her every possible bit of pleasure and sensation before he succumbed.

"Dare!" She sounded almost frightened.

"I'm here, Andrea. I'm here. I'll keep you safe. I'll catch you when you fall." He meant every word.

Her eyelids fluttered, and she arched backward. "Fall with me," she gasped.

"Baby, I fell a long time ago." But he let her pull him down, and as soon as he felt her beneath him he lost it, lost it all. With her legs wrapped around his waist, he fell into a hard, driving rhythm that pushed them to the brink and then over.

"I'm embarrassed."

The muffled words against his shoulder brought a smile to Dare's face. He lay on his side, holding her snugly against him, his leg thrown possessively over her hip. "Why should you be embarrassed?" he asked gently. "Nothing happened here that we didn't do together."

"Mmph."

He chuckled. "You were shameless, Captain."

She groaned and burrowed her face deeper into his shoulder. "I liked it a whole lot. It's what I wanted."

"Well, you're the CO. We aim to please."

He laughed then. "Andrea, Andrea, you're a marvel. You delight me. Everything about you delights me."

Slowly, blushing profusely, she tilted her head back and stole a look at him. "Really?" she asked shyly.

"Really and truly."

Yielding a sigh, she relaxed against him. "I like everything about you, too."

Bending, he kissed the tip of her nose. "Are you ready for your coffee? Shall I bring a fresh cup in here, or do you want to get up?"

"I think I'll get up. I've been decadent enough for one morning."

"I bet I could make you even more decadent."

Green eyes met blue. "No contest," she said after a moment, and grinned her elfish grin. Suddenly she threw her arms around him and hugged him tight. "Thank you, Dare," she whispered. "I'll never be able to thank you enough."

His throat tightened uncomfortably. When he spoke, his voice was rough. "Come on, Captain. Get your pretty little rump out of bed before you miss your coffee again."

Fresh from a shower and wrapped in one of his flannel shirts, Andrea joined Dare at the breakfast table in the kitchen. He'd used the time to rustle up eggs and bacon, having seen Andrea's morning appetite once before. She dug in like a trooper. Smoking a cigarette and drinking coffee, Dare watched her eat.

"How would you like to spend Christmas day, Andrea?"

She set her fork down and picked up her mug, taking a sip of coffee before replying. "I keep wishing there weren't so many complications, but there are." Her green eyes lifted to regard him steadily. "Reality won't go away, Colonel."

Sighing, he stubbed out his cigarette. "I know it won't. I don't live in a fool's paradise either, Captain."

"I never meant to imply that you did."

He arched a questioning brow at her. "Are you turning into Captain Burke again?"

She smiled faintly. "I never stopped being Captain Burke."

"Okay, I get it. I'll take you home."

"No!" She startled him by reaching out and grabbing his forearm. "That isn't what I meant, either! Will you just hear me out?"

Dare settled back in his chair and wondered why the devil he'd been so hell-bent on tangling himself up with a woman. He'd forgotten how confusing they could be. Lighting another cigarette, he sighed. "Burke, you're going to be the death of me. Get to the point, will you?"

"I will, but it's not easy. It's embarrassing."

"I thought we'd dealt with embarrassment."

"We did." Color rose to her cheeks again, and Dare was charmed. God, she delighted him!

"But," she continued bravely, "that doesn't make it easier."

"Just close your eyes and spit it out," he said kindly. "I promise I won't laugh."

"Well, actually," Andrea said hesitantly, "what I want to do today is—live in a fool's paradise."

It took him a moment to comprehend, but when he did, he smiled with such gentleness that Andrea blinked. "Consider it done," he told her.

"You don't mind?"

"Why would I mind? It's exactly the way I'd like to spend the day myself."

"Really?"

"Really." And, Charlie Burke, may you burn for what you did to your daughter, Dare thought grimly. Competent, capable Captain Burke had absolutely no confidence in herself when she shucked the uniform and the role that went with it. Was she such a disappointment, Charlie? Dare wondered. Were you so blind?

"Dare?"

Andrea was looking worriedly at him, and he realized she must have seen some of the anger he felt on his face. At once he stomped down on it and smiled at her. "Sorry, I just got to thinking about something else. Lack of sleep, I guess. What kind of fool's paradise do you have in mind?"

Again her color heightened. "Well, I'm not really sure. I've never lived in one before."

His smile deepened. "Come on, Andrea, you admitted last night that you occasionally indulged in a romantic fantasy or two. Everyone has. Share one of yours."

But her chin took on the stubborn set he recognized, and she shook her head.

"It's hardly fair," he pointed out, "if we only live out *my* romantic fantasies."

"I think yours will do just fine."

He considered arguing with her, then decided against it. "Well, you can't say you didn't ask for it."

That evening, by the light of the Christmas tree, they lay side by side against pillows on the floor. Andrea curled against Dare, her head on his shoulder, and listened contentedly to the slow, steady sound of his heartbeat. Well, she had asked for it, she thought, but never in a million years would she have envisioned a romantic day that involved making Christmas dinner and playing cards. It had been a homey day, the kind of day she'd missed all her life, it seemed. And, surprisingly, it had been very romantic.

Dare lifted her hand from his chest and brought it to his lips. "Tired?" he asked.

"Pleasantly so." Tilting her head, she looked up at him. "Do you have something in mind?"

"Like a starving man has food in mind."

A chuckle escaped Andrea. "You're not starving."

Dare turned a little, bringing Andrea closer. "Oh, yes, I am. I haven't made love to you in ten whole hours."

"Well, *you* were the one who wanted to play games."

"How about a game right now?"

"I might be persuaded," she said demurely.

"What kind of persuasion do you need?"

"Oh, a little of this and a little of that."

"A little of this?" he asked, his hand grazing her breast. "Or some of that?" He slipped his hand between her legs and pressed gently.

Andrea's eyes grew wide. "All of it," she answered, suddenly breathless. "All of it."

But all too soon it was time for Andrea to leave. They both needed their sleep, for tomorrow was a duty day, and neither of them argued against the inevitable. Still, they lingered over a last cup of coffee in the kitchen, watching the clock tick steadily toward midnight, knowing the fantasy was over.

"Andrea?" Dare spoke into a silence that had grown too long.

She lifted her head and gave him a questioning look.

"I just want you to know. Regardless of what your father told you about pilots, I've never gone in for one night stands or casual relationships."

"Oh." Her color heightened a shade.

"In fact," he continued, "this is the first time in my life I've gone into something like this knowing there was no future."

Her eyes shied away from the intensity of his stare, and she concentrated on her coffee cup. "Are you saying it shouldn't have happened?"

"No, I'm saying I don't give myself cheaply. I know you don't, either. So someday, down the road, when you think back over this, don't feel cheapened by it."

Slowly, very slowly, her eyes rose to meet his once again. "No," she whispered. "Oh, no, I wouldn't ever think that. But, Dare..."

He waved a dismissing hand. "Forget it, Andrea. I told you, I already know all the arguments and all the reasons. Your career comes first. Don't worry about it. Tomorrow, when we're captain and colonel again, I just want you to be sure that this is one of my treasured memories. Don't ever doubt it." Standing, he reached for her, pulling her to her feet.

"One last kiss, Andrea," he said. "One last kiss. And if you ever, ever again think you'd like to be with me, don't hesitate to call me. I mean it."

Before she could answer, he covered her mouth with his, drinking deeply of the sweetness he feared he might never know again. One last time he held her close, squeezing his eyes shut against the ache that had taken root in his heart. "This is a relationship, Andrea," he whispered. "Like it or not. We'll do it on your terms, but you can't escape the fact that it exists."

"All quiet on the Northern Front, skipper," Nickerson said to her the following morning as he entered her office. "Nothing happened, and Lieutenant Dolan managed nothing very well."

Halting before her desk, he peered down at her. "And *you* look like the morning after a heavy-duty night before. You get hit by a truck or something?"

"Or something." Andrea managed a travesty of a smile. "Just some trouble sleeping, Nick. Nothing exciting."

"I've seen Marines look better after a forty-eight-hour pass in Saigon."

Andrea chuckled. "I imagine they didn't feel much worse."

"Shoulder bothering you?"

"A little." Which was the truth, although not the truth of why she hadn't slept. No, she'd lain awake all night wishing she were in Dare's bed instead of her own, which was why she should never have broken her own rules by going over there in the first place. And Nick's eyes were too sharp and too wise for her comfort.

Nick poured himself a cup of coffee and sat in one of the straight-backed metal chairs that faced her desk. "You sure nothing's wrong?"

"What could be wrong? Honestly, I just didn't get enough sleep. A few more cups of coffee and I'll pass for normal. So we didn't have any more intruders?"

"Not a thing. Never fear, we'll make up for all the peace and quiet on New Year's Eve. You know, I was talking to Halliday about how somebody could slip past the electronic security system, and he says it can't be done."

Andrea rubbed her forehead. "That's Halliday. Those circuits of his are infallible. *Somebody* got past them."

"I told him that. I think I'm in his black books."

"That'll do it, all right."

"But I was thinking, what if Halliday's right?"

Alerted, Andrea dropped her hand from her forehead and looked at Nick. "What if?"

"*If* Halliday's right, then it's an inside job, right?"

"What's an inside job?"

"Scuttlebutt has it that it wasn't a goose that took out the nose of that B-52."

Andrea gripped the edge of her desk. "I'd be very interested in the source of this scuttlebutt."

Nickerson ran his index finger alongside his jaw. "You know what they say. You can't keep a secret from military wives, and once a military wife knows, it ain't no secret."

"Damn." Andrea slumped back in her chair. Unfortunately she'd experienced the truth of that sexist military aphorism more than once during her life. Like the time the Tactical Fighter Wing had been secretly sent to Cambodia. They were not to tell their wives a thing except that they were flying out for a few days. Before the first plane even took off, all twenty-five thousand people at the air base had known their departure time and destination. Too often GIs felt that keeping a secret didn't mean they couldn't tell their wives. And unfortunately the wives too often felt that rules about secrecy didn't apply to them, because they were civilians.

"I take it," Nickerson said, "that scuttlebutt is true. Which means we've got a king-size problem. What's being done about it?"

"I can't tell you that."

"Well, damn near everybody's talking about it, Captain. If that's a problem, maybe you'd better tell Colonel MacLendon."

Just then the phone on Andrea's desk rang, and she looked at it as if it were a rattlesnake. "Speak of the devil," she said to Nick. "How much do you want to bet?"

"I ain't a betting man, skipper, but I might take this one. Bet his First Shirt's just dumped the same story in his lap."

Groaning inwardly, Andrea lifted the receiver. "Captain Burke."

"Andrea, we have a problem," Dare's voice said into her ear. "I want you and Nickerson over here on the double."

"What's wrong?"

"The rumor mill's running at full speed, and we need to take steps to contain it."

"We're on our way." Replacing the receiver, Andrea looked at Nick. "You would have won this one. He wants us both over there five minutes ago." Rising, she grabbed her parka from the coat tree in the corner. "You know, Nick, I could resign."

"Been a long tour?" Nick asked, matching his pace to hers as they headed for the parking lot.

"No, just a long two months."

"That'll do it."

Already present at Dare's office were the Bomb Wing deputy commander, Major West, and the Wing's First Sergeant, Matt Hawley. Dare was nodding in response to something Hawley was saying, but his eyes followed Andrea as she entered and took a seat. Instantly he saw the weariness on her face and guessed she hadn't slept any better than he had. When her eyes lifted to his, she colored faintly and looked quickly down. Dare forced himself to look away, worried that one of them would give the game away, wishing that he could just go to her and take her into his arms.

God! Andrea thought, clasping her hands to still their trembling. One look at him and her heart started thundering like a stampeding horse. And how was it possible for him to look better this morning than she remembered him? How was she going to survive the next month if she felt this way every time she saw him?

"You've heard the rumors?" Dare asked Nickerson.

"Yes, sir. I was just telling Captain Burke about them when you called."

"Well, we can't have people buzzing about a terrorist attack on this base. First of all, we don't know it *was* a terrorist act. It might have been the act of someone who's mentally ill, or someone with a grudge. Secondly, if the rumor gets off the base, the locals will be upset, maybe panicked. Some of you remember the uproar a couple of years ago when a jet engine fell off a truck and word got around that it contained radioactive cesium.

I don't need to tell you that the Department of the Air Force isn't going to be very happy with us if this hits the pages of the local newspaper. And if it makes headlines here, it'll undoubtedly make the national news. So put your heads to work and come up with a suitably innocent official explanation for what happened to that plane."

"Too bad a goose won't hack it," Hawley remarked. "None of the locals would believe that, though."

"Even if we had feathers?" Major West asked. "What if we showed them feathers and blood and claimed it was a sick goose that hadn't migrated."

"A brain-sick goose," suggested Nickerson. "Maybe the base vet could come up with some disease that could make a goose crazy."

"Something that doesn't kill," Andrea put in. "The geese migrated more than a month before the accident."

Dare nodded. "It would work if he can come up with something legitimate." His eyes lingered on Andrea just an instant too long. "Hawley, get Captain Emory up here, will you?" Emory was the base veterinarian. As he was largely involved in the care of the police dogs and, when time allowed, servicemen's pets, Dare doubted he would know much more than the rest of them about geese. Still, it was worth looking into.

Dare sat back in his chair, steepling his hands on his chest. "You know, the only people who knew this wasn't a goose were a couple of mechanics, Captain Burke, and myself. I guess one of the mechanics must have shot off his mouth. To his wife, probably."

Andrea and Nickerson exchanged amused glances.

Major West spoke. "I'm not sure any of the pilots really believed it was a goose, sir. Somebody could have speculated."

"I guess, but you're telling me that somebody was talking about explosives."

"When you've got a hole that size in the nose of an aircraft, explosives make sense in the absence of other causes."

"Well, the source of the rumor has to be someone in the Bomb Wing," Dare said. "West, you and Hawley see if you can track it down. I know it'll be damn near impossible, but try anyhow."

Dare swiveled his chair suddenly and looked at Andrea. "I know you've beefed up security, but damn it, I want something more than that. I want to get to the bottom of this, Burke."

"We all do, sir."

One corner of his mouth quirked. "Point taken. Sorry. I had trouble sleeping last night."

Andrea felt Nickerson glance at her, but she managed to keep her face impassive, although some perverse part of her took delight in the fact that Dare had been as miserable as she was last night. And what had Nickerson sensed that made him look at her like that? Was she wearing a sign on her forehead?

Availing himself of one of the privileges of rank, Dare lit a cigarette. He should have quit the damn things completely by now, but here he was, still smoking half a pack a day. More, if he got to thinking too much about Andrea. She didn't look as if she'd slept too well, either. He took some satisfaction in that, remembering how only a few short hours ago he'd been standing at his bedroom window wishing for sleep that wouldn't come. He'd been doing too much of that since Andrea popped into his life.

Captain Emory arrived only a few minutes later. "I suppose," he said when he'd been briefed, "there must be something I could come up with." He pushed his glasses up on the narrow bridge of his nose. "You understand, I'll need to research the problem, Colonel. I'm not exactly familiar with Canadian geese."

"But does it sound plausible?" Dare asked.

"Oh, yes, off the cuff, I'd say it's a possibility. Of course, we really don't understand all the mechanisms of migration. It's entirely possible such an event could occur and we'd never know why. As in the case of that whale in Alaska. We may never understand what happened there."

Dare rubbed his chin. "If worse comes to worse, I guess we'll just call it a freak accident, but I'd really rather have something more convincing than that, given the rumors. And goose feathers. I need some goose feathers."

Emory smiled. "Oh, I can provide those, Colonel. My wife makes artsy-craftsy things with them. She'll never miss a couple."

"Just make sure she doesn't know you've taken them. All I need is another wife in on what's going on. Okay, people, that's our story, then. A goose hit the plane. If Captain Emory can come up with a disease, so much the better. If not, we'll just go with the freak accident idea, unless somebody has a better one."

But nobody had a better explanation for a six-foot hole in the cockpit of a B-52.

"What are we going to do about it, ma'am?" Nickerson asked Andrea as they drove back to the security squadron headquarters.

"Do?"

"Well, somebody blew a hole in a plane with plastique. That's not something you overlook. We've got to find out who did it."

"People are looking into it, Nick. I can't tell you any more than that."

"Why aren't *we* looking into it?"

Andrea sighed. "I have it on good authority that we don't have the training or experience to handle this case."

Nick frowned. "Oh yeah? Maybe not the technical end of it, but we know people, Skipper. We need a list of possible suspects, and then we find a motive. Basic police work."

"The suspect list is pretty big. Just about any aircraft mechanic would have unsupervised access to those planes. If it wasn't a mechanic, it could be one of our cops, because it had to be somebody who could get through security. That's another couple of dozen people, even if we allow only a narrow time frame. It could be any one of the aircrews, too. So how long is the list now? A hundred? More?"

Nick scowled. "So we eliminate as many as we can."

"Sure. Who do we eliminate? People without any gripes? *Every* GI has a gripe. Besides, it's hands-off. I told you."

"That doesn't mean we can't *think* about it, ma'am."

"I guess not." Rubbing the back of her neck, Andrea sighed. "Sorry, Nick. Not enough sleep. You think about it. I'll think about it. But frankly, I just can't imagine anyone I know wanting to blow a hole in that aircraft."

"Isn't that always what the next door neighbor says after the ax murder? *He wouldn't hurt a fly.*"

Tired or not, Andrea laughed. It was true, of course. Nobody could ever imagine that somebody they knew would do such a thing. "You're right, Nick. That's what they always say."

Chapter 10

Several afternoons later, Andrea sat at her desk, studying the list of names her staff had compiled. Finding people with the opportunity to get to that aircraft had been easy. What with aircrews, mechanics, and cops, the list held thirty-three names. Discovering who might have a motive was a different matter altogether. OSI had probably compiled this same list of names weeks ago, and they'd gotten nowhere.

Absently rubbing her shoulder to ease the faint ache that still plagued her, Andrea leaned back in her chair and stared off into space. She would probably be long gone before they discovered the culprit, if they ever did. There just wasn't enough evidence to go on.

Why would anyone do such a thing? Greed and revenge were the commonest motivations among people. It was possible that some airman had been paid to set an explosive on that bomber, but that still left the question of the motivation of whoever had paid him. Greed couldn't be behind that, because it was against official policy for the Air Force to give in to extortion. That left revenge and terrorism, and she had trouble accepting the notion of terrorism, because nobody had called the local or national news. Where was the point in doing something like this if you didn't call the news and get your free publicity out of it? On the other hand, if somebody had a grudge against a member of that plane's crew, then there were easier and surer ways of achieving revenge.

So what did that leave? No motive at all?

Frustrated with the circles she seemed to be going in, tired from too many nights of not enough sleep and too much thinking about a certain Colonel who appeared to have forgotten her existence, Andrea decided to leave Dolan in charge for the night. She would have an early dinner at the O-Club, followed by a hot shower, and then she'd hit the sack.

It wasn't steak night, and it was too early for the evening crowd, so the dining room was fairly empty. A group of B-52 crew members on alert sat in one corner eating dinner and laughing together. Their flight suits indicated their alert status and gave them precedence, whether in being served dinner or in the checkout line at the exchange.

In another corner a young couple, looking as if they were barely old enough to be married, argued with quiet intensity. Andrea took a corner for herself and sat with her back to the wall as she nursed a beer and waited for her dinner.

The room was not brightly lit, and Andrea wasn't certain how long she had stared absently at the laughing pilots before she realized that one of them, glimpsed occasionally as another pilot leaned backward, was Dare MacLendon.

What was he doing with the alert pilots? she wondered blankly, and then looked quickly away, unwilling to let him catch her staring. She wouldn't give him the satisfaction, not when he'd ignored her since Christmas. But wasn't that what she wanted? No strings? No messy involvement? Her mind said yes, but her heart kept clamoring for more.

Which was why she should never have broken her own rules. And why she must be sure never to break them again.

"Good evening, Burke."

Well, damn, she thought even as her heart tripped into high gear. Of course he couldn't just leave without stopping to say something. She looked up, and up, and thought that nobody with the extraordinary build and looks of Dare MacLendon ought to be allowed to parade around in a flight suit. He was smiling down at her, a pleasant, friendly expression.

"Good evening, Colonel," she answered politely.

"Can you give me a minute?"

"Of course, sir."

"Good." He turned, looking over his shoulder to answer a remark from the departing pilots, and then pulled out a chair and straddled it. He rested his arms along its back and studied Andrea in silence as she leaned to one side to allow the waiter to serve her dinner.

"Just a coffee for me," Dare said in answer to the waiter's question.

Andrea felt pleased with the steadiness of her hands as she sliced into her chicken breast. She would *not* let him know how his proximity affected her. No way. Absolutely not.

"You look tired, Andrea," he said quietly in a tone so gentle that her throat tightened. When had anyone ever spoken to her with so much concern? If anyone ever had, she couldn't recall it.

She cleared her throat. "I've been busy, sir. Have you been flying?"

"I took up one of the bombers this afternoon on a low-level run. I hear you've started a little investigation of your own."

Her hands tightened on her knife and fork, and she looked across the table at him. "Who told you that?" And why did she have to remember so vividly just how soft his mouth could be?

"One of my people told me that one of your folks wanted to know who in the Wing could have had access to that damaged plane. I don't need somebody to lay it out like a map for me, Andrea."

Anger sparked in her green eyes. Now it would come, she thought. He would tell her to leave it alone and to mind her p's and q's. And if he did she'd—well, she didn't know what she'd do. "So?" she asked, and almost winced at the belligerence of her own tone.

Dare's eyes narrowed. His voice turned soft as silk, a dangerous sound. "You have a problem with the chain of command, Burke?"

"No, sir," she said swiftly, and then sighed. "I'm sorry. Not enough sleep. Right now I think I'm my own worst enemy."

He softened, recognizing her fatigue and admitting to himself that it had been easy for her to misconstrue the direction of this conversation. "I only wanted to know if you've come up with anything."

"Oh." After a moment she gave him a sheepish smile. "Actually," she admitted, "all I've done is chase my own tail so far. I decided there were three possible motives for the bombing—revenge, money, and terrorism—and then I came up with reasons why it couldn't be any of them." Briefly she outlined her reasoning.

He smiled, and the expression melted the last of the steel from his gaze. "Well, if it's any consolation, that's about all OSI has accomplished so far."

"You're kidding."

"Nope. All that muscle and brainpower, and they're still standing around scratching their heads. I'm not supposed to know that, of course, so don't tell anyone else."

"How did you find out?"

"I know a few people." God, how he wanted to reach out and touch her. Wrong time, wrong place. Besides, he'd told her to call him if she ever wanted to be with him again, and she hadn't called. Because of his position, he felt he had to let her set the boundaries on their relationship. He didn't want her ever to feel that he was using his rank to pressure her into anything.

"I can tell you one thing," he said, and fell silent while the waiter served his coffee. He didn't speak again until he was sure no one was near enough to overhear. "The plastic explosive is of U.S. manufacture. It's typical government stock."

"Not a homemade brew," Andrea remarked. "That's interesting."

"Yeah, but it evidently doesn't tell us much. OSI concludes from it that the incident wasn't staged by known terrorist groups, but evidently U.S. manufacturers sell a lot of the stuff to other countries the same way they sell countermeasures and weapons. Theoretically it only goes to friendlies, but who can say for sure?"

"There haven't been any calls to the press about it, either,"

Andrea said. "That's another mark against terrorism. Or have there been calls?"

Dare shook his head. "None. My source would have mentioned it. No, OSI is just about convinced we're dealing with an individual or a small group of individuals. The fact that there hasn't been another incident of any kind in nearly a month even has them speculating that the shooting scared the guy off. That and your beefed up security. They're still impressed with your squadron, by the way."

Andrea smiled. It was nice to hear, especially when she was feeling low and useless. "Well, if it's not terrorism, that leaves sabotage or murder for possible intent, and greed or revenge for the motive."

"That's how it looks." Sipping his coffee, he studied her over the rim of the cup as she took another mouthful of her supper. He knew Andrea's appetite, and he was disturbed to see her peck at her food the way she was right now. "Are you coming down with something?" he asked abruptly.

Startled, she looked up. "I don't think so."

He shook his head and set his cup aside. "You don't look very good," he remarked as he stood. "Get to bed and get some sleep. And call me if you come up with anything new. Good night, Burke."

She watched him stride away and thought once again that he shouldn't be allowed to wear a flight suit. On him it was positively lethal to her peace of mind. With a heavy sigh, she tried to convince herself that she really didn't mind the fact that he seemed to have no further interest in her. After all, she was leaving soon, so it really didn't make any difference.

As soon as she arrived at work in the morning, Andrea buzzed the front desk. "See if you can round up Sergeant Halliday for me, Crocker. I'd like to see him in my office."

"Yes, ma'am. I think he's over at Delta Zulu checking something out. It'll be a few minutes."

"Thank you." What the hell had happened now? Andrea wondered as she replaced the receiver. What was Halliday doing over there?

Twenty minutes passed before Halliday showed up, and he arrived looking cold.

"Warm up with some coffee, Sarge," Andrea told him, pointing to the pot on the file cabinet. "Did something happen over at Delta Zulu?"

"No, ma'am. Just checking on things. It's twenty-two below out there."

"I noticed." Andrea watched Halliday fill a cup and take a seat across from her.

"I worry about the systems," he told her. "Especially after what's been happening. The cold shouldn't affect them, but you never know."

Andrea nodded. "You're very conscientious." Most people didn't volunteer to go out in these temperatures. "Is everything okay?"

"Right as rain, Captain."

"Well, I asked you to come in here because I need your help with something. You know how I pull these little inspections."

Halliday smiled. "Everyone knows about them."

"I think I'm getting a little too predictable. I also think the troops are getting too dependent on the electronic systems. So, what if I wanted to give them a real surprise? How could I bypass the system?"

Halliday looked smug. "You can't."

Andrea shook her head slowly. "No system is infallible, Sergeant. There has to be a way. Think about it."

Halliday shrugged. "I don't have to think about it. I know the system like the back of my hand. Maybe better. Everything is redundant, especially around weapons storage. We've got backups on top of backups. To get around them you'd either have to knock out a whole section of the system at the control center, which isn't easy to do, or you'd have to know where each and every sensor is. If you want, though, I can disable part of the system for you so you can surprise the guys."

"You're absolutely convinced I can't do it any other way?"

Halliday's smile broadened into a grin. "I get the feeling you take that as a challenge, ma'am. You *could* memorize the layout. You might be able to do it then, but why go to so much trouble? It's easier just to have me shut it down."

"Who besides you knows the layout?"

"All the guys on my crew." Halliday frowned. "Look, if something's going on..."

Andrea shook her head. "No. It's just that I was asked about it at staff conference yesterday, and I realized I really don't know as much as I should about how things are done. And that was when somebody remarked that my inspections must be getting predictable if I always avoid the electronic systems."

"Well, ma'am, there's not all that much to it. I'm probably the only one who knows the entire system, because each of my technicians specializes in just one part of it. We're the only five people who have access to the classified plans and blueprints on a routine basis. We keep a copy of all that stuff in the safe in my office. If you want to look at it, I can get it for you, or you can look at the copy the document custodian keeps. Anybody with a need-to-know authorization can look at the stuff. I don't reckon there'd be too many folks other than me and my techs with a need to know, though."

"Certainly not me," Andrea said pleasantly. "Not that I could make much sense out of a lot of circuit diagrams."

Halliday smiled, his eyes pallid behind his glasses. "No, but you could read the map."

"And try to tiptoe past all that stuff?" Andrea laughed and shook her head. "Forget it, Sarge. It was a dumb idea."

Well, Andrea thought, now she could add even more names to the list, and she hadn't eliminated any yet. How many people might be able to gain access to the plans? The document custodians sprang to mind, and there were surely others who had a legitimate need to see them. Nope, she had to come at this from a different angle.

"But," she said, asking one last question, "if I *wanted* to learn the layout, I could get past the system?"

"Sure. It's too damn expensive to carpet all those areas with sensors, so they're scattered in a random fashion that makes it impossible to get by them all unless you know where they're at. Captain, I swear, it's a no-man's-land. It's more difficult to get through than a maze. You have to know what you're doing to stand a chance."

Late that night Andrea lay in bed, restless and strangely sad, and tried not to think about Alisdair MacLendon. Just a few short days had passed since Christmas, but they felt like years. All her nerves seemed hypersensitive. The brush of her nightgown against her breasts made her think of his hands. A tingling ache filled her. A nagging sense of incompletion gnawed at her, and some traitorous part of her mind kept demanding to know why she was in bed alone.

It was during the process of trying not to think about Dare that she had a realization so startling that it brought her upright in her bed: somebody wanted revenge, all right. They wanted revenge against Dare.

The evidence for that was slim, so slim that it seemed almost ridiculous. What did she have to substantiate it? The fact that the trouble had begun with his arrival. The fact that it seemed to be directed against the Bomb Wing. The fact that the charge set in the bomber hadn't killed anyone. And all those little pieces of so-called evidence could be argued against. The fact that the explosive in the bomber hadn't killed anyone, for example, could have been purely accidental.

Slender evidence indeed. Falling back against the pillows, Andrea considered. Her suspicion was so wild as to be embarrassing, but it *felt* right. She wouldn't dare tell anyone without more proof, but she could use the assumption as a starting point. It might make her alert to things she would otherwise miss. And it might also make her blind to other things. Troubled, she tossed and turned well into the night.

On the Saturday after New Year's, Andrea stood in her kitchenette yawning widely and thinking that maybe when she got to Minot she would rent an apartment rather than live in the BOQ. Waiting for the coffeepot to finish brewing, she looked around at her cramped efficiency quarters and decided that it was time she stopped living out of a mental suitcase. If she had more room and owned some furniture, maybe she would feel as if she had a home. It would mean a longer drive when she got a call in the middle of the night, but maybe she wouldn't feel so rootless. Maybe she wouldn't feel like a tumbleweed, rolling here and there and leaving no mark anywhere.

The tile floor was cold beneath her feet, causing her to shiver, and she rubbed her hands up and down the silk sleeves of the peignoir Dare had given her. It wasn't warm enough for the draughty rooms, and it wasn't practical by any stretch of the imagination, but she wore it often anyhow and then lay wide awake remembering Christmas. Remembering how it had felt to be a woman. Time and again she caught herself trying to think up excuses to go over to his house.

Like a teenager with a crush, she thought sourly as she headed for the bedroom. Hadn't she deliberately avoided this all these years? What was it about Alisdair MacLendon that made her forget all her common sense?

She was halfway across the small living area when someone knocked on her door. "Who is it?" she called.

"MacLendon."

Hurrying to the door, she released the lock and opened it a crack to see a very irate-looking Colonel MacLendon. Beneath his olive drab survival parka he wore his flight suit. He must have been flying again, Andrea thought. Rated pilots who'd been promoted to desk jobs were allowed to keep their ratings by flying a certain number of hours every month, and the Air Force provided planes for them, usually T-38 jets.

Raising her eyes to Dare's face, Andrea took an instinctive step backward. There was murder in Dare's face, Andrea took an instinctive step backward. There was murder in those icy blue eyes.

As she stepped back, Dare stepped in, easing through the opening and closing the door soundly behind him.

"Tell me, Burke," he growled down at her, "do your troops *sleep* on the job? Or are they doing dope?"

Andrea blinked rapidly and drew herself up to her full five foot six. "Sir! I can't let you say—"

"I'll say anything I damn well please!"

Andrea stood her ground, chin thrust forward, arms folded across her breasts.

"I almost *died* this morning," Dare said, advancing on her. "I almost augered in at Mach 1 because somebody fiddled with my hydraulics. That upsets me, Burke. That upsets the living hell out of me."

Andrea froze, horrified by the image evoked by his words: Dare's plane nosing into the ground at the speed of sound.

As he spoke, he cast his parka aside and took another step toward her.

"And all the time I was fighting the damn stick and pedals and trying to keep from being splattered all over the state of North Dakota, I could only think about one thing. This!"

Grabbing her with hands like steel, he hauled her up against him, forced her head back, and seized her mouth in a punishing, ruthless kiss.

Andrea fought him, twisting and turning like a wildcat, but he held her effortlessly. Moving with her struggles, he made her feel as if she were wrapped in an invisible net, never once hurting her, but giving her no escape from his ravaging mouth.

Suddenly Dare lifted his head and looked down at her with burning eyes. "What if I'd died?" he asked.

Andrea went utterly still, her swollen lips parted, her green eyes huge. What if he'd died? she asked herself.

Dare saw her lower lip quiver, and then she melted against him where she belonged, closing her arms around his waist in a fierce hug. She cared, he thought, shutting his eyes with relief. Whether she would admit it or not, she cared. At twenty thousand feet, when only brute strength had given him any control at all over his plane, in those interminable minutes when he'd been sure he was about to die, he'd wondered about that. He'd wondered if he would ever find out, and it had seemed incredibly important to know.

Wrapping his arms around her now, he held her as close as he could, as tightly as he could, without hurting her, and wished he could pull her right inside him. "Kiss me, Andrea," he said hoarsely. "Kiss me. Please."

She lifted her face and sought his mouth blindly, seeking the warmth, the passion, the essence, of this man. One of her hands crept upward to cradle his rough cheek, to slide into his hair and then hold on for dear life. Without reservation she gave him the kiss he wanted.

"I need you, Andrea," Dare said raggedly when he let her catch her breath. "We've got to talk. About this. About what happened. About everything.'' His blue eyes were intense as he tilted her head up. ''We can't do any of that here.''

With difficulty, Andrea concentrated on what he was saying. At the moment the only thing that seemed important was that a half-dozen steps would carry them to her bedroom. ''No,'' she agreed, dimly aware that before long everybody in the BOQ would know Dare was here.

''Call Dolan,'' Dare said. ''Tell him he's in charge for the rest of the weekend. Meet me at the Gasthaus in Devil's Lake.''

Andrea blinked, coming to her senses. ''I can't just—''

''You *can*,'' he interrupted her. ''You can damn well do anything you please. When are you going to believe that?''

''But your hydraulics! We need to—''

''We'll talk about that later. Right now there's not a damn thing you can do about that.''

Releasing her, Dare stepped back. ''I'm going to Devil's Lake,'' he said. ''I'll give you until one o'clock to meet me. It's up to you, Andrea. It always is. But I won't ask again.''

Without another word, he left.

Nothing was up to her, thought Andrea miserably. Nothing had been up to her since Dare had crashed into her life. Closing her eyes, she clenched her hands into fists and tried to tell herself that she wouldn't do as he'd asked.

She didn't believe it herself. For an entire week now she'd been lying awake, full of yearnings no amount of argument could quash. In little less than a month she would be leaving for Minot, and in all likelihood she wouldn't see Dare again for years, if ever. Why not have a fling during these few weeks? Why not give in just this once in her life? Chances were she would never again have such an opportunity.

Chances were she would never again meet a man like Dare. Squeezing her eyelids tighter, she drew a breath that sounded like a sob. What was happening to her? Just a few short months ago, everything had been so simple and clear-cut. Now she didn't know where she was going, or why she was doing what she did. She didn't even feel like herself. Why was it when she closed her eyes all she could see was Dare? Where had this wrenching need for him come from, and why was she so helpless against it? Why, when she thought of how close he'd come to dying, did her heart stop?

And how the devil was she going to get on with her life and her career when all she wanted to do was punch out and go along for the ride with Dare?

Drawing another deep breath, Andrea stiffened her spine and opened her eyes. She couldn't let him do this to her. She couldn't let any man do this to her. She had a life and a career of her own, and she was going to keep it that way.

No, she wouldn't go to Devil's Lake. He would get the message then and leave her alone. And the longer she stayed away from him, the dimmer her unwanted feelings would grow.

She squared her shoulders. She would go over to Squadron HQ and see what she could find out about Dare's near miss. It looked like she'd been right about the motive behind what was happening, but it gave her no satisfaction.

The Gasthaus Restaurant in Devil's Lake was a large, Swiss-style chalet with a gleaming wood interior and numerous nooks and crannies for guests to disappear into. Dare had chosen it because it afforded privacy to dining couples but had no guest rooms to imply anything more intimate. He hoped Andrea would agree to stay overnight with him, but he didn't want her to think he expected it. He was discovering that dealing with an emancipated female could be every bit as touchy as dealing with the unliberated types of his youth.

As one o'clock crept closer, his state of tension grew almost intolerable. He hadn't handled his encounter with Andrea very well, he knew. Maybe he'd blown it completely. After his near miss, he'd been so full of adrenaline that he'd acted without thinking. No woman would like being grabbed and kissed the way he'd kissed Andrea, and certainly not on the tail end of such a ridiculous accusation. Worse, he'd practically ordered her to meet him here, which was guaranteed to rouse a woman's perversity. Andrea, he'd discovered, could be perverse with the best of them.

So he watched the minute hand on his watch crawl toward one with a steadily sinking heart. She wasn't coming. She could have been here over an hour ago if she'd really wanted to come.

Yep, he'd blown it. The same experience that had made him realize just how much she meant to him had also driven him to ruin his chances. So it went. Only right now he was in no mood to feel philosophical about it. Staring into his beer stein, he decided to give her fifteen more minutes and then go home and get royally drunk.

"There's no future in this, sir."

Dare's breath locked in his suddenly tight throat. Slowly, hardly daring to believe his ears, he looked up and found Andrea standing by the booth. Her cheeks were pink from the cold, and her hair was ruffled from the wind. Her eyes—her eyes were hazy with both sorrow and yearning. Dare thought he'd never seen a more beautiful sight.

"I know. Sit down, Andrea."

But she didn't obey immediately. "I almost didn't come."

"I know." His heart beat in a slow, painful rhythm.

She blinked. "It'll hurt worse if we don't stop this right now."

"I'll risk it. What about you?"

Slowly, very slowly, she slid into the seat facing him. "I don't want either of us to be hurt, Colonel."

"I've got a feeling it's already too late to avoid it."

"It feels that way." Abruptly she reached out and covered both his large hands with her small ones. Dare immediately turned his hands over and clasped hers.

"I keep thinking," she said in a tense, un-Andrea-like voice, "of what almost happened to you this morning. I've seen it happen before, so it doesn't take a whole lot of imagination—" She looked to the side, blinking rapidly. "It'll be like that when I leave for Minot."

"Do you think if we pretend it doesn't exist that it won't hurt?"

Her green eyes came back to meet his. "No," she said steadily. "It hurts already. I've been lying to myself all along, I guess. I thought I could handle a fling. I kept telling myself that's all this is. That was a really stupid assumption from someone who's never had a fling before."

He squeezed her hands gently. "I told you this wasn't casual. This is no fling."

She drew a deep, unsteady breath. "No, it's not. And it'll hurt just as much when I leave whether we make love again or not. I'd rather have the memories than nothing at all."

"Would you like the menu now, sir?" The waitress's voice startled both of them.

"Yes," Dare answered without taking his eyes from Andrea. "And a couple of beers."

Releasing one of her hands, he pulled a pack of cigarettes from his breast pocket, shook one out, and lit it. "This morning wasn't my first close call, but it reminded me of something I've lost sight of over the past few years. Life doesn't give any guarantees, Andrea. Today is the only day we've got for sure. Tomorrow might never come."

"I know. I was thinking the same thing. I was thinking..." She shook her head as if she couldn't find the words. Dare waited patiently.

"I was thinking," she said presently, "that I've been so busy following this schedule I have in my head that I haven't had time for anything else. I guess I've been missing a lot."

"And so?"

"And so maybe I should accept these next few weeks as a gift and quit trying to fight it. I—I really don't want to miss it."

Dare squeezed her hand.

"But..." Her voice quavered and then steadied. "But I have to know exactly what it is you want from me."

"Exactly what you've offered me."

Andrea drew a deep breath. "I can only give you the next few weeks," she said straightly. "There's no future."

He nodded. "I understand that. Didn't I just tell you that there's no guarantee tomorrow will ever come? I want *now*, Andrea. The moment in our grasp."

She looked into his blue eyes, eyes so close to the color of the North Dakota sky, and it was like racing down a ski slope at eighty miles an hour, like the time she'd gone skydiving and she'd been falling, falling, only this time there was no rip cord.

Letting go of her, he leaned back, allowing the waitress to set two frosty steins of beer on the table along with two menus. "Give us ten or fifteen minutes before we order," he told the girl.

Food? Andrea thought. He wanted her to think about *food?* Wrapping her hands around her stein as if it were the last anchor in the universe, she stared down into the frothy beer and tried to find a rip cord. Any rip cord. Oh, God, she was so scared. She could only fail. She couldn't be what he wanted, even for a few weeks, any more than she'd ever been able to be what her father wanted. She wasn't that kind of woman. She was unnatural.

"Relax, Andrea."

Dare's deep voice beat back her panic a little, and she managed to look up.

"I told you," he said gently, "I don't want anything you can't give, so quit worrying about it."

"You don't know that."

"Yes, I do, and for the third time—Charlie Burke is a horse's ass. Just pick up your menu and think about lunch. Let me worry about everything else."

It was tempting to do exactly that, Andrea thought as she obediently picked up the menu. His shoulders looked broad enough to handle all his own worries and hers, as well.

"I'd like to get my hands on the son of a bitch who messed up my hydraulics," Dare remarked.

The words had a salutary effect. Andrea was immediately diverted, anger rising at the thought of anyone pulling a stunt like that. With her anger came her appetite. She hadn't eaten breakfast, because she'd been too upset by Dare's visit to her quarters. Suddenly everything on the menu looked good.

"I'm surprised you didn't punch out," she said. "Most pilots would have. You couldn't have had much control."

"Barely enough," he agreed. "But if I'd ejected, all the evidence would have been gone."

"And that was worth your life?" Andrea looked outraged.

"I didn't say that. I felt I could make it or I wouldn't have tried."

"Exactly what happened?"

"Slow leak. Slow enough so that I'd been in the air more than an hour before I lost enough fluid to make control extremely difficult. I wasn't doing any fancy flying, just straight, level stuff, so I didn't need much stick, but every time I used the pedals, I squeezed out a little more fluid. I thought I was getting a little mushy, but I couldn't be sure. And then I decided to try a stall and spin out of it.''

Andrea's eyes were wide. ''That's when you knew you were in trouble?''

Dare nodded. ''I fell from forty thousand to twenty thousand feet before I could come out of the spin. By then I had more air than fluid in the system, and every time I hit those pedals I was leaking. Air's a lot harder to compress than hydraulic fluid, and it leaked out the holes a whole lot faster. Still, I had just enough control to make it.''

''Thank God.'' She bit her lip, looking hesitant. ''Has it—has it occurred to you that somebody might have it in for you personally?''

He looked surprised. ''What makes you think that?''

Andrea flushed. ''It occurred to me last week that all this business started right at the time you arrived here.''

Before he could reply, the waitress came to take their orders.

''Well,'' said Dare when they were again alone, ''I imagine I have a few enemies, but I can't think of any who'd have that kind of grudge against me. But then, who can?''

''It's a horrifying thought,'' Andrea agreed. ''Maybe it's just coincidence.''

Dare lit another cigarette, saying a mental farewell to his attempts to quit. Maybe next year. ''You know, Andrea, I fly that trainer every Saturday morning. You could say it has my name on it.''

Andrea sucked a sharp breath. ''Nobody else flies it?''

''Not on Saturday morning.''

Andrea's hands knotted into fists. ''Maybe we should go back to the base and—''

''And what?'' he interrupted. ''Damn it, Andrea, I called in the OSI to handle this, and if you think I like the OSI any better than any other Blue Suiter, you're wrong. I've got those guys tramping all over my bailiwick, poking their noses into every little nook and cranny—God knows what dirt they're digging up to look into another time—and I want you to let them handle this. This is *our* time.''

He looked so irritated that she almost smiled. "Poking their noses everywhere, huh?"

"*Everywhere,*" he said emphatically. "Hell, you've been in the service long enough to know. I'll bet they've got a complete list of every glove that's disappeared from Supply in the last six months."

"Probably." At last her smile broke through. "Okay, Colonel, have it your way. I'll let OSI handle it until Monday. Then, whether you like it or not, I'm getting involved."

"Just what do you think you can do that they can't?"

Andrea shrugged. "My brothers always said I had a mind like Sherlock Holmes. We'll see. Just don't order me to back off, because I won't. My job is to investigate, and that's just what I'm going to do."

Her chin was set like a bulldog's, and Dare decided to let it ride. What would it hurt, anyway? By Monday everybody on the base would know what happened with his plane, and they weren't going to be able to cover this one with tales of sick geese.

"Fair enough," he said. "And if you ask me nicely enough, I might tell you everything I told OSI this morning."

Her eyes widened. "You mean there's more?"

"Actually," he said, letting a smile come through, "the only thing more is that they debriefed me for two solid hours this morning. I'd rather wrestle with a shot hydraulic system any day. It was like a bad scene out of a third-rate movie, the same questions over and over and over."

"Why? They couldn't possibly think you had anything to do with the damage to your plane!"

Dare shook his head. "No. They just wanted to be sure I wasn't overlooking anything. I got away from them by promising that if I thought of anything over the weekend I'd write it down and let them know Monday morning."

"You'll let *me* know if you think of anything, won't you?"

He smiled. "Of course I will. You can count on it."

Chapter 11

The temperature had reached its daytime high of seventeen below zero when Andrea and Dare were ready to leave the restaurant. Standing in the vestibule, they began to zip and button up.

"Where do we go from here, Andrea?"

She paused in the process of zipping her snorkel hood. "I thought you had it all planned."

"I had hopes, not plans."

"Oh." Smiling slightly, she finished zipping the snorkel and peered at him from a small, round opening that was edged in gray fur. "I packed an overnight bag."

She'd packed an overnight bag. Dare felt his face split into a wide grin, the first time he'd felt like grinning since Christmas. "Follow me, Captain."

"Yes, sir."

She drove behind him to a two-story, half-timbered motel on the frozen lake. At this time of year there were few people traveling this way who needed a place to stay, but one wing was open, and they were assured that the dining room served dinner until seven. If they wanted to risk frostbite, they could rent skates and go out on the lake, or they could go tobogganing on a hill two miles up the road. Dare thanked the desk clerk for the information and picked up his overnight bag and Andrea's.

"Do you feel like ice-skating, Captain?" he asked as he and Andrea rode the elevator to the second floor.

"No, sir, not especially."

"Tobogganing?"

"No, sir. It's too damn cold."

The corners of his blue eyes creased as he smiled down at her. "Indoor sports?"

She smiled back. "The best kind."

"Nooky?"

Andrea threw her head back and laughed. "Absolutely."

Dare had splurged on a two-room suite, and in the sitting room there was a fireplace with gas logs. He bent to light it while Andrea shucked her outer gear. When the flame was adjusted to his satisfaction, he straightened and turned to face her.

"Come here, woman," he said roughly, then grinned as she laughed and flew into his arms. Lifting her from her feet, he whirled her in circles. Whatever her reservations, she'd clearly left them behind for now. He was grateful for that, very grateful.

Her nose was still cold from the outdoors when he bent his head to kiss her, but her mouth was warm, so very warm and moist, making him think of those secret places he longed to explore. Later there would be time to take things slow, but right now he felt like a man who'd been starving all his life.

Setting Andrea on her feet, he took one of her hands and pressed it to his swollen manhood. Then, never taking his eyes from hers, he reached for her sweater and began to pull it up.

"Do you know what I'm going to do to you, Andrea?"

Her eyelids fluttered, and a secret smile came to her lips as she raised her arms over her head. "Tell me," she suggested. "In detail."

A choked laugh escaped him as he tugged the sweater over her head. As soon as Andrea freed her hands form the sleeves of her sweater, she reached for him. Her fingers released the snap of his jeans and tugged his zipper down. Bending to place his mouth near her ear, he told her in titillating detail just what he had in mind.

He heard her swiftly drawn breath, heard her smothered moan, felt her tremble beneath his hands as he whispered his intentions and unfastened her bra. The bra went the way of her sweater, somewhere across the room, and his hands went to the fastening of her jeans as he bent lower and took the tip of her breast into his mouth.

"Dare!" She gasped his name and hooked her fingers into the waistband of his pants, yanking downward. She was as impatient as he was now. Electric currents tingled along her nerves, and she felt herself melting, growing liquid and weak. She moaned with disappointment when he tore his mouth from her breast so that he could pull her jeans the rest of the way off. There was a horrible moment of delay while he dealt with her boots, and then she was free of all the restrictions of her clothes.

Before he could prevent it, she fell to her knees before him and reached for his pants to finish what she'd started. He went to work on the buttons of his shirt, but his fingers fumbled and then froze in utter amazement as Andrea pressed her face into his groin. Tremors like an earthquake shook him, and he tried to hold perfectly still for fear a single movement might cause her to pull back.

Andrea nuzzled him slowly, inhaling deeply of his male scent. His hair was so thick there, she thought, and so crisp against her cheek, a sharp contrast to skin as unexpectedly smooth as satin. Then slowly, daringly, she licked him delicately with the tip of her tongue.

That put paid to the last of Dare's self-control. Dropping to his own knees, he eased Andrea swiftly onto her back, and then he was on her and in her, taking her with a driving rhythm as primitive and basic as his hunger for this woman.

Andrea slept deeply and soundly, so deeply and soundly that she didn't wake when Dare lifted her from the sitting room carpet and carried her to the king-size bed in the next room. When he drew the blankets up over her, she sighed and turned onto her side, but her eyes never opened. Dare stood over her for a while, smiling faintly. Clearly she hadn't slept any better this week than he had.

He felt a little embarrassed by the rough, quick way he'd taken her. Hell, he'd come back to himself to discover that he still wore his shirt, and that his jeans were twisted around his ankles, caught on his boots. There was something indecent in that, especially for a man who'd always tried to be a considerate lover. Talk about jumping a woman's bones!

It was just after four, and beyond the windows, daylight was rapidly fading. Soon the northern night would blanket the world. Outside, the wind was kicking up again, and though the windows were double-paned, he could swear he felt a cold draft. Leaving Andrea, he went to close the insulated curtains in both rooms.

He wanted to lie down beside her, but mindful of the fact that the dining room would close at seven, he couldn't risk it. If he closed his eyes, he would be apt to sleep for hours. A long week of sleepless nights and this morning's events virtually guaranteed it. Knowing Andrea's appetite, he couldn't imagine her making it until tomorrow morning without a meal, especially not with the activities he had in mind for later.

A frown came to his brow as he thought about what had happened and the suspicions Andrea had shared with him at lunch. He'd managed to put her on hold, but in fact, the more he thought about it, the more he thought she might just be right about what was going on. But why would somebody be out to get him? He was no saint, but he couldn't remember ever having done anything to make anyone that angry. If somebody really did have that big a grudge against him, they must be a little unhinged.

The thing was, he didn't want to think that whoever had punctured his hydraulic lines had meant to kill him. Scare the devil out of him, yes, but kill him, no. Killing him would have involved no more effort—less, in fact—than making those small, careful holes. A person with access to plastique didn't have to make tiny punctures in hydraulic lines.

Or maybe, like most people, he was just unable to believe that someone had genuinely tried to kill him. Because, if he were to be honest with himself, he had survived only by the skin of his teeth. And when he thought about those endless minutes in the dive as he battled to gain control, it was almost possible to believe that someone had meant him to suffer that excruciating awareness of his impending fate. Whoever had made those little holes would probably be disappointed to know that during those interminable minutes, Dare had been too busy and too full of adrenaline to feel any fear.

Rubbing his eyes wearily, he decided he'd better call room service and have them send up something that would keep for a few hours. He had the feeling that he was going to sleep whether he wanted to or not, so he might as well do it comfortably, at Andrea's side, rather than in uncomfortable snatches sitting up on the couch and fighting it.

Forty minutes later, stripped to the buff, he crawled under the covers beside her. In her sleep she turned into his arms, resting her head on his chest, twining her legs with his. Contented, he let himself sleep at last.

Andrea awoke hours later to a dark room, but she knew instantly where she was. Only once before in her life had she wakened with arms around her, and with Dare's arms around her it didn't seem to matter where on the planet she was.

They were tucked together like spoons, one of his arms beneath her head, one resting heavily on her waist. She could hear his deep, steady breathing above her head, and against her back she could feel the springy hair of his chest and groin. It would be nice, she thought dreamily, if they could stay like this forever.

The memory of their earlier lovemaking was vivid in her mind, and she indulged herself in the luxury of a mental replay. She'd never thought herself the kind to inspire passion in any man, but there was little doubt that Dare had been impassioned. The rough and ready way he'd taken her had been testimony to that, and she hadn't imagined the shudders that had ripped through him. On the other hand, she couldn't be sure *she* had inspired that passion. She'd heard that a close brush with death could cause reactions like that. Maybe it wouldn't have made any difference to him who he'd been with.

He'd almost died. The thought slithered into her mind, poisoning her afterglow. At the age of six, out at Edwards Air Force Base, she'd seen a plane auger in, and no one had thought to keep the pilot's identity from her. Dave Wallace had been a buddy of her father's, and whenever he happened to come by the Burke home he always had a piece of candy for little Andrea, and a place on his lap. Andrea had been fascinated by his ribbons, and Wallace had made up outrageous stories about how he'd gotten them. "I got this one for punching General LeMay in the nose," he would tell her. "And that's for beating Mike Metger at poker. And they gave me this one over here for the time I slammed my finger shut in the canopy." Even at six she hadn't believed him and had giggled until her sides ached.

Dave Wallace had augered in at better than Mach 2, riding a shrieking metal demon straight down out of the sky to end his life in an explosion that sent pillars of flame and black smoke nearly to the clouds. "God!" Charlie Burke had said hours later when telling his wife what he and his three children had seen. "Can you imagine it? He must have felt so alive in those last few seconds!" Andrea had had nightmares for months afterward.

She was having a nightmare right now. With the vivid memory of fountaining flames in her head, she squeezed her eyes shut. He hadn't died. He hadn't died. He was right here with her. The wind rattled the glass in the windows, a forlorn sound, a cold sound. Unconsciously she wiggled backward a little, trying to get as close to Dare as she could.

"Don't move, Andrea" said a sleepy, thick voice above her head.

"Dare?"

"Shh," he whispered soothingly. "Shh. Don't move. Not a muscle."

She held perfectly still.

"That's it," he whispered. His hand left her waist, sliding slowly, ever so slowly, upward, skimming over the skin of her stomach in feathery circles that left a tingling sensitivity in their wake. Andrea's breath caught and held as his fingers glided upward some more, reaching the underside of her breast. Helpless to stop herself, she twisted, trying to bring him more fully into contact with her.

"Uh-uh," Dare said huskily. "Don't move, darlin'. We've got all night, and I want to pleasure you."

His words, the huskiness of his voice, sent tingles arcing across her nerve endings, and she began to grow heavy.

"That's it," he whispered again. "Let me, Andrea. Just let me."

She might try to hurry him, but not even to save her life could she have stopped him. Her muscles were growing syrupy with the feelings he drizzled over her, and when his fingertip brushed her beaded nipple, she could only gasp. Movement was suddenly beyond her.

Dare cupped the weight of her full breast in his palm and kneaded gently, oh so gently, as he found the nape of her neck with his mouth and began to nibble softly. Shivers raced down Andrea's spine, adding to the weight growing at her center.

"Dare..." She sighed his name from the depths of her.

That was how he wanted her to say his name. Again and again. Forever.

"So lovely," he murmured. "So sweet." His hand slipped to her other breast, testing its heaviness, tormenting softly. "They're better than standard issue, Andrea."

A short, breathless laugh escaped her. "You like my breasts?"

It was his turn to laugh hoarsely. "I love your breasts. I especially love to see you in uniform, because nobody but me would ever know how perfect and lovely your body is."

It was true. It still amazed him that she was so perfect in every way. Full breasts, fuller than he'd ever expected, narrow waist, hips that flared just right and joined to legs that were long and slender. Thinking about those hips joining to those legs caused him to sweep his hand downward to the apex of her thighs. They both groaned as he touched her.

"Don't move, Andrea," he said again. "Don't move." He was far from finished with her, but his own control was getting more precarious by the second as he felt the heat blooming in her.

Slipping his hand between her thighs, he lifted her leg and pulled it back over his, leaving her opened to his seeking, stroking fingers.

"So hot," he murmured, a catch in his voice. "So wild and sweet..."

"Dare...Dare..." She began to chant his name on each quickening breath as he parted her with his fingers and stroked her deeper. Her hips began a gentle, helpless undulation against his hand, and this time he didn't try to still her. He couldn't. Each movement pressed that wonderful rump gently against his manhood, and with each touch he became more helpless against his own needs.

"Do you know what it did to me before when you licked me?" he asked her. His voice was rough, hoarse. He heard her catch her breath again at the memory. "I'm going to show you, Andrea."

Pressing her onto her back, he drew a couple of breaths to steady himself, and then he knelt between her legs, pressing her soft thighs apart. It was dark in the room, and she thought he was going to touch her as he had on Christmas, so it came as an utter shock when she realized that it was his tongue that now followed the path he'd blazed with his fingers.

"Dare?" She sounded almost frightened.

"It's okay," he said, raising his head. "It's okay, Andrea."

It was more than okay. It was too much. She was riding a shooting star at transluminal speeds, burning in the heat of the sun, melting, melting....

Dare felt the convulsions take her, and he slid swiftly up over her, filling her, giving her the last ounce of pleasure he could wring out of the moment for her. Holding her snugly within his strong arms, he sheltered her vulnerability and brought her safely back.

"And now," he whispered, when her breathing slowed and her shuddering eased, "now we go together, sweetheart."

She would have said it was impossible. It wasn't.

Champagne, club sandwiches and cherry cheesecake made their dinner before the gas fire. Andrea wore her green peignoir; Dare had pulled on his jeans. There was, Andrea thought, something incredibly sexy about a man wearing nothing but jeans, jeans with the snap suggestively undone. It gave her the freedom to drink her fill of his broad, muscular chest, and from time to time she couldn't resist reaching out to run her fingers through the whorls of dark, springy hair that patterned him. When she did, he invariably sighed and smiled.

Three weeks, Dare thought. In just three short weeks she would walk out of his life. Minot wasn't that far away, and he hoped to persuade her to see him from time to time. He could always fly out there for a weekend. But now wasn't the time to discuss it. She still hadn't really come to terms with their relationship, and he strongly suspected she had come this far only because there was a definite time limit. She felt safe giving in because she knew it would end on January thirtieth.

Charlie Burke had a lot to do with that, he suspected. Old Charlie had been—probably still was—a male chauvinist pig of the first order. While Dare didn't much care for the indiscriminate way a lot of feminists flung that term around, he had to admit there were some men who fit the bill perfectly. On the occasions when Dare had met Andrea's mother, he'd thought he'd never seen a woman so downtrodden. Clara Burke didn't have a thought or a wish of her own, and whenever Charlie said jump, she jumped. Clara might as well have been a dog and Charlie her master. Hell, Charlie probably would have treated a dog better.

Andrea had grown up seeing that. She'd grown up with her father trying to turn her into another Clara. Small wonder that she probably couldn't imagine other men not wanting the same. Dare could only hope that eventually Andrea would realize that a man who fell in love with Captain Burke was hardly looking for a Clara Burke clone.

Nor was now the time to tell Andrea just how much he admired the strength of will and determination that had allowed her to rise above that kind of upbringing. Now she was still too defensive, still too sure that she was somehow different, somehow *wrong*. She would misunderstand what he was trying to say. Later, when she was surer of him and his feelings, surer that he really didn't want to change a hair on her head, then he would tell her how much he admired her.

If she gave him enough time. Later, he told himself sternly. Think about tomorrow later. No sense coloring this weekend with the shadows of losses that might never happen.

Andrea's hands dipped into the hair on his chest again, and Dare smiled.

"I like it when you touch me," he told her, catching her hand and rubbing it over his pectorals. "Are you fascinated by my chest hair?"

Her cheeks colored faintly. "Yes, sir."

"Why?"

"Because I don't have any."

Dare laughed. "You've got something much better."

"That's all a matter of perspective, Colonel."

"I suppose it is." Seizing her about the waist, he lifted her onto his lap. "There. Now you can comb my hair to your heart's content, and I can enjoy your soft little tush." Her blush deepened, and his smile broadened. "Your tush drove me crazy for weeks, you know. If you had any idea how enticing it looks in your uniform slacks, you'd wear skirts forever."

She slanted a look at him from the corner of her eye. "Your tush drove me crazy, too."

"Mine?" He looked disbelieving.

"Yes, sir. Hard and flat. *Very* male. Every time you write on a chalkboard—"

"You little minx! I had no idea you were eyeballing me that way."

"You weren't supposed to. And I was trying very hard not to. The truth is—and I probably shouldn't admit this to my CO—I never heard a word you said when you wrote on the board."

"I love it. And all the time I thought you were utterly impervious."

"If I were impervious, I wouldn't have called you on Christmas Eve."

"No," he agreed, "I guess you wouldn't."

His blue eyes were smiling and warm, their corners crinkled in the way she loved.

"You're going to hate me for this, Andrea."

"For what?"

"I think you look cute in battle dress."

"Cute? In *fatigues?* Colonel MacLendon, sir, may I respectfully suggest that you've gone crazy? Nobody looks cute in fatigues."

"You do." He nuzzled her cheek and blew softly in her ear, enjoying the way she shivered. "And you look adorable in your Academy sweat suit. Promise me one thing, Andrea. Promise me you'll never stand at attention in that sweat suit again. I could hardly keep my mind on what I was saying because your breasts were—"

She clapped a hand over his mouth. "Don't say it! I'll die of embarrassment."

"It's humanly impossible to die of embarrassment."

She ducked her head. "No, it isn't," she said in a smothered voice. "God, I'll never be able to wear my sweats again."

"You can wear them for me," he suggested. "And stand at attention—"

"Don't." But the eyes she raised to his were laughing despite the painful color in her cheeks. "All the while, I thought that wooden expression on your face was because you were mad at me."

"Never. I was trying not to pounce on you."

"I'll bet. You were probably every bit as embarrassed as I am now."

"I don't embarrass. Believe me, embarrassment was the last thing I felt. Actually, I was annoyed with you when I first arrived. Your conduct was unprofessional, you know."

"I know," Andrea admitted. "I should never have called you cowboy. I don't know what possessed me."

"I do. It's that little imp that lives inside you. Every so often your imp gets out. Anyhow, I was annoyed, just a little. Nothing serious. And the whole time I was there talking to you, I was coming to like you more and more. By the time I left, I was laughing."

"You were not!"

"I was. I just didn't dare let you see it. I like your imp, Andrea." He ran a gentle fingertip along her hairline to her ear. "I like every damn thing about you just fine. I wouldn't change one hair, one eyelash, one thought in your head." Which was not strictly true. There was a thought or two he had every intention of changing.

Looking into his eyes, she almost believed him. Those blue eyes were warm, intense, determined. She wished she could believe him, but even so, she didn't see how their careers would sustain any kind of a relationship, and she wasn't about to sacrifice her life's goals for anything. Of course, he knew that. So when he said he wouldn't change one thought in her head, it could only mean that he was content with the way things were, that he accepted that it would all end when she left.

Well, hey, she told herself bluntly. The man's past forty, and he must have had numerous opportunities to remarry, if that was what he wanted. And to women whose career wouldn't be a problem.

Dare saw the sorrow slip across her face. "Did I say something wrong?"

She shook her head. "I was just remembering that tomorrow always comes."

"Tomorrow we're going to stay here," he said firmly. "We'll go back early on Monday morning."

"That isn't what I meant."

"I know. I'm just trying to tell you that you don't need to think about tomorrow. Don't waste today thinking about what hasn't happened yet, Andrea."

Nodding, she tucked her face into the curve between his neck and shoulder. "I'll try not to. But it always comes, Colonel. Sooner or later, tomorrow always comes."

And he couldn't have made it any plainer that he wanted no more than the moment from her. Well, that was what she wanted, too, she reminded herself. That being the case, why did she feel so sad?

Monday morning came all too quickly, the way dreaded tomorrows always do. Once again Andrea was in uniform, sitting behind the polished expanse of her large desk, sipping coffee and trying to relegate the weekend to memory, where it belonged. Images insisted on flashing before her mind's eyes, however, images of Dare stepping stark naked out of the shower and grabbing her, tickling her until she begged for mercy. Images of the way he threw back his head and laughed full-throatedly. Images of the way the hair on his chest arrowed down to the perpetually, suggestively, unfastened snap of his jeans.

Her body remembered things, too: the way his hands felt sliding over her skin, cupping her breasts, grazing their peaks until she ached. The way his buttocks bunched under her hands when he thrust into her.

"Damn it, Burke," she said aloud. *"Quit it!"* Two solid days of lovemaking and laughter, and she was greedy for more. Unbelievable.

It was with great relief that she heard Nickerson's familiar knock on her door. Now maybe she would get her mind on work, where it belonged.

Nick carried a large envelope with him, as well as his usual folder, and he handed the envelope to her.

"For you, ma'am. It arrived just a couple minutes ago."

Andrea recognized Dare's office code in the return address block. "What now?" she wondered, then shrugged, setting it aside. It could wait until after Nick brought her up to date. "What do you have for me, Nick?"

"The usual." He helped himself to coffee and took a seat. "Do you really want the litany?"

Andrea had to smile. "Photocopy it and give me a copy. What's on your mind?"

"Did you hear what almost happened to MacLendon Saturday morning?"

Andrea was surprised that Dare's visit to the BOQ wasn't all over the base by now. The military grapevine usually worked better than this. "I heard. Somebody punctured his hydraulic lines."

Nick nodded. "So he told you. I wondered if it was true."

"Yes."

"Begging your pardon, ma'am, but what the hell are we going to do about it?"

"I told him I was going to investigate whether he liked it or not."

Nickerson nodded. "I'm glad you did, skipper. I don't know who he called in to handle this mess, but I reckon it was OSI, and if you'll excuse me for saying so, they ain't accomplished diddly squat so far. I was going to ask for your permission to pursue an investigation on my own."

"I was going to ask you to join me in mine."

Nickerson smiled. "I'm with you all the way, Captain."

Andrea reached for the envelope and cut it open. Inside, as she had half expected, was an incident report on the events of Saturday morning. A hand-written note was attached.

You said you were going ahead whether I wanted you to or not, so I thought you should have all the available information. Unfortunately I don't have access to everything OSI may have learned, but everything we've been able to give them is here.

Andrea looked up. "It's all here, Nick, everything MacLendon can put together about what happened. After I read it, I'll pass it on to you, but I don't want anyone else to see it or to know that you and I are investigating."

"Yes, ma'am." Nickerson looked satisfied as he rose. "I'll get you a copy of the weekend incident report."

Dare's mood was, to put it mildly, crummy. He and the entire Wing were grounded as a result of Saturday's events. No more flying until the culprit was found. The alert planes, the bombers that stood ready with nuclear weapons aboard, were surrounded by a tight cordon of security guards, some of whom were OSI. Dare had been angry enough on Saturday, but it was nothing compared to what he felt now at having his Wing's operations hampered. One entire SAC bomb wing, an essential link in the nation's defenses, had been brought to its knees by one or two crazies with a grudge. It was enough to make *him* crazy.

The higher-ups didn't like it, either. He had been in some uncomfortable positions in his life, but never before had one so closely resembled the Iroquois torture of roasting a man alive over hot coals. He was under pressure from all directions, yet there wasn't a damn thing he could personally do except ensure that SAC didn't get another black eye by losing a plane and crew. OSI was doing what it could, eliminating suspects one by one, but nothing was moving fast enough to please anyone.

Wednesday afternoon brought the only bright spot to his entire week. During the early afternoon, Andrea called him.

"Colonel, if you can see your way to coming over here, I'd highly recommend it."

Dare looked out his window at the blowing snow and frowned. "What is it?"

"I don't want to spoil the surprise, sir, but you could classify this as a sort of public relations matter. A pleasant one."

Well, he thought, it would give him an opportunity to see

Andrea, even if only formally. Maybe he could even find a private minute with her to discuss the upcoming weekend.

"Give me twenty minutes, Captain." It would take him almost that long to get into his cold weather gear. With the temperature at twenty-seven below and the wind blowing at forty to forty-five miles an hour, it was no day for cutting corners, even for a short trip.

Andrea was waiting for him in the front office of Security Police Headquarters. With her stood a wizened man of about seventy with a ramrod posture that belied his years. Throwing back his hood and peeling off his gloves, Dare strode toward them.

"You wanted to see me, Captain?"

"Yes, sir. Thank you for coming. Colonel, this is Mr. Selfridge. He farms up toward the Canadian border. Mr. Selfridge, Colonel MacLendon, commander of the 447th Bombardment Wing."

Dare shook the old farmer's hand, saying, "It's a pleasure to meet you, Mr. Selfridge."

Selfridge eyed him keenly and then gave an approving nod. "Reckon you've seen combat."

"Vietnam."

"I was in the South Pacific from '41 on. Navy."

Dare smiled. "Then it's an *honor* to meet you. What can I do for you, Mr. Selfridge?"

"Not a thing," said Selfridge, surprising him with a laugh. "Not a thing. Just have something to return to you."

Perplexed, MacLendon looked at Andrea and saw the devil lights in her hazy green eyes. At once he felt the corner of his mouth lift in anticipation. Well, he could use a good joke.

"Mr. Selfridge," Andrea said, "came to return some government property."

"What's that?" Dare asked, totally at sea now.

Andrea pointed to a box at her feet. "This, sir. Mr. Selfridge collected three more boxes as well."

"They're out in my truck," Selfridge assured him.

Andrea's eyes sparkled with humor, and Dare decided to go along with her. Squatting, he opened the top of the box and stared. It was filled with hair-fine, aluminum-coated glass fibers.

"This is chaff," Dare said blankly.

"Yes, sir," Andrea said gravely, betrayed by a faint tremor in her voice. "Four whole boxes of chaff."

"Saw it fall off one of your planes," Selfridge said. "Damn stuff went everywhere. Had a hell of a time collecting it all, but I think I got most of it."

Dare froze in his squatting position and hastily covered his mouth with his hand, rubbing it as if lost in thought. He didn't dare look at Andrea for fear he would be unable to contain his laughter. These fine little fibers, called chaff, were dispensed by aircraft in order to confuse radar. Millions upon millions of these dipoles were often expended in a single evasive maneuver, and they had absolutely no further value once they were emptied from their tubes. Dare almost couldn't bear to think of Mr. Selfridge conscientiously collecting all these little hairs.

Dare cleared his throat. "Ah, Captain Burke?"

"Sir?"

"Why don't you get a photographer over here. I want to thank Mr. Selfridge properly, and I'd like him to have a photograph as a mark of our appreciation."

"Yes, sir." Pivoting, Andrea strode up the hallway.

Slowly rising to his feet, Dare glanced at the two desk cops. That wasn't a safe direction to look, either. From their wooden expressions, he gathered they were close to strangling on their suppressed laughter. The only place left to look was at Selfridge.

"I can't imagine," Dare said to the farmer, "how you ever found all these on the snow."

"Twasn't difficult to see them. They're gray against the snow. It was the devil to collect 'em. Thought they might be secret, though, and I couldn't see letting them blow all over where anyone might find them."

Dare managed a nod. "Why don't we go to Captain Burke's office and have some coffee while we wait for the photographer?"

"Let me get the other boxes of that stuff in here first."

"That won't be necessary. These two airmen will get them for you." The two desk cops no longer looked like laughing, Dare saw. Satisfied, he escorted Selfridge to Andrea's office. She was just hanging up the phone when the two men entered.

"The photographer's on his way over, sir."

"Good, good." Smiling broadly, Dare ushered Selfridge to a chair. "Pour Mr. Selfridge some coffee, Captain." He enjoyed the flash of irritation the order brought to her green eyes.

"What do you raise, Mr. Selfridge?" Dare asked while Andrea dealt with the coffee.

"Durum wheat. My boys do most of the work these days, but it don't hardly seem fair to them. There ain't much money in it, for sure. Not like there used to be. Time was a farmer could expect to make a fair living from the soil, but the price of seed and fertilizer's shot to the moon."

"It's rough," Dare agreed. "My dad and brothers ranch in Montana, over toward Kalispell, and it's a struggle to make ends meet."

Eventually—none too soon, in Dare's estimation—the photographer showed up and snapped a photo of Dare and Selfridge as they shook hands in front of the U.S. flag. The desk sergeant was summoned to escort Selfridge back to his truck.

"You know, Mr. Selfridge," Dare said as the farmer turned to leave, "it's not often that I meet someone as honest and patriotic as you are. I don't think one man in ten million would have gone to so much trouble to return that chaff. I'm truly honored to have met you."

Selfridge actually blushed. "Just doing my duty, Colonel."

When he and Andrea were alone, Dare turned to look at her, fully expecting to find her doubled over with laughter. He was astonished to find her regarding him with wide, dewy eyes.

"What's wrong?" he asked. Damn, she looked as if she were about to weep, and he couldn't stand the thought of Andrea weeping.

"Nothing."

"Then why are you crying?"

"I'm not crying, sir. I never cry. You saw it. I didn't know for sure if you would."

"Saw what?"

"What an adorable, selfless, touching thing that man did. It was funny, of course, but only because we know how worthless that chaff is. What Selfridge did is beautiful. Can you imagine how many days he must have spent gathering that stuff?"

"My back aches at the thought." More than his back ached, right now. His heart ached at the way she was looking at him. He couldn't remember anybody ever having looked at him that way, as if he were the most wonderful man in the world. "Andrea, I—"

"Thank you for coming over here, Colonel," she interrupted. "I felt he deserved some kind of recognition."

"No problem. Andrea—"

"I just couldn't send him all that way back without—"

Goaded by her evident determination to avoid personal conversation, Dare took matters into his own hands. Rounding her desk, he hauled her into his arms and kissed her into quivering submission. When she was finally clinging to him for support, he decided to risk trying to talk to her again.

"About this weekend, Andrea." He sounded a little breathless himself, but that was okay. He wanted her to know what she did to him. Damn all these clothes!

"Yes, sir?"

"We've got to make plans."

Her eyelids lifted a fraction, revealing just a glimpse of her green irises. "Plans?"

"Plans for the weekend," he repeated patiently. "Damn it, Andrea, you can't look at me like that and then tell me to get lost. I want to spend the weekend with you again."

"Oh." Blinking, she made an effort to gather her wits. Why not? she thought. She was already in so deep that one more weekend wouldn't make a bit of difference.

A knock on the door jolted them apart. Andrea turned away from him.

"Burke, damn it, look at me and answer me."

"That's Nickerson," she said breathlessly. "You make the plans and let me know."

Relieved, Dare yielded a sigh. "Okay," he said, just as Andrea called out, "Come on in, Nick."

Dare exited swiftly, leaving Andrea and Nickerson to their meeting.

Nick, who'd stared after MacLendon, turned to look at Andrea, and his face went suddenly and totally wooden. From his unusual and utter lack of expression, Andrea guessed he'd somehow picked up on something in the atmosphere. Hell!

"We've got work to do, Nick," she said abruptly.

"Yes, ma'am."

He glanced at her and then away, but not before she caught the twinkle in his eye. Damn all nosy NCO's, she thought irritably, and snatched up the report she wanted to discuss with him.

Chapter 12

In the early hours of Thursday morning, one of the alert planes caught fire. After recent events, no one doubted that the fire had been deliberately set, but the question no one could answer was *how.* Even under ordinary circumstances those planes were closely guarded, because their bomb bays were full of nuclear weapons. Lately, security around them had been so tight that Andrea would have said even a field mouse couldn't have slipped past unnoticed.

"I want the s.o.b. who did this," Andrea told Nick that morning as she sat bleary-eyed at her desk. "I've got one measly week left, and I want him before I leave."

Nick stood at her window, hands on his narrow hips, and looked out at the bleak morning. The Security Squadron had gone on full alert the instant the fire was reported, and it had been a long night for everyone. He sighed now and rotated his shoulders to ease the tension.

"The fire marshal promised to call me as soon as he knows what caused the fire," he said.

Andrea looked at his back. "But he said it was arson."

"*Thinks* it was," Nick said. "I expect he's right. Merle knows what he's doing. But he won't commit himself till all the evidence is in."

"Sensible," Andrea admitted, rubbing the back of her neck. "Did he tell you how long that should be?"

"He hopes to know by sometime tomorrow. He's in one hell of a hot seat, ma'am. Did you hear the news on the radio this morning?"

"You mean all the uproar in town because there were weapons on the plane? That's the kind of noise politicians get paid to make. And, of course, the locals are nervous about it. Most people don't understand how harmless an unarmed nuclear weapon is. As far as hot seats go, I think MacLendon's must be the hottest."

Nodding, Nickerson faced her. "I hear he's talking to the news people and the city council this morning."

"Probably. I really don't know." Sighing, Andrea stood and went to the file cabinet to pour another in an endless stream of cups of coffee. "I want the squadron to stay on full alert for the time being. And I'm going to activate the Pyramid tonight to make sure nobody's ignoring our status."

The Pyramid Alert System was an ingeniously simple system whereby each person on the pyramid telephoned the two persons below him to pass along information or to bring the squadron to full alert. In less than twenty minutes, Andrea's entire four hundred man squadron could be communicated with individually. In only slightly more time, the Bombardment Wing commander could bring the entire base to alert status through the same system.

"I guess that's it for now, Nick," she said after a moment, dismissing him. "When you go by Lieutenant Dolan's office, stick your head in and tell him I'd like a word with him."

"Yes, ma'am." He departed, shutting the door quietly after him.

Poor Dare, Andrea thought as she settled behind her desk again. Closing her eyes, she leaned her head back against the chair and sighed. Between SAC HQ, the press, and the local politicians, he must really have his hands full. Through it all, he would have to be courteous, concerned, understanding, and firm.

Quite a recipe, especially for a man who'd had no more sleep than he had, thanks to last night's events.

With her eyes closed, his image rose vividly in her mind, and now that there was no one to betray herself to, she admitted just how much she'd missed him this week. She went to bed at night longing for him and woke in the morning feeling empty because he wasn't there. It was a ridiculous dependency, she told herself, especially since they'd only had three nights together. How could he have become a habit so fast? Why was it that after such a short time, such a brief acquaintance, a dozen times a day she wanted to turn to him to share some thought?

And only last night she'd awakened in the dark and mistaken the shape of a pillow for his shoulder. She didn't like to remember how her throat had ached and her eyes had burned when she'd realized it was just a pillow.

Well, she told herself firmly, it didn't matter. January thirtieth was fast approaching. Dare was clearly content to let the relationship end there, and after a time she would get over this ridiculous emotional reaction.

A knock on the door announced Lieutenant Dolan's arrival, and Andrea straightened. "Come in," she called in a brisk, businesslike voice, relieved to have the distraction of work.

"Still working, I see."

It was after ten that evening when Andrea looked up to see Dare standing in the doorway of her office. Her neck was stiff from hours of hunching over lists that refused to shed any light on the case, and her eyes were red and burning.

Dare had never looked so good to her as he did now, leaning against the doorjamb. His unbuttoned parka revealed a teal blue sweater, and his fingers were tucked into the front pockets of snug, worn blue jeans.

"Give it up, Andrea," he said roughly. "You're out of here in a little over a week. It won't be your problem anymore."

"It's my problem right now, sir."

"It's the OSI's problem."

"They don't seem to be getting very far with it."

He looked tired, too, she noticed. And angry and frustrated. The lines of his face seemed to have grown deeper just since yesterday. She resisted a totally feminine and totally ridiculous impulse to smooth them away. Or soothe them away.

"Got any coffee?"

"I just brewed a fresh pot." She watched him lever himself away from the door frame and stride to the coffeepot on top of her filing cabinet. She'd forgotten how big he was, just since yesterday. How tall and lean and hard he was. She always felt a clenching thrill when she saw him for the first time after an absence, however brief. Why was that?

Her eyes never left him as he filled a cup and settled into one of the chairs facing her desk. He crossed his legs loosely, one ankle on the opposite knee, and leaned back, rubbing his eyes wearily.

"The guy doesn't leave a trail," he said. "Not a hint or a sign of what he's up to. What's the point of all this if he doesn't get the satisfaction of telling somebody why?"

"Maybe he gets all the satisfaction he needs just from doing it. Or maybe he's saving up his explanations for some grand finale."

"That thought's cost me some sleep, I can tell you." He sipped the coffee and grimaced. "I've swallowed enough coffee today to float a battleship. At this rate I'll have an ulcer in a week."

Andrea opened her desk drawer and pulled out a bottle of antacids. She tossed them to him. "Help yourself."

"You, too, huh? Thanks."

"I keep thinking I'm missing something that's as plain as the nose on my face," Andrea remarked. "Like I've got all the puzzle pieces but I just can't see how to fit them together."

"Well, if you're right that I'm the target, he's doing a damn fine job. My career's getting more tenuous with every passing minute."

"But why, Dare? You've done everything you can to stop him."

He shrugged. "The buck stops here, as they say. They're starting to ask some tough questions at the top, like why the devil everything's gone to hell in a handbasket since I took command here."

Andrea ached for him. "Everything has *not* gone to hell since you took command. Everything is just fine, except for some loony, and you can't be responsible for loonies."

"That's not how it looks if you're sitting up at SAC headquarters and one of your bases is all but out of commission, and the guy in charge out there isn't doing diddly about it."

"That's not fair!"

"Who said life was fair?"

"Who said it shouldn't be?"

A faint smile came to Dare's mouth, lifting the corners slightly, as he took in the pugnacious set of Andrea's chin.

"I need a cigarette," was all he said, but he was thinking how badly he needed her in his arms right now, needed to feel her warmth and the gentleness she kept so well hidden.

Andrea pulled open yet another drawer and retrieved an ashtray, setting it down on the desk between them. "So smoke," she said.

"Prepared for all eventualities, I see," he remarked as he pulled a pack of cigarettes from his parka pocket.

"Yes, sir. We try." She rose and refilled her own cup with coffee, then started to pace around her office, unaware that Dare spared a few moments to admire her bottom in the ugly blue Air Force slacks.

"What have we got?" she asked rhetorically a few minutes later. "I was shot by somebody who was evidently trying to get through the perimeter fence. That doesn't fit with the rest of it."

"Why not?" Suddenly he looked over his shoulder at the door to her office. "Andrea, maybe I'm paranoid, but if you want to discuss this mess in any detail, maybe you should close your office door."

"There's plenty of reason to be paranoid lately." She even glanced into the hallway before closing her door and, after a moment's hesitation, locking it.

"So what doesn't fit about you being shot?"

Andrea perched on the edge of the desk and set her mug down so she could rub the back of her neck. "It's not just me being shot that doesn't fit. It's that at this point I'm not sure our loony is an intentional murderer."

"Why not? Want me to rub your neck for you?"

Andrea looked at him, her green eyes growing smoky.

''Maybe later,'' she said. ''I don't think too clearly when you touch me, and right now I want to think.''

There was no way he could repress the grin that seemed to rise from the tips of his toes and banish his fatigue. From Andrea that was one hell of an admission. The lady admitted very little, he'd learned.

''I'm having trouble with the idea that this guy is a mad killer,'' she said, ''because nobody has died. Anybody who's been around B-52s for a while knows how hard it is to knock one out of the sky. That charge didn't knock out anything essential to the aircraft's survival. That may have been deliberate.''

''It could also have been an accident,'' Dare pointed out.

''But don't forget last night. Setting fire to a plane on the runway was hardly designed to kill. It seems to me that it was designed to give you a hard time. Tell me you haven't had a hellish day today, with more to come.''

He smiled faintly. ''I can't. It was awful, start to finish. What about my hydraulics? For a while I believed that hadn't been intended to kill me, but I've had a lot of time to think about it since Saturday, Andrea. Nobody messes around with an aircraft's hydraulic system if he *doesn't* want to kill.''

''He could have intended for you to punch out, which any pilot in his right mind would have done, Dare. I still can't believe you didn't eject as soon as you knew you were in trouble. My God!''

''A pilot has to believe he's got no other option before he'll punch out, honey. I didn't believe it.''

For a long moment she appeared to be incapable of speech. Dare watched the way her eyes sparked with outrage and darkened with remembered fright. God, he needed to hold this woman.

''Anyhow,'' Andrea continued when she had a grip on the surge of unwelcome emotion, ''I was shot because I scared the guy. I can understand that. No, my problem is that it just doesn't fit with the rest of what's been going on. We've agreed that our man must be somebody who can get past security, who probably has a legitimate reason to be on the flight line. Halliday keeps telling me—''

''Halliday?''

"My electronic security expert. He keeps telling me the perimeter is a no-man's-land of sensors, that nobody who doesn't know the location of those sensors could get through without detection—unless the sensors are turned off. If we agree to that, and I don't see any reason why we shouldn't, then I can't understand why anyone was trying to get through the perimeter. And even if somebody could get through the perimeter, he'd have to get past all the security guards, which brings us right back to someone who has a legitimate reason to be out there—"

"And therefore has no need to cut the fence and dodge the sensors."

"Exactly."

Dare rubbed his chin and then took another swig of coffee, steeling himself for the fire when it hit his stomach. Life dealt rotten hands sometimes, and right now he was feeling that the most rotten hand was that he couldn't take Andrea home with him and fall asleep wrapped around her. Instead he forced himself to consider what she was saying.

"Maybe," he said presently, "we ought to look at it another way. Say our man has a legitimate reason to be out there, but not one legitimate enough to cover multiple visits to the flight line. Say he doesn't want anyone to know he's been there if he can avoid it, but if he gets stopped his cover story is good, just once."

"Just once?"

Dare shrugged. "Well, not enough times to explain repeated visits, but good enough that he'd be overlooked once or maybe twice."

Andrea nodded. "He still has to get past all the sensors."

"There must be people who can do that."

"Not according to Halliday. According to him, only he and his technicians know anything about the layout of the sensors. He said each of them knows part of it, and only he knows all of it."

"So maybe Halliday's wrong. Maybe he just likes to think he's the only one—"

Andrea shook her head. "I looked into it. The plans are highly classified. There's one copy in Halliday's safe and one copy with central document control. Nobody on the base has checked out the copy from document control, and none of the document custodians has enough technical background to understand the stuff, so that rules them out. That leaves only—'' Andrea's head snapped up. ''Dare!''

He leaned forward. ''What?''

''Maybe he *is* the only one.''

''Who? What? Run that by me again, Andrea.''

''Maybe Halliday *is* the only one who can get by all the sensors. And he'd have a legitimate excuse to be on the flight line, but not too often.''

''How so?''

''He could say he was checking out the security systems. My guys know who he is. They'd let him pass without a second thought. But if he was out there too often, they'd get suspicious.''

''Well, I guess he's a possibility, then, but that doesn't prove anything, Andrea.''

She sighed. ''I guess not. I can't imagine why he'd do this, anyway.''

''That's been a problem all along—no apparent motive. Look, maybe it wouldn't hurt to keep an eye on him.''

''Damn straight,'' Andrea said briskly, standing. ''I'll talk to Nickerson in the morning. Honestly, Dare, he sat right here and told me he was the only person who could bypass the electronic surveillance. I thought he was bragging, but it never occurred to me that he might be laughing at me.''

''Maybe he wasn't.'' Dare stood, too. ''Maybe we're too tired to think straight.''

''Yeah.'' She gave a short laugh and rubbed her neck again.

Dare moved around behind her and put both his hands on her shoulders, rubbing deeply but gently. Andrea released a soft groan of satisfaction.

''Feel good?'' Dare asked.

''Mmm.''

''You know what I want more than anything, Andrea?''

''Hmm?''

Bending his head, he closed his teeth gently on her earlobe. ''To take you home with me and go to sleep with your head tucked under my chin and your legs all tangled with mine.''

He heard her softly indrawn breath and waited for the anticipated refusal.

"Okay," she said.

Stunned, Dare froze, his hands locked on her shoulders, his mouth near her ear. He had to clear his throat before he could find his voice.

"What did you say?"

"I said 'okay.'" Turning, she faced him.

Dare drank in her face, noting that her eyes were incredibly weary, but also incredibly soft. This Andrea was the one who'd reached in and plucked something from his heart that he'd thought himself incapable of giving. He was fond of all the Andreas, but this one, so rarely in evidence, held a special place in his soul.

"Are you sure?" he asked, daring to touch her hair, her cheek, with the gentleness she so easily evoked in him.

"I'm sure." She met his look squarely.

"You won't regret it?"

"I'll regret even more spending tonight alone," she said steadily. So little time. So very little time. It was suddenly important not to waste even a minute of it.

"I'll get you back before the world is up."

She nodded. "I know you will, Dare." The words conveyed her trust, surprising them both, for neither of them had realized just how much she trusted him.

"Give me ten minutes to warm up the Bronco, then come out," he told her. Not for anything would he have the cops at the front desk see them depart together. It wouldn't bother him, but it would bother Andrea.

A short while later, Andrea snuggled into Dare's embrace, her head tucked under his chin, her thigh caught between his, just the way he'd wanted her so badly.

"Now," she murmured, "I don't want to sleep."

"You should. You're pooped."

"So are you. Are you sleepy?"

"Only a little."

"I needed this," she sighed. "God, how I needed this."

"You only had to tell me."

"I know. That scares me."

He slipped his fingers into her short hair and stroked her scalp gently. "Why does that scare you, Andrea?"

She was silent for so long that he began to think sleep had claimed her, but then he heard her draw a deep breath.

"I've never had anyone want to please me before," she said finally.

"But why should that scare you?"

"Because it's so different. Because it changes the rules."

"How does it change the rules?" Patiently he caressed her, waiting for her to work her own way through her feelings.

"It's a responsibility," she said. "A big responsibility."

"How so?"

"I could hurt you."

He sighed heavily and hugged her tighter. "That's not your responsibility, Andrea."

"Maybe. Maybe not. I don't think I'm explaining myself very well."

"Take your time."

"It doesn't matter."

"Yes, it does," he said. "It's as important as hell because it bothers you. Are you afraid you'll disappoint me?"

"Yes!"

The way the word burst out of her told Dare more about Andrea's real fears than any number of words could have. So she wasn't terrified of being turned into another woman like her mother; she wasn't terrified of being devoured by him. She was terrified of disappointing him the way she'd disappointed her father.

Dare had a sudden painful image of Andrea the way he'd seen her at chapel when she was all of what—thirteen? fourteen?—in that ridiculous, frilly dress. Had she been trying to please the father who could never be pleased? Had she given up finally, burying the hurt deep inside, and gone her own way, thinking she couldn't please any man, that she was a failure as a woman?

He had no difficulty imagining Andrea even younger, five or six maybe, with her freckles and pert face, being hollered at because she was dirty, or because she'd been playing with the boys. Because she wasn't Charlie Burke's notion of a female.

"Andrea," her name came out hoarsely, torn from some place deep inside him, "you won't disappoint me."

"You don't know that, Dare."

"Sure I do." He tried to keep his tone light enough that she wouldn't pull away from the depth of the feelings she'd just drawn out of him. Rolling onto his back, he pulled her with him so that she lay on top of him and hugged her so tightly she squeaked a protest. "You can make me mad," he said, "and you can make me hurt, but you can't ever disappoint me."

Andrea told herself it was because she was so tired, but tears sprang to her eyes and dropped onto Dare's chest.

"Andrea, honey, don't cry. You're worrying me."

"I'm just tired," she said, sniffling forlornly. "It's one of those stupid female things I do sometimes."

What could he say to that? Not knowing what else to do, he kissed her soundly.

"Now sleep, darlin'," he said, once again tucking her securely into the curve of his large body. "I'll wake you in time to get you back."

Andrea woke at the first sound of Dare's alarm clock in the morning. Still tucked against his shoulder and side, she waited while he cursed softly and felt around his night table. The buzzing stopped, and he relaxed back into the bed with a sigh.

"Andrea?" His voice was hushed. "Time to get you back."

"What time is it?"

"Five."

She snuggled closer. "How about a quickie, cowboy?"

"I was going to feed you breakfast."

"I'll eat at the O'-Club."

"A quickie, huh?"

"Very quick," she said, nuzzling his nipple. "I can't believe I climbed into bed with you last night and *slept.* Not when all I've been able to think about all week..."

With a growling laugh he rolled over onto her. Moments later he was sheathed in her moist warmth. "That quick enough for you?"

Andrea rolled her hips suggestively. "Not quite, cowboy. You forgot the rest of it."

"The rest of wha—" The words died in a groan as she tightened herself around him. "Now you've done it, woman," he growled. "Now I'm going to—" He whispered the rest of the words into her ear, very earthy words. Andrea might have giggled except that he was doing exactly what he'd threatened, and it felt so damned good....

"You can talk dirty to me any time you want, sir," Andrea told him breathlessly a few minutes later. "Just as long as you follow through."

Dare was still chuckling when he drove her back to the BOQ.

Nickerson knocked on her office door almost before she settled into the chair behind her desk.

"Oh hell, what now?" she asked on a sigh as she watched him close the door and come to stand in front of her.

"The fire marshal called me at three this morning, ma'am. I thought you'd want to know what he said."

Andrea was silent, thinking the only thing she really wanted to do was curl up in some cozy corner and enjoy the glow Dare had left her with. He always left her feeling good, she realized with a dawning sense of wonder. He always made her feel good about herself.

"Ma'am?"

Nickerson's voice called her back to the present with a thud.

"Sorry," she said. "I guess I'm not really awake yet." Looking up at Nick, it suddenly dawned on her that he had probably tried to raise her as soon as the fire marshal called him, but she'd left her radio on her desk because Dolan had taken the command, and she hadn't been in the BOQ to answer her phone. Her cheeks began to heat, and the oddly wooden expression on Nickerson's face didn't help.

"What did the fire marshal say?" she asked, hoping he wouldn't notice her rising color.

"The fire was definitely arson, Captain. Merle says it was started by a homemade electronic fire starter that was hidden behind the instrument panel in the cockpit. He also said that whoever built and hid the ignition device has a fairly sophisticated knowledge of electronics.''

``You could say that about half the airmen on this base, Nick. This is the high tech Air Force, remember? Anything else?''

Nick shook his head. ``That's the big development. Not real helpful.''

``I'm beginning to think this is one case where we'll have to make our own breaks.''

``Ma'am?''

Andrea waved her hand dismissingly. ``Just thinking aloud, Nick. Never mind.''

When Nick had gone, she found her thoughts straying away from business again and back to Dare and the warm glow he'd left her with. Maybe she was in love with him.

The thought trickled into her mind almost casually, forming fully before it really registered. When it did, shock caused her heart to slam. Love? Why that, of all things? In all her planning and dreaming for her future, that was one contingency she'd never considered, one possibility she'd never reckoned on. She didn't want to be in love, for crying out loud! But the more the word turned in her mind, the more realistic it sounded.

If she was in love with Dare now, then she had certainly been in love with him even before Christmas. Maybe, she thought with a reluctant smile, ever since the moment he'd come marching up to her at gunpoint the night her cops had brought him in for loitering near the weapons depot. Maybe since the moment he'd told her that he would be grateful if she wouldn't go around addressing people as ``cowboy.'' Certainly at least since he kissed her at Thanksgiving, because after that he'd begun to seriously preoccupy her thoughts.

And what difference did it make exactly when it had happened? There was a deep certainty in her that it *had,* happened and for the worst possible person at the worst possible time. Her departure for Minot had been looming unpleasantly for some time, but now it yawned before her like a step into a black pit. She didn't want to give up her career, and she wasn't certain any longer that she could give up Dare.

What now?

* * *

Dare spent the day in a considerably more optimistic frame of mind. SAC might be breathing down his neck for a resolution to the problem, OSI might be crawling into every nook and cranny on the base, but his night with Andrea had persuaded him that he was winning on that front. She had finally confided her fears to him, a sign of trust he valued fully. She'd wept in his arms, slept in his arms, and played this morning with a blossoming confidence in her womanhood. What more could he ask?

A commitment. The word nearly made him break into a cold sweat, and his confidence took a sharp dip. She'd certainly given him no indication that she no longer considered their relationship temporary. For all he knew, she was still planning to leave for Minot free as a bird and without a backward glance. How could he possibly persuade her that he was capable of giving her the freedom she needed for her career while nailing her down to permanence in a relationship?

Because he wanted that kind of permanence. All his life long he'd wanted it, except for a brief spell after his first marriage. He could have had it a half-dozen times over, too, except that he was particular about things like companionship and friendship. And love? If the day ever came when he was sitting in a rocker and leaning on a cane, he wanted to be with someone he liked, not someone he tolerated. And, by God, he *liked* Andrea. There wasn't a shadow of a doubt in his mind that she would still be zinging him when he was ninety.

It was too soon, he decided with a sigh, to press for a commitment from her. For now he'd better stick with persuading her to let him visit her out in Minot on weekends. Then, when she saw he was willing to commute any distance to be with her, maybe she would consider more. Maybe all she needed to know was that they could make it work whatever the difficulties.

With that thought, he felt a resurgence of optimism, and he was still feeling pretty good when he closed up his office and headed over to the Security Squadron. It was the weekend at last.

"Hi," Andrea said with a shy smile when Dare appeared in her doorway.

"Hi," he replied, stepping inside and closing the door. "It's

Friday.'' Why did she look so shy? he wondered. What had happened?

''So it is,'' she agreed. ''What are your plans?''

''Our plans,'' he corrected gently. ''How about options, instead? There are a number of places we can go.''

She bit her lower lip, lifting her eyes hesitantly to his. ''Would you—would you mind very much if we didn't go anywhere?''

Dare wouldn't have believed he could plunge so far so fast. ''What's wrong?'' His tone was sharper than he intended, and he regretted it instantly when he saw her head snap up and her chin thrust out.

''Nothing's wrong, sir,'' she replied coolly.

Dare started backpedaling immediately. ''I didn't mean to snap at you, Andrea. It's been a long week. Has something come up?''

Little by little her chin softened and the flare in her green eyes died. ''I just don't want to be out of touch this weekend. I need to be accessible if something happens.''

Well, he thought, here's your chance to prove you can let her career come first. It didn't thrill him. ''All right. Maybe we can squeeze in a little time together.''

Andrea gnawed her lip and darted a couple of uncertain looks at him.

''Andrea, is something wrong?''

Only that he hadn't even argued with her, she thought miserably. Her feelings were so new, so fragile and so frightening, that she needed the reassurance of knowing they were returned, at least a little.

''Actually,'' she said after a moment, then cleared her suddenly dry throat, ''actually, I thought maybe—if it wouldn't be too much trouble—that I could—that is—''

Dare couldn't stand it another minute. His hopes for the weekend were dashed, and now Andrea was acting like she was afraid of him. Damning the consequences, he rounded her desk, pulled her up from her chair, and kissed her soundly. When he lifted his head, her green eyes looked glazed.

''Spit it out, Andrea,'' he coaxed. ''If *what* isn't too much trouble?''

"Can I stay with you this weekend?" The words came out in a breathless sigh.

He couldn't help it. He kissed her again, then tucked her head against his shoulder. "You can stay with me any weekend, every weekend, and every night in between if you want, honey. You don't even have to ask. But someone might find out. I thought that bothered you."

"Nobody will know." She lifted her head and looked up at him with eyes so soft that Dare felt his heart turn into instant mush. "I just have to be reachable by radio."

"Done." He brushed a stray tendril of strawberry blond hair back from her forehead. "Do you want to come with me now?"

"I need to pack an overnight bag first. I'll walk over later."

"Andrea, sweetheart, it's twenty-three below outside."

A smile rose from her lips to touch her eyes. "That's okay. I've got the gear for it. Besides, nobody will ever recognize me all bundled up like an Eskimo."

Dare shook his head. "Uh-uh. I'll pick you up in front of the base library at seven. You're not going to walk more than half a block in this."

She tilted her head. "If you're going to come out anyway, then you might as well pick me up in front of the BOQ."

"Aren't you worried there might be gossip?"

Andrea shrugged. "Let 'em talk. I'm leaving in just over a week."

A cold fist clenched Dare's heart. She sounded so damn cool that it hurt. "Yeah," was the only reply he could manage. "Yeah."

Chapter 13

Dare's romantic streak showed that evening. While a polar air mass moved in, sending the temperature ever lower and obscuring the world with blowing snow, he and Andrea ate by candlelight in his dining el. Afterward he put a tape on the stereo, and the sadly haunting strains of "The Tennessee Waltz" filled the room.

"Dance with me, Andrea."

"I can't dance," she protested, feeling shy again.

"It doesn't matter," he coaxed, his blue eyes as warm as the candle flames. "Just lean on me."

She ought to be wearing some beautiful gauzy creation, Andrea thought, not jeans and a sweater, but it ceased to matter the instant she stepped into his arms. She felt as if she were floating, and as she relaxed it became easier to follow Dare's slow movements. Before long they were waltzing slowly around the room.

With a deep sigh, Andrea rested her head on his chest and gave herself up to all the good feelings. Through the soft wool beneath her cheek she could hear the steady beat of his heart, and she was surrounded by the soapy, musky scent that was particularly his. He felt so strong and solid against her, made her feel so secure and cherished when he held her. It was going to hurt badly when she left next week. She sighed again.

"That sounded sad." Dare's voice rumbled deep in his chest.

"I guess it was, a little."

"Anything I can do to help?"

Tell me it won't be all over in twelve days, Andrea thought. "Not really," she said.

Bending, he pressed his face to the top of her head. "Just let it all go, Andrea," he murmured. "Don't think, don't worry. Just *be.*"

It was a tempting invitation, and Andrea tilted her head back, seeking his mouth with hers. Finding it, she kissed him with every bit of longing in her heart, pressing closer to him, wrapping her arms tightly around his neck.

Dare felt her desperation and wondered at it. Her kiss, however, was evoking thunder in his blood, and he didn't feel like thinking right now. Reaching down, he cupped her delightful derriere and drew her snugly up against him. Slipping his leg between hers, he pressed against her and felt her thighs tighten around him.

Andrea leaned back a little and smiled hazily at him. "You always manage to teach me something new."

He flexed his thigh again and smiled when she drew a deep breath. "I like dancing with you, Captain."

"Is that what this is? Dancing?"

Dare tightened his grip on her, rocking her suggestively against his leg. "Maybe it's flying," he said. "It sure feels every bit as good."

Andrea buried her face against his sweater. "Maybe we should go fly in the bedroom, Colonel."

"Not yet." He drew his leg from between hers and began again to move in time to the music. "Right now, Captain, I just want to enjoy holding you and dancing with you. We've got all weekend."

"Yes, sir."

"I don't get to hold you enough, Andrea. I don't get to be with you enough."

He expected her to stiffen, to withdraw in that subtle way she had when she was uncomfortable. Instead she seemed to soften even more against him, and Dare began to really relax.

"I remember you at Mather," he told her. "I used to see you in chapel. You had a pink dress with flounces and ruffles all over it."

Andrea groaned. "I hated that dress. I hoped there wasn't a living soul who noticed me in it."

"Why'd you wear it?"

"My father made me. He told my mother to get me something feminine to wear to chapel so I wouldn't embarrass him. My mother had terrible taste."

"Maybe she just knew what your father considered feminine."

"That's entirely possible. It used to drive me crazy, the way she always buckled under and let him dictate everything."

"You're certainly not the type to let anyone do that."

She looked up at him, a teasing glint in her eye. "And here I thought I was the model of an obedient subordinate officer."

"You've never been insubordinate, Captain. You have other methods."

She dropped one of her hands from his neck and slipped it up under his sweater, finding the soft mat of hair on his chest. There was no way, she realized, that she would ever get her fill of touching him.

"Are you into my chest hair again, Captain Burke?"

"Yes, sir." She curled her fingers, giving it a playful tug. "I don't suppose I can persuade the Colonel to ditch his sweater?"

"What's wrong with my sweater?"

"It's in my way."

So he ditched it, and while he was at it, he ditched hers, as well. And he discovered that Andrea could still blush when he looked at her.

"Save the blushes for when I remove your bra, Captain."

She looked at him from beneath lowered lashes. "And when are you going to get around to that, sir?"

"Soon, Captain. Very soon."

But he continued to dance with her, holding her close and stroking her back from neck to hip. Andrea pressed her cheek to his chest and closed her eyes.

"Tell me about where you grew up," she said.

"My dad has a ranch near Kalispell, Montana. A few years back I bought some acreage farther west, closer to the mountains. When I retire, I hope I can spend more time there."

"You want to ranch?"

"No." He kissed her temple and cuddled her ever closer. "I just want to spend a little more time enjoying life. I see it more as a vacation place."

"What'll you do with the rest of your time?"

That'll depend on you, he thought. "There's always a market for retired generals," he said. "I'll see what develops."

Andrea looked up at him, the devil light in her eyes. "You're pretty sure of that promotion."

"I'm positive about it."

"Nothing like a pilot's ego, I always say. Has something to do with the 'right stuff,' I guess. Maybe it adds lift to the plane."

Chuckling, he stole a kiss. "Actually," he said, when she was suitably breathless, "I got the word this morning. I pin on my stars April first."

"Dare! That's wonderful!" Her green eyes shone as she looked up at him.

"I guess that means I'll outrank you for at least a couple more years."

But Andrea was in no mood to joke about it. Her joy for him seemed to swell until she felt she could barely contain it.

"I'm so pleased for you," she said softly.

That softness got him every time. Forgetting his determination to drag out every moment of this evening, he scooped Andrea up into his arms and carried her to his bedroom.

"Celebrate with me, Andrea," he said as he lowered her to his bed.

"I've never made love with a general before," she whispered, drawing him down with her.

"Big deal. You'd never made love with a colonel before, either."

The soft smile lingered on her lips and in her eyes as he hovered over her.

"I'd never made *love* before," she answered.

"Me either," he murmured as he released the clasp of her bra.

Before she could wonder at his meaning, he closed his lips and teeth over her swollen nipple and sent shock waves of pleasure radiating outward to join with the ache that had been building all evening.

He had one intention and one intention only: to love Andrea so well, so perfectly, that if she never again allowed him to give her anything, he would already have given her the best he had in him. In seemingly no time at all, she reached a fever pitch, but he refused to give in to her pleas and tugs. Instead he trailed his mouth in lazy, tormenting spirals lower, across the sensitive skin of her stomach. Millimeter by millimeter, he drew down the zipper of her jeans, teasing her with hesitations. And finally he sent his hand foraging where she wanted his mouth, then his mouth where she wanted him.

All he wanted, all he needed, all he sought, was her pleasure. Only when he at last could please her no other way did he join himself to her and give her the gift of his own pleasure.

Sunday afternoon came all too swiftly. Andrea sat between Dare's legs on the floor of the living room, her back resting against his chest. They'd been sitting in companionable silence for some time, and she found herself thinking how nice it was to be able to share a comfortable silence with someone else.

She also found herself thinking about the swift passage of time. She was racing against it neck-and-neck now. One more weekend. Nine more days. The more she dreaded her departure, the faster it bore down on her.

Looking back over the past two years, she had the uneasy realization that time had been racing past her all along but she had been too busy to notice it. Hadn't she promised herself when she arrived here that she would make the terrible climate tolerable by taking the time to go cross-country skiing? Not once in two years had she taken her skis out of the closet. Instead she'd put her nose to the grindstone, determined to make her squadron the best in SAC.

And what had that gotten her? A slightly bigger squadron in the same execrable climate. Two years had passed in the blink of an eye, and the next two years would probably pass even faster, and maybe she would garner a somewhat bigger command with all its attendant extra headaches. By then she would surely have made major, and she would immediately set her sights on light colonel.

Some morning, inevitably, she would wake to discover that twenty years had flown by in the blink of an eye. Would she look back at those twenty years and think that the only time she'd ever really lived was during her last few weeks here, on these too-short weekends with Dare?

As for Dare, Andrea was no fool. She knew very well that men like him didn't grow on trees. He was strong enough to be gentle and secure enough not to be threatened by her. In her experience, that was a very rare combination.

"Something wrong?" he asked when she stirred restlessly against him.

"Time," she said obscurely, but he understood.

"Little enough of it in a lifetime, let alone a week."

Slowly, she tilted her head and looked up at him, wondering not for the first time if he could read her mind. "Yes," she said on a soft sigh.

No time like the present, Dare thought, to take that forward step and see if his foot landed on solid ground. "I'll visit you on weekends, Andrea. If you want me to."

"Will you?"

Her misty green eyes held a flare of hope, and he smiled as much from relief as pleasure. "Yes."

Andrea turned over, still lying between his legs and against his chest, and kissed him. "Thank you," she said.

He wrapped his arms around her, holding her snugly. "My pleasure. You won't be that far away. I'll just avail myself of one of the prerogatives of my position and fly out there. Things can almost always be managed if you want to badly enough."

"You won't mind?" she asked him.

"Are you kidding?" Tilting her chin up a little more, he looked into her eyes. It still shocked him to realize that his calmly confident Captain Burke was truly confident only in her job and her uniform. If he'd had a magic wand, he would have used it to give her all the personal self-confidence she lacked.

But there was no magic wand, and all he could do was hope she would eventually get the message.

"Andrea, darlin'," he said gently, "the only thing I'd mind is never seeing you again."

Her eyelids fluttered closed, and he was horrified to see a silvery tear squeeze out from beneath one lid.

"Andrea? Andrea, what's wrong?"

"Nothing," she said shakily, and managed an unsteady smile. "Damn, every time I turn around, you're making me cry. I *hate* to cry."

"Then don't."

"I can't help it. You say the damnedest things sometimes. Nobody's ever said so many nice things to me."

He gave her a bruising hug. "I'm just being truthful, sweetheart." And only partially truthful, at that.

For a long time they sat like that, her head on his shoulder, arms wrapped around one another, but finally Dare's stomach started rumbling. Reluctant as he was to disturb the cocoon of closeness they shared, he was going to have to do something about dinner.

"Give me a few minutes to get dinner started, Andrea."

"Can I help?"

"Nope." He kissed the tip of her nose. "When I come to visit you, you can do the honors."

"Every time?"

He caught the wicked sparkle in her eye. "Well, maybe just sometimes."

She let him go reluctantly and stretched out on the floor, unwilling to disturb the warm glow she was feeling. He was going to fly out to see her. She hugged the thought to her, more relieved than she could say. Even though he wanted nothing but an affair, at least he wasn't casual in his feelings about her. He cared, or he certainly wouldn't be willing to visit her in Minot.

Now, if she could just catch their homegrown saboteur. Why couldn't there be some way to smoke him out, right into a trap?

Toying with the idea, she wandered out to the kitchen and helped herself to one of the carrot sticks Dare had set out on the counter.

"I can almost smell smoke," Dare remarked as he lifted a

steak off the electric grill. ‘‘What’s got your brain on overdrive?’’

Andrea shrugged. ‘‘Just wondering if there isn’t some way to lay a trap for our saboteur.’’

‘‘To lay a trap you need some kind of enticement to draw your quarry out. We don’t know enough about him to come up with the right bait.’’

‘‘That’s what has me stymied. But maybe we *do* know enough and just can’t see it.’’

‘‘You keep saying that. Pull the milk out of the fridge, will you?’’

Andrea complied. ‘‘I keep saying that because I can’t shake the feeling that the answer’s staring me in the face. It just keeps nagging at me.’’

‘‘Maybe you ought to let it rest awhile.’’

‘‘I’ve let it rest all weekend.’’ Walking up behind him, she wrapped her arms around his waist from behind and leaned against him. ‘‘You smell so good.’’

‘‘Better than steak?’’

‘‘Always.’’ Sighing, she nuzzled his spine. ‘‘I keep wondering, if the culprit really is Halliday, why he’d be doing this. I always thought he seemed pretty happy with his niche. You haven’t served with him before, have you?’’

‘‘Not to my knowledge. We might have been posted to the same base at some time or another, but we’ve never been in the same unit.’’ He flipped the second steak off the grill. ‘‘Come on, let’s eat. You still think I’m the target?’’

‘‘Well, you’re the only person being consistently harmed by all this. It makes more sense than the entire Bomb Wing being the target, or SAC.’’

‘‘I guess.’’ Dare held out her chair for her and snagged a quick kiss as she sat. He rounded the table and took his own seat, then unfolded his napkin. After a moment he shook his head.

‘‘Nope, I can’t remember ever knowing a Halliday. Now back in Nam there was this kid named Holi—’’ He broke off abruptly, his eyes growing distant with recollection.

‘‘What is it, Dare?’’ Andrea asked impatiently. ‘‘What kid?’’

"Holiday. I thought his name was Holiday, but maybe it wasn't."

"What kid?" Andrea demanded.

For a long moment he didn't answer. "Just a kid, an airman. He was in my ground crew. He got hit in a firefight one night at Tan Son Nhut, and I tried to get to him, but I couldn't. I wrote to his family afterward, but there wasn't much to say. He'd been out there exactly one week, he was eighteen years old, and he was dead because he was on mission for me when the firefight broke out."

Andrea set her fork down, aching for him, for the shadow of old sorrow she read on his face. "It was war, Dare," she said after a moment. "You can't hold yourself responsible."

His blue eyes focused on her. "I don't. Oh, maybe that was my first reaction when it happened. You're bound to think *if only* when something like that happens, but nobody is responsible for the accidents of war. No, I was just wondering if his name was Halliday, not Holiday. It's possible, I guess. It's been a long time. My memory could be playing tricks." He shrugged. "And where does it get us if his name *was* Halliday?"

Andrea pushed a piece of steak round and round on her plate. "Well," she said presently, "maybe a younger brother grew up thinking you were responsible for his older brother's death because you sent him on an errand."

"That's sick."

"So's poking holes in your hydraulic lines and blowing a hole in the nose of a flying B-52. We're clearly not dealing with a normal mind here. And it would fit with this feeling I can't shake that you're the real target."

"Then why didn't he kill me?"

"Damn it, Dare, he almost did! If you weren't as physically strong as you are, you would probably never have come out of that nosedive. I know you don't want to believe it. I sure as hell don't want to believe that somebody is trying to kill you. But I think we're both going to have to accept it. This creep wanted to kill you, and he wanted to be sure you were aware every agonizing moment of your approaching death."

Dare shoved his plate to one side. "I just lost my appetite. Andrea, we're really reaching with this."

"You mean *I* am." She'd lost her appetite, too. And then slowly she raised her head, looking at him. "I've got it."

"Got what?"

"An idea for a trap." Suddenly she was excited. "Say this guy wants to ruin you."

"I thought he wanted to kill me?"

"Say he does, but say he wants to get you into hot water before he does you in. Look, he put a hole in one bomber cockpit and set fire to another. Neither one of those incidents was physically dangerous to you, but both of them have made your life miserable."

Dare sighed and looked truly dubious. "All right, I'll agree with that for the sake of argument." He pulled out his cigarettes and lit one.

"Well, if he wants to ruin you, I bet he couldn't resist a chance to do it spectacularly."

Dare exhaled smoke. "How spectacularly? Why do I get the feeling I'm not going to like this?"

"You'll like it. Listen, let's use the grapevine. I swear it works better than the base paper. Schedule a generation for Wednesday or Thursday."

"I can't do that. We're grounded until—"

"You can always cancel it right beforehand," Andrea interrupted. "Say you schedule a generation, and then we put it on the grapevine that some important congressman or other is going to be on base—unofficially, of course—and that the generation's being held for his benefit. We can even increase security under the guise of protecting this congressmen."

"And then?"

"And then we put somebody on each and every one of the bombers from now until then. If our man can't resist the opportunity to give you a black eye in front of the world, he won't be able to resist this. And we'll catch him."

"We haven't caught him so far," Dare pointed out. "Despite stepped-up security."

"Dogs," Andrea said. "Let's use the K-9's. Put one on every plane with a handler."

Dare gave a grudging nod. "I can almost believe dogs might work. But Halliday, if it is Halliday, is bound to hear about it."

Andrea shook her head. ''Nick can handle it. He can order the dogs out on some kind of maneuver, keep the entire unit out of contact with the rest of the squadron. Once it's dark they can move around the airstrip without anybody being the wiser. There's not even a moon this week.''

''Somebody will hear about it.''

''So I'll slap a classification on the whole damn thing. Nick can pick guards who he trusts to keep their mouths shut. The group of people who'll know what's really going on will be small enough that they'll know I can court-martial every one of them if word gets out.''

Rubbing his chin, Dare thought about it. The plan was a rough sketch, of course, and a lot of details needed to be worked out, but it was a hell of a lot better than no plan at all.

''Okay,'' he said. ''First thing tomorrow, I'll schedule a generation for Wednesday.''

Andrea grinned. ''Thanks.''

''Thank me when it works.'' And it just might. At least they would be *doing* something, which agreed with him a hell of a lot more than sitting on his hands waiting for events to unfold. In fact, it gave him back his appetite.

''Eat up,'' he said after a moment. ''And tell me how you're going to manage the security on this trap.''

Dare ate and listened, thinking that Andrea had a tactician's mind. Steadily, piece by piece, she outlined a covert operation in which handpicked troops would move in and occupy all the bombers without tipping off the other guards. She'd learned well at the Academy, he thought, and displayed a natural talent for applying the things she'd learned. If she were a man…

The thought brought Dare up short. *If she were a man.* How many times must Andrea have thought the same thing and been forced to face the fact that she had to work harder and perform better and yet would never have the same opportunities? If she were a man, she wouldn't have set her sights on making colonel. No, she would be aiming for brigadier, at the very least, and he would have put his money on her to make it.

It was no wonder she was so fiercely independent, so determined to let nothing affect her career, so reluctant to let her femininity come forward. She worked under a major disadvantage and had to struggle continuously to overcome it.

He hadn't really thought about it like that before, but then, he'd never really been burdened by notions of what women should and shouldn't do. If an officer was capable, Dare didn't particularly care if the officer was male, female, black, or white or green with purple polka dots. Finding women in positions of command responsibility was a relatively new experience, a facet of the changing Air Force, and one that still caught him unawares at times, but he never held gender to be a mark against someone. Unfortunately he doubted that all his fellow officers felt the same.

When all was said and done, he decided, it was pretty remarkable that Andrea had let go as much as she had with him. And the fact that she *had* must mean that she felt something for him, something strong, because Andrea obviously wasn't the type to be led astray by mere hormones, not levelheaded, sensible, virgin Andrea Burke.

When Andrea at last fell silent, it was nearly nine. Dare was already thinking of taking her to bed for some long, lazy lovemaking that would still leave time for a good night's sleep before he took her back to the BOQ. She, however, was clearly revved up, thinking over her plans for the trap. He watched her for a while, but his patience began to wear thin as the minutes ticked by.

"Captain Burke."

She looked up from the pad she was making notes on. "Sir?"

"It's getting late. Are you planning to make notes all night?"

Andrea blinked, obviously coming out of her preoccupation with difficulty, but then a smile appeared, warming her hazy green eyes. "Do you have a better idea of what I should be making tonight, sir?"

"A much better idea. Can I interest you?"

Andrea crossed the living room and slid onto his lap. With a smile, she wrapped her arms around his neck. "I might have a few ideas of my own."

The ache that never entirely left him when he was within sight of her began to deepen. "Have I told you just how special you are?" he asked, capturing her face so she couldn't look away.

A faint blush stole into her cheeks, and her eyelids fluttered. "I'm not special," she protested in a smothered voice.

"Oh, yes, you are," he said gently, never taking his eyes from hers.

Unable to bear the intensity of emotion she was feeling, Andrea ducked her head, wiggling until she was able to tuck it into his shoulder. "No more, please," she begged in a small voice.

"All right, darlin'. No more. Just know that I think you're pretty damn special."

He felt her arms tighten convulsively around his neck, and he smiled against her ear. She was so small, so soft, so sweet, his lovely Captain Burke. And she would probably kill him for even thinking such a thing.

"Let's go to bed, sweetheart," he said. "I need to get as close to you as I can."

Much, much later Andrea said, "You never told me about your childhood."

They lay snuggled together under a down comforter, basking in the afterglow while the wind keened noisily around the corner of the house and rattled the windowpanes.

"There's not much to tell. I grew up with three brothers, working hard and playing harder. It was a good life for a kid. Plenty of fresh air and open space, horses to ride and a creek to fish in. My brothers are still on the ranch, and their kids are playing in the creek now."

"How come you didn't stay on the ranch?"

"I just always wanted to fly. To hear my father tell it, I was plane crazy from the age of two. I can't remember ever wanting to do anything else."

"Did it ever wear off?"

"A lot of things wore off, especially in Nam, but I still love being all alone at forty thousand feet in a clear sky." Turning onto his side, he wrapped his other arm around her.

"What about you, Andrea? When did you make up your mind to go to the Academy?"

"As soon as they announced they were going to take women as cadets. Before that I'd planned to go ROTC in college."

"But why?"

"Oh, I don't know. Maybe I wanted my father to have to salute me."

There was a laugh in her voice, and Dare smiled. "But you could have done so many things. Why this?"

"I just never seriously thought about doing anything else. I don't know why. Maybe it was because I grew up with the Air Force. I just wanted to do it, and do it well."

"You certainly do it well. Why didn't you want me to notify your family when you were shot?" As he spoke, he stroked the puckered scar on her shoulder with a gentle finger.

Andrea sighed. "Because my dad would have gotten on my case again about resigning, settling down and having a family. Because he would have said I wouldn't have been shot if I'd been doing my job right."

"You don't believe that, do you?"

"No. I know better. That's just my father."

Dare kissed her. "Do you want a family someday?" He nearly held his breath.

"I never thought about it."

"Never?"

"Never. Why? Do you?"

"I think about it." Though she didn't move a muscle, Dare could feel her withdrawal. "You *could* have a family, you know," he said quickly. "Lots of career Air Force women do these days."

"Child care would be a pain," Andrea said distantly. "Base day-care isn't open in the middle of the night."

"Are you planning to do this without a husband?"

"I'm not planning anything at all!"

She was rigid in his arms now, and he could tell she felt cornered, but he couldn't understand why.

"Easy, honey. This is just a theoretical discussion." With one hand he kneaded her shoulders, willing her to relax.

"It may be theoretical," she said stiffly, "but I'm a realist. You can't expect me to believe any man would tolerate being a baby-sitter while his wife went running out in the middle of the night."

Dare held his peace, stroking her soothingly.

"Well," she said after a moment, "it doesn't matter. It's all academic."

He wanted to shake her then, shake her until her teeth rattled. *It doesn't matter? It's all academic?* Never had mere words cut him so deeply or hit him so hard. Take it easy, MacLendon, he warned himself. Take it easy or you'll drive her away.

Andrea bit her lip, sensing that she'd angered him, stunned to realize that she wanted him to argue with her, to tell her it wasn't academic. To say he wanted her to have his children.

But he hadn't said it. He'd been the one to say the discussion was theoretical, and he hadn't argued with her. All of a sudden she was terrified in a way she'd never been terrified before. Everything was out of whack, as if she'd become a person she hardly recognized. All those things she'd never thought she would want had suddenly become paramount. She wanted to talk about them, argue about them, hammer them out until she'd built a modified version of her future that included Alisdair MacLendon.

"You're mad at me, Dare."

"No, I'm not mad." Just frustrated all to hell. He forced himself to relax and resume caressing her back.

Presently he remarked casually, "You know, I learned a long time ago that if a person feels they're sacrificing too much they become bitter. I had a bitter wife."

"That wasn't your fault."

"I could have given up the Air Force. I didn't. I wouldn't. And I wouldn't ask anybody else to do what I won't do."

"But some compromises have to be made."

"Sure, but the compromises can't be all on one side."

Unsettled, Andrea moved even closer, seeking comfort. Dare turned a little to accommodate her. What compromises would she be prepared to make, she wondered, if she could have Dare? Could she set her sights a little lower and not work quite so hard? Well, of course, if she had a home to come back to each night she might be a little more eager to knock off at the end of the day. And a little less eager to go to work on weekends. But that couldn't possibly be enough, could it?

"Take it easy, Andrea," Dare said. "I was just talking generally, not trying to upset you."

"Weren't you?" The challenge was out before she could stop it, and they both froze. Dare spoke first, his tone dangerously silky.

"Do you want a confrontation, Captain?"

Andrea pulled out of his arms and sat up. "Yes!" And then, swiftly, before he could respond, "No! No, I don't."

Dare sat up, facing her, and saw the minute quiver to her lips and chin. God, she *was* upset! He really hadn't meant to upset her. "Andrea—"

"I'm sorry," she said unsteadily. "I don't know what's wrong with me."

Her distress tugged at his heart, creating an ache deeper than any he'd ever felt before. Reaching out, he lifted her onto his lap and cradled her close.

"Don't worry about anything, Andrea," he said gently. "Just let me love you. Everything will be all right."

Before she could register his words, he bent his head and captured her mouth in a deep, soul-searing kiss. His tongue teased hers, incited hers, until hers followed his blindly into the consuming, hungry warmth of his mouth. She became his willing prisoner, surrounded by arms that were powerful yet gentle, held by hands that were strong yet caring. When he lifted her so that he could capture her breast with his lips and teeth, she groaned and threw her head back in utter surrender.

"Dare," she begged. "Dare…"

Carefully he lowered her to the bed, his every muscle trembling with the strain of his restraint. Her hand blindly sought and found the rigid proof of his hunger for her. He groaned, nearly losing his grip on his massive self-control.

"Not yet, honey," he whispered hoarsely, and gently removed her stroking hand. "Not yet."

Surprising her, he captured her small feet in his large hands and kissed each of them gently on the arch and instep. Then his mouth found her delicate ankles, his tongue her shapely calves.

"I'm going to kiss you from head to foot," he said in a passion-rough voice. Turning her, he found the backs of her knees and the sensitive undersides of her thighs.

"You're beautiful, woman," he said roughly. "God, you're beautiful!"

She writhed and whimpered, everything forgotten in the tidal waves of yearning his caresses caused in her. Her hands gripped wildly at the bedsheets, at the headboard, and finally at him. When at last Dare covered her, she was so open, so receptive, so defenseless, that it was as if there was no skin to separate them. His pleasure was hers, and hers was his. They sighed as one, and cried as one, and found completion as one.

Chapter 14

Dare's parting kiss was still warm on Andrea's lips when she settled behind her desk on Monday morning of her last week. *Her last week.* Those simple words held all the threat of a death sentence. She didn't know how she would bear the separation, let alone the inevitable end of the relationship. For it would end. How long would he continue to fly out to Minot to visit her when, right here, there were any number of warm and willing women? Women who were more feminine, who could provide all the things that men seemed to want from women.

Andrea couldn't begin to imagine what it was that had drawn Dare to her in the first place, and being unable to imagine that, she couldn't imagine that he wouldn't swiftly tire of her. She must simply be a novelty to him, she thought. He was caring and kind, but that was because he was a decent human being. He treated her with the same consideration he would show anyone. Their relationship wasn't casual, because he wasn't a casual person, but that didn't mean he cared about her the way she cared about him.

And so she would leave, and time and distance would slowly sunder them. How was she ever going to bear it? Yet how could she not? She couldn't sacrifice everything she'd worked for, everything she believed about herself, every need of her own.

"Morning, skipper," Nickerson greeted her as he entered her office. "We had a surprisingly quiet weekend, all things considered." He set his list on the desk in front of her and poured coffee.

"Nick, skip the weekend incident report. I want to discuss something with you."

Last night, Andrea thought, it had all been so clear and certain. Now she was uneasily aware that she might be making a gigantic mistake, one that could conceivably stain her career. Her conviction that Halliday was involved in these incidents was a guess supported only by the slenderest thread of evidence. The entire premise behind her idea of setting a trap was equally shaky. There was certainly no sort of discernible logic behind the sequence of events.

For a long moment she hesitated, uncertain whether to go ahead with this. She would be leaving in a week, after all. No one would condemn her for letting events unfold in their normal course. No one would condemn her for failing to risk everything on a last-ditch attempt to solve the mystery before she departed.

But she would condemn herself, Andrea realized. Looking at Nickerson, she plunged ahead.

"Nick, we're going to set a trap for the saboteur."

Nickerson nodded approvingly. "Who's in on it?"

"You, me and MacLendon. I don't want anybody else to know what's really going on. We're going to use the dogs, because it's a hell of a lot harder to slip past a dog than a tired human. And I'm going to need you to handpick me a group of the most trustworthy cops in the squadron."

Nickerson chuckled unexpectedly. "Now ain't that ironic, skipper?"

Andrea looked blankly at him. "What's ironic?"

"Oh, it's just that Halliday and his crew have really ticked off the dog handlers a few times. Halliday's always insisting that the dogs are a waste of government money, that his electronic gizmos can do the job a hundred times better. I finally shut him up by asking if he had a gizmo that could sniff drugs or explosives half as good as a dog."

"So why is that ironic?" Andrea asked, wondering if Nick also suspected Halliday.

"Because," Nick said, "when push finally came to shove around here, his electronic gizmos failed and we're turning to the dogs. He's not gonna like it."

"He damn well better not know about it," Andrea said sharply.

Nickerson lifted a brow. "No, ma'am. Not until it's over. You made that clear."

Asking for input, Andrea laid out her plan to Nick: the dogs on each plane to prevent any more sabotage to them; the phony news of a congressman's impending visit; the staged generation. Nick was concerned that the magnitude of the security preparations alone would tip the perpetrator to the trap. Andrea had already considered that.

"He's got to pick up on something or this whole thing will fall through. Look, Nick, if a congressman were really coming on Wednesday and a generation were planned, we'd be up to our eyeballs in security preparations after what's happened around here. I suggest you just start arranging additional security and fit the real briefing to the dog handlers somewhere in the middle so it doesn't stick out. Once our man thinks he knows what's going on, he'll buy whatever cover story you give our operatives."

Nick nodded. "I figure I'll order the dogs out on night patrol in the family housing area. Then, during shift change tonight, we can move 'em onto the planes. It'll sound okay that we're putting the dogs in the housing area, because we'll be calling in every available man for added security."

"What about patrols in the housing area? We can't leave every family on this base without police protection. I realize almost nothing ever happens out there, but if we leave them unprotected, you can bet your boots something will happen."

"I thought of that. I plan to peel off a couple of regular patrols to replace them. The problem is explaining why we're mobilizing all the dogs, and a patrol in family housing is the best I can come up with that doesn't sound suspicious."

"Okay. You get started on preparations, Nick. I have to go to staff conference."

The weather, which had turned thoroughly inhospitable on Friday night, remained so. Dry crystals of snow blew in a hazy, hissing cloud that resembled a light fog. The drift at the end of the building had reached ten feet in height, but the walk in front of the building was dry, with the snow snaking across it in undulating lines. Andrea unplugged her truck's engine block heater from the pole in front of her parking slot and ran the engine until the cab was warm enough that she could pull off her snorkel hood. While she waited, her breath formed a mist of ice on the driver-side window, and she had to scrape it off.

Boy, did Florida sound good right now, Andrea thought as she wheeled out of the parking lot. Instead she got Minot.

Twenty minutes later, Dare dropped his bomb at the staff conference.

"Well, people, on Wednesday we're receiving an unofficial visit from Bill Thomas. In case some of you don't know, he's the senior member of the House Armed Services Committee. He'll be on base for approximately two hours, and for his benefit I'm scheduling a generation."

The reactions were immediate and negative, but Dare waved them aside.

"Look, folks, this one's on my head. SAC left it to my discretion, but I think you realize the higher-ups aren't going to be very happy if Thomas discovered that an entire bomb wing is out of operation thanks to what seems to be a solo saboteur."

"The rock and the hard place," remarked his deputy commander. "Damned if you do and damned if you don't."

"Essentially," Dare agreed. "Anyhow, this visit is not to be officially announced. The fewer people who know, the better. Maybe we can keep our troublemaker from finding out. Burke?"

"Sir?"

"I expect you to step up security accordingly. Even if we can't catch this guy, I want things tight enough that we'll get wind of anything unusual. If there's a whisper of anything out of line, I'll cancel the generation."

"Yes, sir."

"Maybe we'll luck out and have a blizzard," Captain Bradley remarked.

Dare snorted. "That would be lucky only if it kept Thomas from getting here. Those planes are supposed to be able to take off under all conditions, Bradley." He looked down at the pad on the table before him. "I think that covers everything I've got. Anything else, people?"

No one had anything else to bring up.

"Dismissed, then," Dare said. "Burke, I want you in my office to discuss security."

"Yes, sir."

Dare's office was larger and more impressive than Andrea's, complete with wood paneling, and his desk dwarfed hers. Perks of rank, she thought as she closed the door behind them.

As soon as the latch clicked, Dare turned and tugged her into his embrace.

"God, woman," he said gruffly, "it drives me crazy to be in the same room with you and have to stay cool."

Resting her hands on his upper arms, she smiled up at him. "Me, too." It did indeed, and it thrilled her to know he felt the same.

"I want like hell to kiss you, but I can't have you walking out of here looking thoroughly kissed."

"Just a little one, then," Andrea said, rising on tiptoe to brush her lips lightly against his. She felt the tension in him, the control, and everything inside her clenched with the pleasure of knowing she was desired.

Dare sighed and released her. "Okay, back to business." He rounded his desk and took his chair, then motioned her to do the same. "I've cleared this little operation of yours with SAC HQ. We've got the go-ahead for just about anything short of actually launching a generation."

"Good." Andrea nodded her pleasure, but suddenly had one of those schizophrenic moments when she saw everything from a different perspective. She was busting her behind to try to reach Dare's position, yet he was sitting here and telling her that he'd had to clear everything with *his* superiors. She'd cleared it with him, he'd cleared it with them, and maybe they'd cleared it with somebody even higher. In other words, no matter how high you got, there was always somebody higher to appease. Was it worth the effort? Unsettled, she shook herself.

"Are you with me, Andrea?"

Blinking, she looked at him. "Yes, sir."

"This is the part you'll like. SAC HQ notified OSI that this is your baby. They can cooperate at your request, but they're not to interfere in any way."

Andrea *did* like that. She grinned. "Yes, sir." Dare must have had a great deal to do with this, she realized. After all, what would SAC HQ know about her except what Dare told them? Her heart swelled.

"Andrea, you do realize that your neck is on the block now?" His expression was disturbed. "I made it clear that there are no guarantees this operation will work, but you know how that goes. They want a resolution, and if they don't get it, they'll be looking to lay the blame somewhere. When I called OSI in, I took you off the firing line, but now you're right back in the way of all the flack that'll fly if this falls through."

Andrea's stomach did an unpleasant little flip, but she nodded serenely. "It goes with the territory."

"Yes, it does. We can still call it off."

She shook her head. "No, sir. This is how I earn my keep. Risks go with the job."

Damn, but he admired this woman! "I wish all my officers were like you, Andrea," he said gruffly. "I'm speaking as your commanding officer when I say that."

Rising, he came around the desk and bent over her. "Speaking as a man, I want another quick kiss before you go. But just a quick one, or I'll forget you can't walk out of here with swollen lips, mussed hair, and a rumpled uniform."

But oh, how she wished she could, she thought as his lips nestled against hers, caressing gently.

"I guess you'll be too busy to stay with me until this is over," he murmured regretfully. "Thursday night?"

Andrea nodded. "Thursday night."

He smiled and straightened. "Go get him, Captain."

Andrea had a few doubts before the day was over, the worst of them having to do with the number of assumptions they'd been making. She was flying on instinct, and she knew it. Assuming Halliday was the culprit was the least problematic of all her assumptions, because they could just as easily catch someone else with this trap as Halliday. A shakier assumption was the notion that their man would move at night, based solely on the fact that she'd been shot at night. What if the incidents were unrelated? What if the guy wasn't interested in ruining anyone at all? What if he was just a crazy who was striking out in random, pointless ways? What if this bait didn't tempt him? What if it scared him off?

Doubts notwithstanding, she sat on the edge of the flight line in her truck at eleven that night while Nickerson positioned the dogs and their handlers. Shivering as much from tension as cold, she waited impatiently and tried not to envision the dozens of things that could go wrong. She had to try equally hard not to think of how she could be lying in Dare's arms right now if only she weren't so pigheadedly determined to catch this guy before she left. There just wasn't enough time!

At twenty minutes after eleven the passenger door opened, and Nickerson climbed into the cab of the truck with her.

"Done," he said, pulling back his hood and blowing a cloud of frozen breath. "You know what really bugs me?"

"Tell me." Leaning forward, Andrea turned over the ignition.

"I just moved fifteen men and dogs past supposedly tight security, and not one damn sentry challenged us."

"Well, they can't sit under the planes, Nick. It's too cold. You had the advantage of knowing when the patrols would be passing."

"True, but it still bugs me. You still planning to come back later tonight?"

"About 4:00 a.m.," Andrea confirmed. "Just when everybody's at their lowest ebb."

"Might be the time our guy pulls his pranks. If I was doing something like that, that's the time I'd pick for it. Do you want me to come get you at MacLendon's?"

Andrea paused in the process of shifting into reverse and looked at Nick. How had he known? It was a question she didn't dare ask. His half smile was evident even in the dim glow of the dash lights.

"Go for it, skipper," he said.

Ten minutes later she stood in front of Dare's house, watching

Nick drive off down the street. The sound of the truck's engine faded, leaving only the hiss of the blowing snow, loud on the dark, deserted street. Drawing a deep breath of frigid air, Andrea looked up at the starless sky and then turned to face the house.

Her stomach fluttered nervously as she took in the dark windows and drew another deep breath. What if he was annoyed at her for waking him up? Well, she'd burned her bridge behind her when she sent Nickerson on his way. It was either ring Dare's bell or take a long, cold walk to the BOQ. Gulping yet another breath, she squared her shoulders and marched up the sidewalk to the front door. Her hand trembled only a little bit when she punched the doorbell.

Two minutes later Dare, wrapped in his terry robe, opened his front door and peered through the storm door at a not-very-large figure in anonymous survival garb. Andrea? he wondered.

"Andrea!" Flinging open the storm door, he grabbed her unceremoniously by the arm and tugged her inside as he swiftly closed both doors behind her. "What's wrong?"

Pulling back her hood, she smiled uncertainly up at him. "I got lonely," she admitted in a small voice.

God, he looked good, she thought. Had it only been twelve hours since she'd left him in his office? His short dark hair was tousled, and there was a crease in his stubbled cheek from his pillow. His eyes were wide awake and alert, however, those wonderful blue eyes that seemed to see right into her heart.

"I was too lonely to sleep," he told her, a smile deepening the creases at the corners of his eyes. Reaching out, he began to unfasten her parka, buttons first and then the zipper. "That damn bed feels so big and empty without you. I keep wanting to roll over and put my arms around you. Are you here for the night?"

"Nick's coming back for me at a quarter to four." She pulled off her mittens so he could tug the parka down her arms.

Dare hung her parka carefully on the coat tree, but then he turned and gathered her into his arms, lifting her from her feet and burying his face in the curve of her neck.

"My boots," Andrea protested weakly as he carried her down the hall to his bedroom.

"I'll get to them," he laughed, raising his head and looking down into her eyes. "I intend to get to every damn thing you're wearing, one piece at a time."

"You don't mind that I just dropped in like this?"

"Mind? How can you even think that?" Still smiling, he lowered her to the bed, leaving her feet dangling over the edge. He paused to drop a kiss on her lips before turning his attention to the laces of her boots. "Come and go as you like, sweetheart." He pulled her boots off and dropped them beside the bed. Next he went to work on her snow pants.

Andrea's response was little more than a whisper. "I don't want to go."

Slowly his eyes rose to meet hers.

"I've never felt like this before, all confused about what I want to do and where I'm going. Everything seems all mixed up."

"Maybe you're just making things too complicated." Grabbing the cuffs of the snow pants, he pulled them off and then sat beside her, reaching for the button of her slacks. "It's really not all that complicated, Andrea, unless you get bogged down in the details. You just have to look at the big picture."

"What's the big picture for you?"

He paused in the act of removing her slacks. "Enjoying what we have together whenever we're able to be together."

"You make it sound so simple." *And so terminal,* she thought miserably. Whatever they had for however long they had it. Until next week was all they had.

"That's because it is, when you get down to what really matters." He stripped away her slacks and reached for the fastenings on her blouse. "Like this. Once you get past all the games, all the worries and doubts, all the false starts and hesitations, it's really quite simple—two people wanting and needing each other. Me needing to feel your arms around me, your skin against mine. Me needing to hear your sighs and needing to please you as much as you please me. What could be simpler, Andrea? Yet how much did you agonize over this?"

A whole lot, she thought as he cast aside his robe and stretched out beside her, gathering her into his warmth.

"Make love to me, Dare," she begged. "Just make love to me, please."

So he did just that, loving her with his lips, his hands and finally his whole body. Andrea felt the silken threads of his caring tighten about her, but that was all right, for now. His caring made her feel safe, and then it drove all the worries from her mind until the only reality was the gentle one he created for her.

"Reveille, Andrea," said a deep, husky voice in her ear. "It's 0300. The coffee's brewing, and the eggs'll be ready by the time you dress."

Andrea was lying facedown. With a groan, she rolled over onto her side and pried one eye open. As many times as she'd been rousted out of bed in the middle of the night, she'd never gotten used to it. Invariably her stomach and eyes burned, and there was a sense of unreality to everything.

"Did you say coffee?" she mumbled.

"Hot and black."

"Nobody ever woke me up with coffee before." She yawned and pushed herself up onto one elbow. "God, I hate getting up in the middle of the night."

"We all do. Are you really awake?"

"I won't go back to sleep, if that's what you mean." She shoved herself up into a sitting position and rubbed her eyes, unleashing another groan.

Dare thought she made a fetching sight as she sat there, blinking herself awake, completely unaware that the sheet had fallen to her waist, exposing the tempting white globes of her breasts. He damned Halliday for making it impossible for him to succumb to the temptation. No way would he ever get enough of this woman.

"I'll go start the eggs," he said, wrenching his eyes from her and standing up. "Ten minutes, Captain."

Stifling another yawn, Andrea looked over at him as he walked out of the bedroom and realized he was wearing battle dress. "How come you're dressed?"

"I'm going with you," he said over his shoulder.

"Oh." It was nice, she thought as she tossed back the blankets and climbed out of bed, to wake up in the middle of the night to find breakfast and coffee waiting. He had the damnedest way of making her feel cherished.

He was going with her?

"You're not going with me," she said ten minutes later, facing Dare over a generous breakfast. She refused to touch it until this was settled, but her stomach gave a betraying growl.

Dare grinned. "Eat up, Andrea. I know your appetite."

"I said you're not going."

"I heard you."

She regarded him suspiciously. "And?"

"And I'm still going."

"You'll get in the way."

"No, I won't." He spread marmalade on a piece of toast. "Save your breath, kiddo. My mind is made up."

"Nickerson and I know what to do," Andrea argued. "We'll split up and check things out. You'll just make it more likely that somebody will spot us."

"Did I ever tell you about the time I evaded the Vietcong for six weeks?"

Andrea ground her teeth. "There isn't a jungle out there to provide cover."

"The same principles still apply. Eat, Andrea. I promise I won't mess anything up."

"But—"

He looked at her, and all the gentleness was gone from his face. There was a steely, implacable look to him now, a glimpse of the man who'd made general. "Don't make me pull rank, Andrea," he said quietly.

"But *why?*" She had to know that, at least.

Dare shoved his plate aside and lit a cigarette. "The last time you went after this guy you got shot. He was armed, and he used that weapon on you rather than be caught. He tried to kill me. In the expert opinion of some people who examined my hydraulic system after it was tampered with, the holes were a very cunning way of leaving no trace, because if I'd augered in from forty thousand feet, it would have been impossible to tell what caused them."

"When did you hear that?"

"The report came in this afternoon. The investigators concluded that it *was* an attempt to kill me and I was damn lucky to have survived it. He's no sick little mind trying to ruin my career, Andrea. This guy *means* to kill, and he's not particular about who. You get in his way, you get killed. You accused me of not being able to accept the fact that somebody wants to kill me, but you've been treating this the same way, babe. You haven't really believed it, either. Not really."

Sickened, shaken, Andrea looked down at her untouched plate. Here he'd gone to all the trouble to make sure she had breakfast and she wasn't even eating it. "If he's trying to kill you, you should stay away as far as possible."

"Absolutely not. I'm not letting you go out there alone to face a killer."

"If you weren't involved with me—"

"Damn it all to hell, woman. That makes absolutely no difference in what I'm doing! Do you think I'd let *anyone* go out to face a bullet that's meant for me?"

Looking into the icy blue chips his eyes had become, Andrea knew she'd said exactly the wrong thing, made exactly the wrong assumption. As well as she felt she knew him, she knew him not at all. She kept making assumptions about him and what he was doing based on something that wasn't Alisdair MacLendon at all. The realization shook her.

"We need to clear the air on something, Andrea," he said sternly. "I may care about you, but that has absolutely no bearing on my judgment. I didn't clear this operation of yours with the brass hats because I'm fond of you. I did it because, in my judgment, it's a good plan and stands as much chance of success as we could hope for. I would have done the same if you were Captain Joe Blow. I'm going out with you tonight because, whether you like it or not, I'm your CO and I've got oversight on this operation, and because I never send anybody else where I won't go. This is my usual mode of operation, and I'm not changing it for you or anyone else."

"I'm sorry," Andrea said. "I didn't mean to insult you."

He puffed on his cigarette, still frowning. "You're too damn defensive. You've got to stop filtering everything I do through your idea of how men treat women. I trust you to do your job right. Give me the same respect. Trust me to do mine."

He stubbed out his cigarette. "Now eat, damn it. It's cold out there, and you need the energy."

Instead she reached across the table and covered his larger hand with hers. "I'm a pain in the neck."

A faint smile banished his frown. "Sometimes, but that was one of the first things I liked about you." Turning his hand over, he squeezed her fingers briefly and then released them. "Now are you going to eat, or do I get to be a pain in your neck?"

Nickerson arrived promptly at three forty-five, and Andrea sandwiched herself between the two men in the cab of the truck. If Nick was surprised to see Dare, he betrayed no sign of it, merely greeting him with a laconic, "Morning, sir."

Nick had barely pulled away from the curb when the radio crackled to life. "Bravo Bravo One, this is Tango Four Two, do you read?"

"Roger, Tango Four Two, this is Bravo Bravo One. What's wrong? You guys got frostbitten toes? Over."

"Ah, Bravo One, we've got a breach at Zulu Delta three-oh-one. Request backup and suggest you alert the duty officer."

Andrea yanked her brick off her belt and broke into the conversation. "Bravo One, this is Alpha Tango Niner. Tell those yokels to get on a secure frequency and then patch me through. Over."

"Roger, Alpha Tango Niner. Tango Four Two, do you copy?"

"This is Tango Four Two. I copy. Changing frequency, now."

Andrea punched in the new frequency on her radio in time to hear, "Alpha Tango Niner, this is Bravo One. We've got you patched. Go ahead, ma'am. Over."

"Tango Four Two, this is Alpha Tango Niner. Tell me what you've got."

"The perimeter fence has been breached about four hundred yards from the guard shack at the west end of the strip, ma'am. There's a boot print in the snow on the other side, but after that the ground's frozen and there's no more snow. We're waiting for backup, but if we go in there, we'll trigger all the alarms."

"Are you mobile or on foot?"

''On foot, ma'am. It was only going to be a short walk. Man, it's cold.''

''We'll get a truck out to you, Tango Four Two, but you stay put in case the intruder tries to exit the same way.''

''Yes, ma'am.''

''Bravo One?''

''Bravo One, I read you, ma'am. Mobile backup is on the way to Tango Four Two. Anything else?''

''Notify all units to go to secure frequency and be alert. I'm on my way to the strip to check things out.''

''Damn,'' said Nick. ''Maybe this is it.''

Andrea wondered the same thing as tension coiled in the pit of her stomach. ''Still not a betting man, Nick?''

''Maybe this time, skipper. Maybe this time.''

Yes, maybe this time. Andrea glanced up at Dare and found him looking steadily at her. He seemed to be waiting for her next decision, and nothing could have impressed upon her more clearly that he considered this to be her show. It was as if blinders fell from her eyes and she finally saw him unshadowed by memories of other men. Dare MacLendon looked at her as an equal.

''Where to, ma'am?'' Nickerson asked as he neared the flight line.

''The guard shack near the alert planes,'' Andrea responded. ''If the intruder's on the flight line, he'll be less alarmed to see a truck pulling up there.''

When she stepped out of the truck, a gust of wind blew up the snorkel of her parka and stung her eyes to tearing.

''Damn, it's cold,'' Nickerson muttered as he caught her arm to steady her. He reached back into the truck and pulled out two M-16s, then handed her one.

Andrea felt the familiar heaviness of the rifle in her arms but looked at it as if she'd never seen it before. Was this really necessary? Looking up, she felt as if Dare were staring intently at her, but his snorkel shadowed his eyes completely, and she couldn't be sure. For a long moment she stood utterly still, and then she squared her shoulders, hefting the rifle more securely.

''Let's find out if the sentries have seen anything,'' she said briskly.

The guard shack was heated, allowing them to dispense with their hoods. In the dim red night lighting, Andrea could see that her troops were sleepy looking but alert.

"No, ma'am, we haven't seen anything," the senior airman answered her question. "After we heard the fence was breached, me and Lewis went out to look around, but we didn't see anything unusual. Sergeant Nickerson said we weren't to go close to the planes, though."

"That's right." With a dog and its handler on each plane, the bombers should be secure. Even if the handler fell asleep on the job, the dog would be guard enough, alerted by the faintest of noises.

"Has there been any trouble with the electronic systems?" she asked.

"No, ma'am. Not since we came on duty. Maybe earlier, though. Want me to check the logs?"

"Please."

While she waited for the sergeant to scan the logs by the illumination of a penlight, Andrea turned to look out at the B-52s as she had the night Halliday claimed to have found the fault in the system that had caused the intruder alert. The night Alisdair MacLendon had arrived on base. No way could she have guessed then just how much he would shake up her life. Apart from small whirlwinds of blowing snow, everything looked just as it had that night four months ago, yet Andrea felt the woman she'd been then was a complete stranger. What had she thought as she stood here that night so long ago? What had been uppermost on her mind then, except the loss of sleep?

"Ma'am?" said the sergeant from behind her. "Sergeant Halliday was out here at nineteen-thirty hours. The log shows he did some work on the system. There was an intermittent circuit failure."

"Where have I heard that before?" Andrea mused aloud, remembering that Halliday had used those same words four months ago. "Nick—" She broke off and leaned forward. "Nick, something's moving out there."

"Douse that light, Kavitch," Nickerson said sharply to the sentry. "Where, Captain?"

"Three planes down and to the right. I could swear I saw something."

It was gone, though, and after thirty seconds of staring intently into the night, Andrea gave up.

"Let's go, Nick. Kavitch, get on the radio and tell everyone to look alive. Our man is out there, and he's going to be trying to get away very shortly."

"Yes, ma'am."

"Andrea."

Dare's voice drew her up short just as she was about to go out the door. Wheeling, she glared at him as she struggled to zip her snorkel with one hand.

"Damn it, Colonel, stay here," she said shortly. "Don't get in my way." She heard Nickerson draw a sharp breath, but she was past caring. The intruder was out there, and every moment's delay increased the chance he would escape.

Dare's voice reached her, deceptively mild. "I was just going to say that I saw a shadow moving under the fourth plane down. Take it easy, Captain."

"Damn fool thing to say, skipper," Nickerson remarked near her ear as they stepped out of the guard shack.

"I'll apologize later. Stow it, Nick. Let's split up and move in on the third and fourth planes from opposite sides." She kept her voice low even though they were downwind from the planes and their voices shouldn't carry.

"I'll take the left side," Nick said. "Likely he'll try to make a break toward the perimeter, and I'm bound to be at least as big as he is."

And I'm not, Andrea admitted silently, bowing to reality. "Okay. Let's move out."

Just then the door of the guard shack opened and closed quickly. Turning, Andrea recognized Dare's large shape. In his gloved right hand was his pistol.

"Not a word, Burke," he said flatly. "I'm pulling rank."

She should have known, Andrea thought. Right from the start he'd been the kind of CO to stick his nose everywhere and get involved where he wasn't wanted. She should have known. She wanted to get angry, but she couldn't, because part of her warmed to the fact that somebody in the world wanted to stand shoulder-to-shoulder with her. ''How do you want to proceed, sir?'' she asked stiffly.

''It's your show,'' he said levelly. ''Just get it through your head that it includes me.''

She could live with that, Andrea thought. ''Okay. Nick, you go ahead to the left. The Colonel and I will come up along on the right. Let's move out.''

Chapter 15

Andrea crouched, keeping low, and moved swiftly across the tarmac to the right of the parked planes. She hadn't gone a dozen steps before a sense of déjà vu assailed her, reminding her of the night she'd been shot. Her neck and scalp prickled with unexpected fear, and her step faltered, but only for an instant. Nickerson was out there, depending on her to do her share, and he could be in serious danger without backup. There was no choice but to go on, and no point in thinking about what might happen.

Suddenly and unexpectedly, she was extremely grateful for Dare's presence at her side. He moved stealthily, reminding her of a jungle cat, but when she inexplicably reached out for him, he paused and caught her hand in his.

What the hell am I doing in this business? The thought came out of nowhere, stunning her with its ferocity. She'd lied when she told Dare she'd never considered anything else, lied to him and to herself. Somewhere along the way all those other ideas had gotten lost in a burning desire to prove herself as an Air Force officer, but not even then had she imagined herself in this situation. Law Enforcement had never been her goal; it had been thrust on her, and she'd been making the best of it ever since.

Now here she was in the dead of night, stalking a killer with an M-16 in her hands. If she had an ounce of sense, she would be back in the guard shack directing this operation, the way a commander should. No, she had to get into it up to her neck. She always had and wondered if she always would.

"Andrea?" Dare's whisper was barely audible, although he'd turned so that his mouth was only several inches from her ear. "Something wrong?"

Andrea drew a deep breath and managed to shake her head. An instant later she released his hand a crept forward again. A faint rustle told her that he was following her.

Approaching the third plane, she slowed up and crouched lower. With her teeth, she pulled the mitten off her right hand and let it fall to the tarmac. The liner glove wasn't nearly as warm, but she had to be able to wrap her finger around the trigger. As quietly as she could, she released the safety and crept forward. The dog wouldn't be able to smell anyone under the planes, not when the wind was blowing at a stinging thirty-five miles an hour, and the same wind would carry away any reasonably quiet sounds. Andrea didn't want to chance it, though, for fear of scaring away their quarry. Those dogs were squirreled away on the sealed-up planes, but she had no idea whether their barking might be audible to someone on the tarmac below.

Seeing nothing around the undercarriage of the third plane, she edged forward to the fourth. Her heart was beating wildly now, and adrenaline soured and dried her mouth. Pausing, she pushed back her snorkel to widen her field of view. Now only a knit stocking cap covered her head, and the cold made her scalp ache.

A sudden groan and clatter to her left brought her swinging sharply around, and she peered intently into the shadow of the bomber. Lord, it was dark under there. Turning, she sought Dare.

"Did you hear it?" she barely whispered.

He nodded. "Nick."

That was what she thought, too. Dare gestured with his hands, indicating that if she moved to the left, toward the sound, he would swing around from the right and try to come up from the rear. Andrea nodded her agreement.

Licking her cold lips, she changed direction, creeping toward the bomber's rear wheels. Those tires were big, big enough to hide a crouched man easily. And she was exposed, mercilessly exposed. Cautiously, she eased into the protection of the big plane's shadow. Maybe the dog in the fuselage above her had heard the clatter, too. Maybe he was even now alerting his handler, who was under orders to immediately radio for backup. Straining her ears, she couldn't hear a thing except the ceaseless wind and her own ragged breathing.

She approached the bomber's right rear tires from the outside, then edged around them and nearly tripped over Nickerson's crumpled form. Dropping immediately to one knee, rifle cradled in her left arm, she shook him.

"Nick?" she whispered, and was relieved when she heard a faint moan. Reaching under his head, she made sure his cheek wasn't touching the frozen pavement. He needed help, but he would have to wait a few minutes.

Her eyes zeroed in on the other set of rear tires. There was only one place the intruder could be now, otherwise she would have seen his shadow as he ran in one direction or another. But between her and the concealment of the other tires, there was only open space. No way could she simply cross it.

She would have to brazen it out.

"I know you're over there, Halliday. Come on out. You won't get out of here."

There was no response.

"The perimeter's been sealed, Halliday. We know what you're up to. You can't run far enough."

A shot cracked on the wind, and chips of tarmac flew up at Andrea's face.

"Damn it!" she swore, and threw herself protectively across Nickerson.

Dare's voice suddenly cut through the night. "She's not alone, Halliday. Put your hands up and come out."

Dear God, don't let him be exposed, Andrea prayed as she huddled over Nickerson. Lifting her head, she looked in the direction Dare's voice had come from and saw his bulky shape striding slowly, almost casually, across the tarmac and into the plane's shadow. "Oh, my God," she whispered. "Oh, my God." He couldn't have made a better target of himself, his shape clearly silhouetted against the background light of the vapor lamps.

Another shot rang out, and this time the bullet smacked the pavement in front of Dare. His step never faltered.

"I'm the one you want, Halliday," he called out. "Come on out and fight like a man. I'm not even armed."

Halliday was going to kill him! The certainty settled in Andrea's stomach like a cold lump of lead. Grabbing her rifle, she waited for Dare to speak again.

"Come on," he said. "This is what you really want. You really want to slug it out with me, not with the whole Air Force. Well, I'm here, Halliday. Here's your chance."

There was no way Halliday could watch both herself and Dare and keep himself concealed from them both at the same time, she figured. Those tires were just too big. Resting her rifle on her forearms, she began to crawl forward on her stomach.

"Don't move another step, MacLendon!"

It was Halliday, all right. Andrea recognized his frightened voice.

"Why not?" Dare asked almost pleasantly. "You want to have it out with me. Well, you can't do it from behind those tires. Come out and face me. We can talk about what's bugging you."

"You killed my brother!"

So that *was* it. Andrea's stomach lurched sickeningly, and she crawled faster. From the sound of Halliday's voice, he was wired on fear and anger. There was no telling what he would do. Damn Dare for sticking his nose into this.

"Tell me about your brother, Halliday," Dare suggested, halting and standing with his hands in plain sight. "I don't remember your brother."

He was buying time, Andrea realized. He was buying time for her to reach Halliday. Ignoring the frozen ache of her ears and nose, ignoring the way her muscles ached from her unaccustomed crawl, she hurried toward those tires.

"He was in Nam with you. He was just a kid."

"I don't remember him," Dare insisted. "I never knew a Halliday."

"Sure you did," Halliday said on a sobbing laugh. "I figured you'd forget him. No reason the big pilot should remember a kid in his ground crew."

Oh, God, Andrea thought sickly. Six more feet. Just six more feet and she could come around behind Halliday.

"Tell me what happened," Dare said gently. "Tell me about it. There's no point in killing me until I know what I'm dying for, right?"

"You sent him out into a firefight at Tan Son Nhut. You sent him out to carry some stupid message."

"Oh. I remember him," Dare replied slowly. "Only you got it wrong, Halliday. The firefight broke out *after* I sent him with the messages. He got caught in the first salvo."

"You're lying!"

Andrea reached the base of the tires and eased up cautiously to her feet.

"I'm not lying," Dare said calmly. "I remember very distinctly that I sent him before the fight broke out. There was no rush. He could have waited until morning for all I cared, but he was young and eager to please. Thirty seconds after he walked out the door, the bombardment started. I didn't send him into it."

Andrea whipped around the tires and shoved the barrel of her rifle into Halliday's back.

"Drop it, Halliday," she said coldly. "Slowly, very slowly, put your hands on your head."

But he turned and pointed his pistol straight at Andrea. Even in the dark she could see the wildness in his eyes. He'd cracked. He'd cracked badly.

"You don't have the guts to shoot me," he said flatly.

He was right, Andrea realized with a sick sense of horror. She couldn't shoot him. But she couldn't let him know that.

"It sure would be messy," she said harshly. "Pieces of you would scatter all over the place. And you'd better not pull that trigger, because my finger's on *this* trigger and the rifle's on automatic. Have you ever seen what an M-16 can do to a man?"

"Stand-off, Captain?" Halliday asked, and laughed wildly.

But it wasn't, not quite. Beneath her layers of winter clothing, Andrea's muscles tensed, and she eased her finger from the trigger. Suddenly, without any warning at all, she swept the barrel of the rifle around and knocked the pistol from Halliday's hand.

A yelp of surprise barely escaped his lips before a dark shape hurtled out of the night and knocked Halliday to the ground.

"Got any cuffs, Andrea?" Dare asked with a grunt as he wrestled Halliday onto his face and pulled his arms up behind his back.

"Yes, sir! Somewhere under all these clothes."

"Use mine, skipper," said Nickerson.

Whirling, Andrea let out a happy cry as she saw Nickerson sagging against a tire but on his own feet. "Nick! Are you okay?"

"One hell of a headache, ma'am, but I've had worse after a night—"

"In Saigon," Andrea completed. "I know. I know."

"Damn it, Andrea," Dare said breathlessly. "The cuffs! Give me the damn cuffs. This guy won't quit."

"I was gonna say after a night of shore leave, ma'am," Nick said as he handed Andrea the cuffs that dangled from his hand.

Yanking off her other mitten, Andrea knelt beside Dare and the writhing Halliday. Together they managed to get the handcuffs on him, and then Halliday grew instantly, surprisingly still. The fight was gone from him.

Andrea's earlobes ached so sharply that she rubbed them and almost groaned from the pain. Tugging up her hood with one hand, she pulled the radio from her belt with the other and called for backup.

"I feel like such a jerk," Nick said. "I can't believe I let him get to me like that. I should have known he'd be hiding there."

"Things happen," Dare remarked, rotating the shoulder he'd bruised in his flying tackle of Halliday. "Worse things could have happened." Permanently engraved on his mind was a stark snapshot of Halliday's pistol aimed right at Andrea's stomach. Adrenaline-induced nausea churned in him. "Burke, if you ever go off half-cocked like this again, I'm going to hang your hide out to dry."

"Half-cocked!" Andrea leapt to her feet, still super-charged on her own adrenaline. "I did *not* go off half-cocked!"

"You sure as hell did!" His stomach kept sinking at the

thought of what might have happened to her, and adrenaline was making him act like a damn fool, but he didn't care. This woman had scared the wits out of him. "Do you think you're supersoldier? You and Nickerson should never have come out here alone to deal with an intruder who was probably armed and dangerous. You should have waited for backup."

"If I'd waited for backup, he might have gotten away! There was no time—"

"There were two guys in the guard shack you could have taken with you."

"So write me up!" Andrea said hotly, glaring at him. How dare he!

"I just may. You scared me out of ten years of life! I don't know whether to shake you or—"

Nickerson cleared his throat noisily. "Beggin' your pardon, sir, ma'am, but there are two trucks headed this way and more comin'. These fellows might not understand your, uh, disagreement the way I do."

Andrea clamped her teeth together, but she couldn't resist snapping, "And I told you not to get in my way, but *you* had to pull rank. You could have been killed." That thought scared her half to death.

"So could you," Dare growled back, keeping his voice low. "It's a damn good thing I came with you. And who's the ranking officer here, anyway?"

"I told you," Andrea murmured too sweetly, "that I couldn't kiss you at night and act like it never happened the next day. If you think I'm going to kiss your—"

"Skipper," Nick interrupted quickly, "someone might hear."

This time Andrea sealed her teeth with an audible click, and she took satisfaction in hearing Dare grind his. They were both acting like irrational idiots, some objective corner of her mind noted. It was the adrenaline, of course, but she was too incensed to care.

In midafternoon, when the first rush of details and paperwork had been cleared out of the way, Andrea returned to the BOQ to clean herself up before her meeting with Dare. She was sure he'd been handling his end of things just fine all day, since he knew everything anyway, but a phone call at noon had informed her that "The Colonel expects Captain Burke in his office at 1530 to deliver her report."

Standing under the needle spray of the shower, Andrea battled bone-numbing fatigue and promised herself that just as soon as this meeting was over, she was coming back here to sleep straight through until tomorrow morning. Dolan could have the command and all the joys that went with it.

Time for another haircut, she thought as she dried her hair in front of the bathroom mirror. And suddenly, from out of nowhere, came a memory of the long, long hair her father had never allowed her to cut. It had fallen below her hips, and she had always caught it back in an impatient ponytail to keep it out of her way. How fiercely glad she'd been when she arrived at the Academy and had it all cut off. Now she wondered, actually wondered, if she should let it grow out.

"You're crazy from lack of sleep, Burke," she told her reflection sourly. She didn't have time to mess with her hair.

Dressed in a pressed, creased and impeccable uniform, she presented herself in Dare's office promptly at three-thirty. Her weary eyes devoured every detail of his appearance, from the lock of hair that tumbled onto his forehead to the broad shoulders that stretched his uniform shirt. No two ways about it, the man looked good enough to eat.

Placing the typed report on his desk, Andrea sank into the chair he indicated.

"I've talked to SAC HQ," he said without preamble. "You're the hero of the day, Andrea."

"Me?" She kept remembering how her goose would probably have been royally cooked if Dare hadn't followed her out onto the tarmac.

"You. I know I sounded off this morning, but I'm convinced you would have handled matters even if I hadn't involved myself."

Andrea blinked. "That's very generous of you, sir."

"Just the truth." She looked exhausted, he thought, and troubled. What was troubling her? "I wanted to warn you that they're sending out a reporter from the *Air Force Times* to do a feature story on you. He'll be here tomorrow."

"Oh, no." She was horrified. "Do I have to?"

"I'm afraid so, Andrea." He smiled faintly. "They just can't pass up the opportunity to show you off. Female Academy graduate turns hero. If you ask me, they'll want a picture of you in battle dress and toting your rifle."

"That's ridiculous!"

"Why? The Department of the Air Force just dropped its enlistment quotas. Now everything's based on ability. Truly an equal opportunity environment. Do you really think they're going to pass up a chance to justify their decision by showing that women can do the job just as well?"

"But I can't do it just as well," she burst out.

Astonished, Dare sat back in his chair and studied her intently. "You *can,* Andrea. What makes you think you can't?"

"I'm a sham," she said tensely, and leapt up from her chair. "The only question is what I'm going to do about it."

Dare watched her pace, a frown on his face. "Tell me about it."

"Last night Halliday pointed a loaded gun at me and told me I didn't have the guts to shoot him. And he was right. I didn't."

Dare rubbed his chin, never taking his eyes from her. "I don't think," he said carefully, "that it takes guts to shoot somebody."

"Whatever it takes, I haven't got it."

"You did once before, not that I'm saying that's a good thing."

"And that's why I can't do it again. If I'd done more than graze him that first time, I don't know if I could live with myself. That's been hard enough to deal with. All I know is that I can't do it again. What kind of soldier does that make me?"

A wounded one, Dare thought, watching her. Nor did he feel he should be arguing in favor of shooting anyone. "You don't think the circumstances had something to do with it?" he asked after a few moments. "After all, you were face-to-face with the guy, and he's somebody you've known for a couple of years. I don't think most of us would have been able to pull the trigger under those circumstances."

"Maybe. Maybe not." Coming to a halt, Andrea wrapped her arms around her waist and bowed her head. "I'm not sure I want to be able to pull the trigger. I told you that once before. I guess I've been ignoring the question, but I think it's time to face it. I've got to decide whether I have what it takes to be a soldier, or even if I want to have what it takes. It's not a game anymore, Dare. Twice, now, it's been real."

"I don't think any of us want to have what it takes, or to like it, Andrea. We just do what we have to when we have to. That's the bottom line."

"Well, I'm not sure I can do what I have to." She raised bleak eyes to look at him. "Some cop."

"I don't know about that. You handled yourself admirably last night, and you managed to do it without bloodshed. That's something to be proud of. And I don't know if you should be worrying because you couldn't shoot a man who's been a friend of sorts for the last couple of years. I don't think we want soldiers who are capable of shooting people they know. I know I don't want any in *my* command."

He rose and came around his desk, then folded her into his arms, holding her snugly against his chest. "Don't beat yourself with this, Andrea. Honest to God, I don't think I could have pulled the trigger, either."

The green eyes she lifted to his were bright with unshed tears, and the sight sent an aching shaft through his heart.

"Come home with me right now, Andrea," he said. "The duty day's over in fifteen minutes anyway, and after the night we put in, we're entitled to take off. Come home and let me take care of you."

Home. The word made her throat ache with yearning. Unable to speak, she simply nodded.

They walked together out of the building, neither of them caring any longer who saw them and what they might speculate. Dare's only concession was that he didn't put his arm around Andrea until they were in his Bronco.

"Let me fix you something to eat," he said when they entered his house.

"I'm not hungry," Andrea replied listlessly. "Really. I just need to sleep." And I need to be held. Desperately.

He seemed to know. He helped her out of her clothes and into bed, and moments later he joined her, tucking her into the sheltering strength of his large body, stroking her hair and back with gentle hands.

"Sleep, sweetheart," he murmured. "Sleep."

Her hands were clenched into cold fists against his chest, and every muscle in her body was drawn tight with tension, but gradually fatigue battered down the last of her resistance. Dare felt her relax against him finally, growing soft and yielding as sleep claimed her. He brushed a light kiss against her forehead and closed his own eyes, welcoming the end of a day that had been too long and too difficult.

Andrea woke with a start in the dark, her heart racing.

"Easy, babe," said a drowsy voice near her ear, and powerful arms surrounded her, hugging her. "It's over."

She turned toward him, burrowing into his warmth and strength, afraid that she was coming to depend on him too much, afraid that she wouldn't be able to stand being alone when the time came. The person she'd thought she was didn't seem to exist anymore. The last thing on earth she wanted to be was a dependent, clinging female, yet here she was clinging like mad and grateful she had Dare to cling to. "I'm scared," she admitted in a whisper. "I'm so scared."

"You've had a rough couple of months," he rumbled reassuringly. "Anybody would be having a crisis of confidence."

As always, he went right to the root of things. She could have sworn he was able to read her mind.

"You know," he continued, "we all go through life running on automatic most of the time. Every so often, though, something comes up. Maybe it's something that happens, or something someone says, but it shakes us up and makes us look at things differently for a while. I guess it's good for us in the long run, but it sure isn't fun."

"It sure isn't," she agreed, nuzzling his shoulder and filling herself with his scent. It felt so good to be held this way, to feel his skin against hers. Why was she so afraid of what felt so right?

"Are you getting hungry?" he asked. "I am. Why don't I go make some soup and sandwiches? I'll even let you pick the soup."

She was so long joining him in the kitchen, however, that he went back to the bedroom to find out what was wrong. She was sitting on the edge of the bed, wrapped in his terry robe, a pair of his black wool socks flopping on her feet.

"Andrea?"

She looked up slowly and gave him a sad smile. "You know what I'm going to say, don't you."

A fist clenched around his heart, and for a moment there didn't seem to be any air in the universe. "I guess so," he said finally. He couldn't even make himself move. "Come on and have something to eat, and then you can tell me. And I'll argue, anyway."

Not until they were seated at the table in front of steaming bowls of soup did Andrea speak. Dare took what consolation he could from the fact that it clearly wasn't any easier for her to say what was on her mind than it was going to be for him to listen to it.

"I need to stop seeing you for a while," she said through a throat that had become painfully tight.

"I know." Yep, he'd known. Damn it, he'd known.

"I've got to find myself, Dare. I've lost me somewhere." The smile she gave him was pathetic. "I don't know myself anymore."

He lit a cigarette and managed a short nod. "I don't quite see how I'd prevent you from finding yourself."

"Because you're so strong that you're easy to lean on. Too easy. And you'd let me lean, just the way you did earlier."

"Everybody needs to lean sometimes, Andrea. It doesn't mean we're weak when we do."

She hadn't touched her soup, and now she pushed the bowl aside, a sure indicator of how lousy she was feeling. Even as he tried to manage the pain of his own impending loss, he felt sympathy for her.

"You've got to understand the dimensions of the problem," she said presently. "You're part of it. I've come to need you. I've never needed anybody in my life before, and suddenly I need you the way I need air to breathe. That's scary enough, but that's what makes leaning on you come close to dependency.

I don't want to become a limpet, and I don't think you want one clinging to you."

He wanted to argue, but she was making sense. He didn't want to see her damaged and gutted, not even if it meant losing her entirely.

"So, okay," he said, and took a steadying breath. "What's the plan?"

"I won't see you again until I figure out who I am and what kind of future I really want."

"And just how long might that take?"

She sighed heavily. "I don't now. The first thing I have to do is figure out what kind of future I have with the Air Force. Or even *if* I have one. I'll go to Minot and take it one step at a time. That's all I can do."

"Will you at least write?"

Suddenly tears were running down her cheeks, huge, silent and heartbreaking. "I'll write," she said brokenly. "Will you?"

Dare stood, knocking his chair over with a crash, and scooped her up into his arms. Jaw working, he carried her to his bedroom and lowered her gently to the mattress.

"You remember this, Andrea," he said as he flung his clothes around the room and then stretched out beside her. Catching her chin in his hand, he turned her face toward him and looked deep into her wet eyes. "I...I care about you, woman. Body and soul. And I'm going to miss you like hell."

She threw her arms around him and clung tightly, pierced by his unexpected declaration, but she didn't answer it. Both of them were aware of her silence. It hung in the room around them as Dare made love to her, adding desperation to his desire and sorrow to hers.

Never had Andrea hated getting dressed the way she did that morning. Each item of clothing she donned removed her that much farther from Dare and brought the moment of separation that much closer. During the night, moments had become infinitely precious, each one to be treasured and drawn out. Andrea clutched every one of them to her heart against the long, lonely days ahead.

Maybe she really had lost her marbles. Trouble was, she kept remembering her mother and how she had depended on Charlie Burke. Andrea had grown up feeling scornful of her mother's utter dependency, and while adulthood had made her more sympathetic to her mother's weakness, she was terrified of becoming a similar shadow. It was a wonder that Clara Burke had managed to get dressed in the morning without Charlie's direction. She had depended on him for everything else, every decision, every opinion, every action beyond the woman's work of household chores.

It wasn't that Dare would want or even try to turn her into that kind of person. Andrea honestly believed he would never knowingly do such a thing. No, she was afraid of the weakness in herself, the desire to curl up in Dare's sheltering arms and let him face the world for them both. In that weakness she felt like her mother, and once and for all she had to prove she could stand on her own.

"Almost ready?"

Andrea looked up from smoothing her slacks over her hips and caught her breath. God, he was magnificent! He stood tall and straight in the doorway, turning the ordinary cut and color of his uniform into something far more. In every inch, he was a soldier, right down to his firm jaw. That jaw was set, containing all the arguments he hadn't voiced, all the emotions he hadn't unleashed.

"Dare..." She spoke his name faintly, uncertainly.

"No talk," he said flatly. "Except for one or two notable occasions, I've never pushed you in any way, and I don't want to start now. You've stated your position. I accept it. End of discussion."

His withdrawal was a tangible thing, leaving her feeling colder and more abandoned then she'd ever dreamed was possible. If he cared about her, how could he let her go like this, so coldly?

He broke the silence between them only when he pulled up in front of the BOQ. Setting the car in neutral, he turned to face her one last time.

"Goodbye, Andrea," he said in that same flat, emotionless tone.

Standing in the dry snow, with the icy predawn wind whipping around her, she watched him drive away. Now she knew what it meant to be truly alone.

Chapter 16

I care about you, woman. Body and soul.

Andrea jerked bolt upright in bed, surfacing from a restless sleep with her heart pounding and her breath coming in ragged gasps. Dare's words rang in her ears as if he'd just spoken them. When she realized she was alone once again in her bed, she flopped back onto her pillow with a groan.

Call him.

No. No. If he really cared about her—if he loved her—he wouldn't have let her go so easily.

But you love him, and you were the one who walked away.

She'd had to. It was a matter of self-preservation.

Oh sure…

Rolling onto her side, she hugged her pillow tightly and fought back the tears that had been close to the surface for the last several days. He could have called, but he hadn't. He'd made no effort to get in touch with her at all.

Except for one or two notable occasions, I've never pressured you. I'm not going to start now.

Andrea drew a shuddery breath. He didn't really want her. Not if he could let her go so easily.

But had he? Had he really let her go easily?

I care about you, woman. Body and soul.

What did he want from her? She'd never understood that. He'd never told her, never explained what it was he needed from her. She'd made assumptions, but…

Once again she sat bolt upright, this time to throw aside the covers, to rise and pace her small quarters. When she passed by the open door of the bathroom, her reflection in the mirror caught her eye. Andrea Burke in green silk. Andrea Burke looking like the woman who Dare MacLendon had seen in her.

Halting, she faced her reflection and tried to see herself as he must have seen her. A man who gave such a gown to a woman was saying something. Well, of course, she'd already recognized that he'd seen the woman inside, the woman who hid behind the officer. That had been evident to her the first time she'd looked at herself in this gown, just a few short weeks ago at Christmas. He'd seen a woman who wanted to be beautiful for a man, and he'd made her feel beautiful.

Staring at herself, Andrea suddenly drew a sharp breath and held it. He hadn't given her this to make her feel beautiful or because he knew she wanted to feel like a woman. He had given her this because she *was* a woman, because to him she *was* beautiful.

Turning swiftly, she hunted up her jeans and sweater. No more guessing. No more assuming. Damn it, she was going to find out what it was he really wanted from her. An affair? A long-term relationship? Or nothing at all.

The latter possibility terrified her, but she would face it. She would face the truth of this relationship at long last. No more hiding, no more running, no more avoiding.

The frigid predawn air was unnaturally still when Andrea climbed out of her car in front of Dare's house. It was so cold that by the time she crossed the short walk to his front door, the moisture of her own perspiration had frozen into a thin sheen of frost on the legs of her jeans, stiffening them.

Afraid to hold still lest she grow hypothermic, she hopped from one foot to the other as she rang the bell and waited. Several minutes passed, and by then she was certain something must be frostbitten.

On her third ring, the door abruptly flew open and Dare stood there, eyes widening as he recognized her through the storm door.

"Andrea!" Throwing open the storm door, he seized her hand and tugged her indoors. "God, woman, you feel like ice," he said as he closed both doors behind them. "What's wrong? Why are you here?"

For a long time she said nothing. Instead she stood there silently, shivering from head to foot and drinking him in with her eyes as if she could fill her soul. He was rumpled from sleep, stubbled with a day's beard growth, wrapped in the frayed blue terry robe he'd once let her wear. He was, simply, the most beautiful sight she'd ever seen.

Dare stared back at her, noting the tremors that shook her, recognizing that she was cold but at a loss as to what to do about it. Once he would have touched her, warmed her with his body. Now he simply didn't know if he was any longer entitled to such intimacy.

What had brought her out in the middle of such a cold night? he wondered. What couldn't wait until morning?

"Andrea," he said gently, "what's wrong? Has something happened?"

Shivering, she stepped toward him. "Hold me," she whispered. "Please hold me."

He was more than willing to oblige. Closing the last bit of distance between them, he unbuttoned her parka with swift fingers and flung it aside. He started to bend so he could lift her, then suddenly paused. Taking her trembling shoulders in his hands, he looked down at her, forcing her to meet his gaze.

"No more games, Andrea," he said gruffly. "I'm in no mood for another scene like Wednesday morning. If you're planning to kiss me off again—"

"No..." she said hoarsely. "Oh, no. Dare, please..."

He obliged, sweeping her trembling body up into his arms. She coiled her arms around his neck, clinging with a fierceness he'd never felt in her before as shivers continued to rack her.

"Damn it," he said roughly as he laid her on his bed, "why didn't you call me before you came? How long did you stand out there?"

She didn't answer, watching him with hazy green eyes as, by the light of the small bedside lamp, he tugged her boots and then her jeans from her frozen body. His scent rose around her from the very sheets, warming the coldest place of all: her heart.

"Come on, honey," he said, lifting her. "Let's get this sweater off so I can warm you."

Finally, at long last, her naked, shivering body was wrapped in the heat of his, swaddled in his arms, in his blankets, in his bed. He stroked her hair and shoulder, tucked her head under his chin, covered her legs with his.

"What happened, darlin'?" he asked gently. "Tell me what happened."

The endearments, the tender caresses, his concern, thawed her as much as his heat. She'd feared he might have come to hate her for the way she'd left him, but he didn't hate her. Of that much she was sure. Now she had to face whatever it was he really felt, and she had no right to ask that of him until she'd given him her own honesty.

"I'm sorry," she said in a small voice, her breath stirring the soft hair on his chest.

"Sorry for what?" he asked, his soothing hands never hesitating in their caresses.

"Leaving you."

Now his hands did hesitate. Noticeably. "You did what you felt you had to," he said gruffly, and resumed stroking her shoulder.

"I was afraid," she admitted. "I was terrified."

"Of me?" He was stunned by the notion.

"No, not of you. Of me. Leaving you was the hardest thing I've ever done, but I was afraid to stay."

Something in him started to unknot, just a little, and made it possible for him to drop a kiss on her forehead. "I kind of got that feeling," he said in what he hoped was an encouraging voice.

"I was afraid of myself," she admitted in a voice that was barely above a whisper. Her heart had climbed into her throat, and she knew that this time there was truly no rip cord. Closing her eyes tightly, she stepped out into space. "I was afraid of how much I love you."

Dare was electrified by her words. He had practically given up hope of ever hearing them. He closed his eyes and hugged her nearer. "Just how much do you love me?" he heard himself ask huskily.

Andrea's voice quavered. "I love you so much that I don't want to imagine life without you."

"I love you, too," he managed to say gruffly through a tightening throat. "For the last couple of days my future had been looking about as barren as the prairie in January."

"But what do you want from me?"

The cry pierced his heart. Bending his head, he sought her mouth with his and kissed her with aching tenderness. "Sweetheart, what I want from you is you. Just the way you are. I never hoped I'd find a woman who can give me as much as you do. You're a friend, a colleague and a lover. I couldn't ask for more."

There was more she needed to ask, but for the moment she was overwhelmed by the need to show him her love. Pushing him gently backward, she rose above him beneath the tent of the blankets. On hands and knees she straddled him, then lowered her head to take hungry possession of his mouth.

At first Dare was content to let her lead, but before long the hunger she always evoked in him began to pulse through him, and he reached for her, wanting her closer, much closer.

Andrea caught his hands, lacing her fingers with his. "No," she whispered huskily, smiling almost drowsily down at him. "Let me. This time, let *me.*"

This was the first time he had ever taken the passive role in lovemaking, and he found the experience at once gratifying and torturous. In relinquishing control, he began to learn the awesome dimensions of the need this woman could arouse in him.

Because Dare had always taken charge of their lovemaking, Andrea knew very little of what he liked for himself. Aware of her lack of experience, she moved slowly, listening attentively to his breathing, heeding the responsive movements of his muscles. She found a sensitive spot behind his jaw, a cord in his neck where a nip could make him groan. She already knew that his nipples were as sensitive as hers, but when she found one hard little button in the soft fur, she set about discovering just what pleased him best.

"Oh! Andrea..."

She wriggled away from his hands and sought lower, as excited by his responses as she had ever been excited by his touches and kisses. She loved everything about this man, she realized. Everything. His rough-soft contrasts, his hardness and smoothness. The hair on his chest and legs, and in his groin. The way his muscles bunched beneath her hands, the way his hands grasped her and held her and guided her...

The way he groaned and caught her hips, this time refusing to let her escape. The way he showed her how to lower herself onto him, the way he reached out and touched her most secret place, depriving her of any will at all except the will to be his.

The way he made her his woman. The way he completed her and filled her and let her know she was all this man would ever need.

The way he held her to his chest with trembling arms afterward. The way he kissed her and stroked her hair back from her damp face, the way he pulled the comforter over them but wouldn't let her move away. The way he fell asleep with her, their bodies still joined, his arms snug around her, her weight a reassurance on his chest.

"Wake up, darlin'," a husky male voice growled in her ear. "It's noon, and I've run out of patience."

Andrea was smiling even before she pried open her eyelids. A gentle kiss on the lips broadened the smile even more.

"Tell me I didn't dream last night," she murmured, fully opening her sleepy eyes.

"I was going to ask you to tell me the same thing, sweetheart." His face just inches from hers, he ran a finger along her cheek and smiled into her eyes. "Did you really say you love me?"

"I love you." She said it positively, in a soft, sleepy voice. "With my whole heart."

"Enough to discuss marriage?"

Her breath caught, and the sleepiness vanished from her eyes. When she didn't say anything immediately, tension began to grow in Dare. He honestly didn't know if he had the patience to wait her out again.

"Okay," he said. "Too heavy before coffee."

He rolled out of bed, and Andrea saw that he was wearing jeans and a white T-shirt. He grabbed his blue terry robe from the back of the closet door and tossed it to her.

"The coffee's ready. I'll make some eggs for you."

"Dare—"

But he'd already left the room, closing the door behind him.

"Damn!" Andrea said in frustration. "Double damn!" He'd caught her by surprise, and now she'd hurt him. Disappointed him.

By the time he heard Andrea come into the kitchen behind him, Dare was feeling pretty annoyed with himself. Just because proposing to her had him all uptight was no reason to be short with her. He *knew* how hard all of this was for her.

"I'm sorry," he said, turning as soon as he heard her step. "I shouldn't have—"

She covered his mouth with her fingertips. "Shh," she said softly. "Shh. You just took me by surprise." For a long moment she stood and simply looked up at him, her expression growing softer.

"I wanted to tell you something about my career goals," she said finally, running her index finger back and forth across his lower lip in a way that made it difficult for him to concentrate on her words.

"You keep touching me like this," he said huskily, "and we're going to wind up in bed pursuing a few physical goals."

A breathless laugh escaped her, and she dropped her hand. "Sorry."

"Never apologize for that, honey." Catching her hand, he astonished her by pressing a kiss into her palm. "What's this about your career goals?"

"Well..." She looked down and to the side, and then stole a look at him from the corner of her eye, as if worrying what his reaction would be.

"Go on," he prompted.

"Well, I decided that I don't really want to be Colonel Andrea Burke after all."

He thought his heart was going to stop right there. She couldn't give up her career. He wouldn't let her. Choosing his words carefully, he asked, "What do you want to be, then?"

The corners of her mouth twitched upward. "How does Colonel Andrea MacLendon sound?"

Understanding crashed through him, overwhelming him. "Are you proposing to me?" he asked, hardly daring to believe it.

Andrea bit her lower lip and looked up at him, shaking her head slowly. "No, sir. I thought about it, but then I decided you should propose to me."

He was beginning to believe. "Why?"

A smile quirked the corners of her mouth. "I imagine I'll never again have a chance to bring a general to his knees."

A snort of laughter escaped him. "I'm not a general yet," he reminded her, struggling to restrain the urge to crush her to him.

"Close enough," she argued with apparent satisfaction. "Well?"

"On my knees?"

She nodded. There was a wicked sparkle in her eyes that quickly gave way to something much softer, much warmer, when, without the least hesitation, he dropped to one knee and took her hands in his.

Tilting back his head, Dare looked up at her, and now there was a teasing glint in his blue eyes. "I always wondered what would happen if I double-dared you."

Andrea smiled. "Try me."

"Captain Burke, I love you with my whole heart and soul. Will you marry me?"

She blinked rapidly as tears welled unexpectedly to her eyes. "Yes, sir, I will," she said and dropped to her own knees to throw her arms around his neck and hold him close. "I love you, Dare," she whispered fiercely. "I love you more than I can possibly say."

He kissed her thirstily, then lifted his head to look down at her. "It doesn't scare you anymore?"

"No." She shook her head. "I was afraid that I'd wind up being like my mother, totally dependent. And then I realized that I had the strength to walk away from you when I needed you most. I'm not weak. I'll never be like my mother."

''I can guarantee that, love,'' he said, cradling her cheek in his palm. ''And what about the rest of it?''

''My problems with being a cop and a soldier, you mean?''

Dare nodded, his gaze skimming her features as if he didn't want to miss a single nuance of her expression.

''I figure I'll always have a problem with that,'' Andrea said frankly. ''There would be something wrong with me if I *didn't* have a problem with guns. It hasn't kept me from doing my job yet, and I don't see any reason why it should. You were right about why I didn't shoot Halliday, and since I didn't have to shoot to protect someone, that's not something I should have to apologize for.''

''Thank God!'' he sighed with heartfelt relief.

Much later, in the intimacy of his big water bed, Dare tilted her face up to his. ''Have you ever refused a dare?''

Andrea shook her head. ''Never. You said you were going to double-dare me. You forgot.''

''Uh-uh, I didn't forget. I saved it up.''

Andrea's eyes sparkled. ''Well then? I'm waiting.''

Under the blanket, he crossed his fingers. ''What would you say if I double-dared you to start a family?''

Andrea stared at him solemnly for a long time, so long that he began to think he'd really blown it bad. Finally she spoke.

''I'd better warn you that twins run in my family.''

He started breathing again.

''Do you still want to dare me?'' she asked.

He never answered. He just held her so close and so tight that she got the definite impression she'd made him a happy man.

''I love you,'' he said a long time later. ''I'll love you with my dying breath.''

Andrea had no doubt that she would love him just as long.

* * * * *